'No one could accuse you of having either a timid nature or a sheltered background,' Deveril said. 'Are you offering yourself in Isobel's place?'

'Of course I'm not! Do you expect me to submit to a lifetime of being bullied and brow-beaten? You much mistake me if you do!'

'Is that how you see marriage?'

'No, sir, it's not. It's how I see marriage to *you*! No wonder poor Isobel was terrified! But I am not so easily frightened—and neither have I a brother to plan my future for me, for which I am eternally grateful!'

'Your brother's problem would be to find a man willing to take on such a virago as you,' Deveril commented. 'It had occurred to me that it would be amusing to seduce you. Now I think my pleasure would be in bringing you to heel.'

As her mouth opened to retort, his own descended on it, hard and unyielding, forcing her head back as his hands pulled her roughly towards him. His arms slid round her body in a grip that lost none of its strength in the change, and she was disconcertingly aware of the power of his body against hers . . .

Janet Edmonds was born in Portsmouth and educated at Portsmouth High School. She now lives in the Cotswolds where she taught English and History in a large comprehensive school before deciding that writing was more fun. A breeder, exhibitor and judge of dogs, her house is run for the benefit of the Alaskan Malamutes and German Spitz that are her speciality. She has one son and three cats and avoids any form of domestic activity if she possibly can.

Janet Edmonds has written four other Masquerade Historical Romances, *The Polish Wolf, The Happenstance Witch, Count Sergei's Pride* and *Wolf Girl*.

SCARLET WOMAN

Janet Edmonds

MILLS & BOON LIMITED
ETON HOUSE 18–24 PARADISE ROAD
RICHMOND SURREY TW9 1SR

*First published in Great Britain 1987
by Mills & Boon Limited*

© Janet Edmonds 1987

*Australian copyright 1987
Philippine copyright 1988
This edition 1988*

ISBN 0 263 76012 X

*Set in 10 on 10pt Linotron Times
04–0288–81,850*

*Photoset by Rowland Phototypesetting Limited
Bury St Edmunds, Suffolk
Made and printed in Great Britain by
Cox & Wyman Limited, Reading*

HISTORICAL NOTE

THE MONMOUTH REBELLION and the so-called Bloody Assize that followed it are well-documented events. Of the characters in this book, the Duke of Monmouth, Lord Grey and Judge Jeffreys really existed. The question of whether Charles II did marry Monmouth's mother when he was Prince of Wales has never been satisfactorily answered. Monmouth was undoubtedly his favourite son, but Charles would have been bound to deny his legitimacy in order not to prejudice any offspring of his dynastic marriage to Catherine of Braganza.

Judge Jeffreys must surely be one of the most handsome men—as well as one of the most notorious—in English history, as a visit to the National Portrait Gallery will reveal. He must also be the most maligned man since Richard III. In fact, he had a remarkably astute legal brain, and a dry wit which gained him many friends as well as enemies. I know nothing of his youthful peccadilloes, but in fairness to him feel bound to point out that his first marriage, to the daughter of a relatively poor clergyman, was a love match, and he was extremely happy until seven years and seven children later, when his wife died. His second marriage was entered into to extend his range of influence, but it seems to have been successful within those terms.

Judges at this time were appointed by the King and owed their loyalty to him. Therefore, in trials concerning matters of state, such as treason, they were expected to make sure the jury delivered the verdict the King wanted. There was no nonsense about an independent judiciary! It was also standard practice for judges to cross-examine witnesses and defendants, and very few defendants were legally represented. Jeffreys has been much criticised for the way in which he handled the Bloody Assize, but he was, in fact, doing no more than any other judge of his day would have done. He was rewarded by being made Lord Chancellor and died—of a gallstone—five years later. I have tried to capture the flavour of his cross-examination (the Public Record Office has transcripts of the trials) but have felt it necessary to modernise his speech: he invariably *thee*'d and *thou*'d those who came before him, partly because it was still the custom, and partly, no doubt, to accentuate their inferiority, since it was a form of address used to children and subordinates.

The punishments for treason depended upon sex and rank. Men were hanged, drawn and quartered, women burnt at the stake; aristocrats of both sexes were beheaded.

The Antelope, its exterior vastly changed, still exists, and the Oak Room, where the Dorchester session of the Assize was held, can be seen virtually unchanged. The hangman's peep-hole is still there, as is the door that is said to have led into the cellars and thence to the Judge's lodgings. It now opens into a cupboard revealing the beginnings of the staircase. Judge Jeffreys' lodgings is now an attractive restaurant of that name in Dorchester's main street, and the Judge's chambers upstairs are still there, though the panelling has been painted cream, which completely alters the appearance of the room.

Taunton Castle has been so altered in the eighteenth and nineteenth centuries and by its recent transformation into a very good little museum that it is virtually impossible to imagine what the Great Hall must have looked like in 1685.

The battlefield of Sedgemoor is clearly signposted at Westonzoyland, but the modern rhines (drainage ditches) are not necessarily in the same places as the old ones. The mists still rise off them as they did in 1685, and it is all too easy to imagine them concealing the ghosts of the soldiers buried in the gravefield. The inn is there —and serves a good lunch!—and so is the church. All the other buildings are figments of the imagination.

CHAPTER ONE

MANDALA SORN DREW rein and looked about her. The sun glinted on the burnished copper ringlet that hung roguishly over one fashionably tailored green broad-cloth shoulder, enchancing a complexion which had sufficient cream in it to avoid being declared pale. A broad-brimmed hat, its mannish lines softened by a profusion of ostrich feathers as well as the rakish angle at which it was worn, protected that complexion from any offensive rays that found their way down through the trees that were now increasingly a feature of the landscape.

The little party of riders wended its way through the bracken and down into the deep, tree-clad combe that stretched below. They had been travelling for some time through this landscape, only rarely coming across a cluster of small thatched cottages, each consisting of one room and a cow-byre. Nothing was visible from here, though Mandala thought she detected a faint trail of smoke that might have come from some hidden chimney below them.

She turned to her companions. 'Here?' she asked. 'Is this it?'

Her old nurse, perched pillion behind a burly man-servant, nodded. 'Yes, this is it. Abbas Manor's down there.'

The fourth member of the party was a small, fussy man of middle years who might have felt at home in Exeter or Bristol, but in fact came from London and wished himself safely back there. 'I am happy to say we can have very little further to go. In fact,' he went on, referring to some papers he extracted from the leather pouch slung across his chest, 'if my memory is correct, we've been riding through Sorn land for some little while.'

'Over half an hour—unless you've been selling land

off,' the old nurse told him.

The little man blenched. 'Not at all; Leafield and Leafield would never dream of such a thing, Miss Rissington! I assure you, Miss Sorn, that neither in your mother's time nor during your minority have we sold so much as one clod of earth.'

'I know that, Mr Leafield, and so, I suspect, does Martha, who is usually at least as well informed as anyone else when it comes to my affairs. You have been most assiduous in your care of my estates. If I can manage them only half as well, I shall have cause to be satisfied.'

The lawyer bridled with professional pride. 'As to that, I'm sure you'll manage very well. You've a good head on your shoulders. No doubt inherited from your mother. A most remarkable woman . . . if a shade unconventional,' he added doubtfully.

Mandala laughed, but not unkindly. 'She was certainly that. I would never have imagined that running a bawdy-house—even one on the road to Versailles which, if you consider the matter, is bound to be a good location for such an enterprise—could be so lucrative. Nor would I have guessed that selling it would realise such a considerable sum. To be perfectly honest, I was sorely tempted to keep it but, alas, I hadn't the slightest idea how to run it and I rather fancy it would have been difficult to find a manageress who would have been trustworthy.'

A shocked Mr Leafield could barely repress a shudder. 'Your mother never intended you to run it yourself!' he exclaimed. 'Her intention was always to distance you from it as far as possible, and I make no bones about the fact that I was very unhappy—*very* unhappy—that you insisted on hunting about until you had found out that part of your mother's story. She would not have wanted it to be so, and if you have the slightest interest in my advice—which I strongly suspect you will ignore when it suits you—you will not let it be generally known where the bulk of your very considerable fortune came from.'

Martha Rissington sniffed disparagingly. 'I'll be very

surprised if no word of Purity Sorn's career has filtered back here,' she remarked. 'It's remote enough, to be sure, but spicy gossip was never something that failed to get into the most unlikely nooks and crannies. The very fact that, when she was sent away, her old nurse went with her must have been enough to create some very accurate speculation as to the cause.'

'I fear you may be right.' Mr Leafield nodded. 'I have heard the occasional hint myself on my rare visits here.'

'I had no idea you had been here before,' Mandala exclaimed. 'I thought it was your father who dealt with the family's affairs.'

'While he lived, he did indeed assume that responsibility. He could hardly continue to do so after his death, however,' the lawyer replied with some asperity. 'I have been here only twice before. Once was when your grandfather died, to arrange with Jonah Swinbrook, your steward, that he would be answerable to me, and again on your mother's death to advise him of the new situation. Apart from that, he met me once a year in Dorchester to render account of his stewardship. A good man, Jonah Swinbrook. You could do much worse than listen to him and follow his advice.'

'Thank you. I shall do so—as I hope also to retain the advice of you and your brother. The advice of your family's practice has stood this estate in good stead over the years.'

'We shall be happy to continue our association with the Sorns of Abbas Manor,' he replied gallantly and truthfully. 'Shall we proceed?'

But Mandala was not yet ready to introduce herself to her peasantry. She turned in the saddle and the summer sun glinted on the diamond pin that secured the ends of her Steinkirk cravat to the lapel of her military style riding-coat. 'Do I have neighbours in this remote part of Devon?' she asked. 'Whereabouts are they?'

Martha Rissington, born and bred in Abbas St Antony, was better able to answer that question than the lawyer. 'None handy,' the old woman told her. 'That's to say, none within strolling distance. Over there is Courtenay Place—you can't see it when the trees are in leaf. A nice old house, it was, but they were saying in Dorchester as how young Sir Nuneham Courtenay had pulled it down and built a new one, all of Purbeck stone. He was a nasty child, I recall, and there's bad blood there. Doubt if he's improved with time. Way over to the north there's Haddenham Hall. A bit too far for a comfortable visit, but it's possible. A good Puritan family, the Haddenhams. Probably won't approve of the likes of you, either. That's all. If you want more company, there's the rector, of course, but beyond that you've got to go further afield—to Axminster or Honiton. And it's my guess you'll find them all a sight too provincial for your taste, my girl.'

Mandala was unperturbed at the maidservant's comment and made no reply except that implicit in putting her spur to her horse's side and moving down the track into the relative darkness cast by the trees. Scarcely half a dozen paces into the unaccustomed dimness, her little mare suddenly snorted and shied at the unexpected appearance of a horseman on the path in front of them. It took Mandala a few minutes to bring Fatima back to hand, minutes which gave the newcomer plenty of time to form his own appreciative opinion of the distinctly unprovincial figure before him.

Mounted on a solid-boned, heavy-necked beast of so dark a brown as to be almost black, he towered over Mandala's little Barb and reined back to allow her room to bring her mare back under control. When he could see that she had done so with the expertise of long practice and would need no help from him, he removed his unadorned wide-brimmed hat and swept her as deep a reverence as the pommel of his saddle and his horse's neck permitted.

'My deepest apologies, madam. I should not for the world have risked disconcerting your horse had I realised it bore so beautiful a burden.'

The flowery words were at variance with the ironic tone in which they were uttered. Mandala liked neither, but was uncertain how best to reply. She decided to ignore both flattery and tone and consider only the apology. 'You are very kind, sir, but I am very familiar with Fatima's little ways. She may have been disconcerted, but I was not.'

The stranger inclined his head in appreciation of a comment that implied this was no shy schoolgirl who could be easily flustered. Her voice intrigued him, too: it was deeper than most women's and had a husky quality about it which he could not recall having encountered before.

Mandala for her part looked at him with frank curiosity. Was this one of her neighbours? Sir Nuneham Courtenay, perhaps? Martha had said there was bad blood there and that he had been an unpleasant child. It was not difficult to believe that both comments might apply to the tall man whose horse blocked the way forward. Mandala was built on generous lines herself, but she suspected that this man would tower over her on foot as he did on horseback: his mount was huge, but even so, his booted and spurred foot came below the line of its rib-cage. He was not a young man—Mandala reckoned him to be well in excess of thirty and very likely as much as thirty-five. She was not close enough to ascertain the precise colour of his eyes but they were light and seemed to be neither grey nor blue but somewhere in between. There was a certain sardonic humour in his face but very little kindness, and it was a face that made her feel uneasy, as if it perceived more than it was meant to and disapproved of much that it saw. It was a lean, almost ascetic, face that would have looked more fitting had it been accompanied by the Puritan fashions of years gone by. The cheekbones were high and deep lines of dissipation ran from the aquiline nose to the well-shaped, if rather thin-lipped, mouth. His height, and a sense of strength held in check, was enhanced by broad shoulders under a riding-coat of midnight-blue broadcloth. Black leather gauntlets held the reins, and black hair, rather shorter than was strictly fashionable and which appeared to be his own, did not quite reach his shoulders. The effect was severe, almost sinister, and Mandala was both intrigued and a little frightened. Her curiosity urged her to ask him his name, but there was something in his manner which stopped her.

The stranger had, by this time, taken full account of the rest of her party and inclined his head towards them before reining his horse back into the trees.

'How thoughtless of me to continue to obstruct your progress,' he said. 'I beg your forgiveness.'

The words were humble but the tone was not, and Mandala felt that something more was needed than simply to bid him good day and ride on. Nothing more occurred to her, however, so she put her heel and her whip to Fatima's side and proceeded along the track. Several hundred yards further on, the path widened and she drew rein, waiting for the others to come up with her.

'Who was that, Martha?' she asked. 'Was it the wicked Sir Nuneham, do you think?'

Martha sniffed. 'Do you expect me to identify someone I haven't seen since he was a child, over twenty years ago? All I can tell you is that I doubt it. For one thing, I'd say that man is too old. For another, if that's Sir Nuneham, there's precious little family likeness he's inherited. If I were his father, I'd be suspicious, and that's a fact.'

Mr Leafield plainly disapproved of such comments. 'I have never met Sir Nuneham,' he said, 'but I can tell you that that wasn't he. I know that man. That's not to say I'm personally acquainted with him but I have seen him many times. That was Deveril York.'

He produced the name with a flourish that was clearly intended to creat an effect. It failed. The name meant nothing at all to either Mandala or Martha.

'And who may Deveril York be?' Martha enquired. 'If you'd said Prince William of Orange, now, or His Grace the Duke of Monmouth, it would have meant something. I can't say the same for—what was it?—Deveril York.'

The lawyer looked a trifle disappointed. 'I suppose, living abroad for so long, you might not have heard of him.' He frowned. 'I'd like to know what he's doing here, that's all. It's very strange.'

'This is all very cryptic,' Mandala told him. 'Martha and I are none the wiser, though. Who is he?'

'It's difficult to answer with any precision,' the lawyer began hesitantly. 'He lives in the fashionable world, yet is never truly a part of it. No one seems to know anything about his background or his family, though he must have one, one presumes. Nor does anyone seem to know how he acquired what is generally believed to be a very considerable fortune. He was a very close friend of the late King, whose acquaintance he appears to have made when His Majesty was in exile in France. Mr York certainly shared a not dissimilar life of dissipation, though he seems to have managed his affairs rather better. If, like his monarch, there are a number of his bastards scattered about, no one seems to know about them.' Mr Leafield coloured and turned to Mandala. 'I do not seek to embarrass you by such a reference, Miss Sorn. I merely wish to answer your question.'

'I'm not the least embarrassed,' Mandala assured him. 'I know what I am, and not mentioning the matter won't alter it. Pray continue: the story becomes fascinating.'

The lawyer frowned. Fascination with Deveril York was not an effect he had sought to produce. 'It is said that Mr York disappears for considerable stretches of time. People assume he goes abroad and he has certainly been encountered in the Low Countries on occasion, but I have never heard an explanation of either his disappearances or his presence abroad, though it is not unreasonable to assume that he may well have acted as King Charles's messenger from time to time.'

'And now that King Charles is dead?' Mandala asked.

'I can't imagine that a man who was so very acceptable to His late Majesty would be similarly favoured by King James. There are many factions at work in the kingdom these days, and it wouldn't surprise me to learn that a man like Deveril York had thrown in his lot with one of them. Why on earth he should be riding on Sorn land in a remote part of Devon is something that defeats my imagination—a fact that I find a matter of some concern.'

'Oh, come,' Mandala protested. 'You impute too much to his actions! If his relationship with the royal brothers is as you suggest, what would be more natural than that he should have bought an estate remote from fashionable society in order to live retired until, perhaps, a more estimable monarch sits on the throne?'

Mr Leafield shook his head. 'Not Deveril York,' he said in so decided a tone that Mandala knew it was not something about which he had the slightest doubt.

The village of Abbas St Antony nestled, cosy and prosperous, at the bottom of the combe, the well-maintained thatch of its roofs evidence of the estate's good management. Here and there a cottager had even replaced the wooden wind-doors with small glass-paned casements, thus securing a maximum amount of light in winter without letting in the cold winds that sometimes blew even in this sheltered valley. There were one or two larger houses such as might accommodate yeomen or even merchants, but the cottages of the poorer folk predominated.

Abbas Manor was an old house built at the beginning of the previous century and added on to subsequently, although nothing had been added in the last fifty years; those additions that had been made had been for the purpose of increasing the number of rooms and not to keep abreast of fashion. As a result, it rambled over a wide area, a multitude of low ceilinged, dark-panelled rooms leading one into another and all of them on different levels. This was hinted at from the outside by windows that did not always quite match in size or alignment. The impression created on someone beholding the house for the first time was of a certain charming eccentricity which would have been condemned by the advocates of the present fashion for the Baroque.

Mandala rode down the avenue of clipped yews, and was charmed. 'So this is where my mother grew up,' she said. 'I don't quite know what I expected, but it wasn't this. I shall be content if the inside is only half as delightful.'

'Whatever it's like, if you'd sent word you were coming, at least it would have been clean,' Martha warned her.

Mandala's mouth set in a firm line that was an echo of the determined expression Martha had so often seen on the face of her mother. 'It has been the housekeeper's task to see that it is always ready to receive visitors,' Mandala said.

'That's as may be, and I don't deny it. The fact remains that you can't deny human nature, either, and it's years since any owner set foot here. It will hardly be surprising if the dust and cobwebs have been allowed to settle.'

The heavy oaken door was opened by a neatly dressed woman whose greying hair was held back under a stiffly starched cap of plain linen. Her surprise at seeing visitors was evident, but she held the door wide as if such things were an everyday event. The heavy chatelaine hanging from her belt told Mandala that this must be the housekeeper, Kate Swinbrook, whose husband managed the wider domain of the estates.

The woman recognised the lawyer. 'Mr Leafield? What brings you here? Jonah made no mention of it. Not that you're not welcome,' she added hastily, and paused as she scrutinised his companions. Her eye dwelt with some curiosity on Mandala's elegant figure and passed quickly over the manservant before coming to rest on Martha. 'I know you from somewhere,' she began doubtfully, and then recognition sprang to her eyes. 'Of course! Martha Rissington! You left here with Miss Purity and were never heard of since. What brings you here now?'

The lawyer had dismounted by this time and helped the old maidservant down from the pillion-saddle. She dusted herself down before answering. 'You've put on weight, Kate Swinbrook. Must be comfortable living at Abbas Manor these days?'

'It always was—I see a long absence hasn't dulled your waspish tongue! Besides, Jonah says he likes a comfortable armful. Why are you here, Martha? And who is this?' She nodded her head towards Mandala.

'This is the reason I'm here, and you might as well show a bit of respect. This is Miss Purity's daughter—Mandala Sorn. She's come to take up her inheritance.'

Mrs Swinbrook immediately dropped a deeply

respectful curtsy. 'Forgive me, Miss Sorn. I wasn't expecting . . . I should have guessed . . . But, in truth, you resemble your mother very little.'

'Why should you expect me when I gave you no warning?' Mandala said cheerfully. 'Help me down, Bostwick, and then take the horses and find the stables, which I imagine cannot be far.'

'Indeed, no,' Mrs Swinbrook hastened to assure her as the lawyer's burly groom helped her new mistress to the ground. 'Round to your left—follow the drive and you can't miss them. Come in, mistress. You'll be wanting refreshment, I dare say.'

Agreeing that this was a truly excellent idea, Mandala followed her into the house and could not repress a triumphant smile in Martha's direction as she took note of the gleaming furniture and spotless flagstones. 'You've looked after the house well, Mrs Swinbrook,' she remarked.

The housekeeper looked surprised. 'It's my job to do so, but I'm none the less gratified, for all that, that it should be noticeable. Had I known you were coming, I'd have had fires lit. We keep them burning during the winter, for nothing deteriorates faster than a cold, damp house, but in summer we don't normally trouble.'

'I should appreciate one in my bed-chamber,' Mandala told her, 'and perhaps where I sit this evening, but there's no need to light them in every room.'

Her mistress might declare there to be no need, but Kate Swinbrook was not going to have her inspect the house without everything being exactly as her housekeeper's pride insisted it should be, and so, by the time Mandala and Mr Leafield had partaken of some refreshment and Mandala was ready to be conducted over her new domain, a crisp, new fire was burning brightly in every grate and the old house seemed the more welcoming as a result.

That initial tour of inspection was both efficient and, given the rambling nature of the house, confusing. Its purpose was as much to introduce Mandala to the politely curious stares of her household as to acquaint her with its geography, and consequently, after she had seen Mr Leafield and his manservant on their way back to London next morning, she decided to take a more leisurely survey of the old house that had been home to the Sorns for two hundred years.

It was, Mandala thought, a happy house, one from which emanated a feeling of great serenity and calm. This atmosphere was enhanced by the evidence of loving care that had clearly been lavished on every aspect of it. The furniture gleamed with the deep patina of age and beeswax, and Mandala noted approvingly that no one had been allowed to forget that table-legs were just as much in need of being polished as the tops. At many windows and round several beds the curtains bore witness to the skilled needlewomen who had embroidered them in past generations, and Mandala, who had never displayed any great interest in the house-wifely skills—though she had naturally been taught them—found herself planning to add her own contribution to the domestic furnishings. Her slim fingers lingered on polished oak and gleaming silver and caressed the comfortable shapes of pottery and porcelain that previous owners of the Manor had imported from strange lands as well as from skilled English craftsmen. She was particularly taken by a large Delft vase which depicted Adam and Eve. Not only was its shape singularly satisfying, but the characters had about them a naïve innocence which seemed particularly fitting.

It struck Martha Rissington that her mistress was uncharacteristically subdued that day, and she debated whether Mandala was, as she put it, 'sickening for something', or whether she was merely thoughtful. When the old nurse joined her erstwhile charge that evening by the fire in the pleasant sitting-room that Mandala had decided to use, she brought some sewing and sat mending linen by candle-light while the younger woman gazed into the fire without, Martha suspected, gaining much satisfaction from the activity. It was a long while before Mandala spoke.

'You were my mother's nurse from the cradle,' she said at last. It was half statement, half question.

'You know I was,' Martha said with an apparent lack of interest in what lay behind the question.

'You must have known her very well,' Mandala continued.

'That I did.'

Mandala glanced round the room, cosy in the light of the fire and the candles. 'I imagine she must have loved this house very much.'

'She was devoted to it.'

There was another pause, which her old nurse made no attempt to break. 'There's so much I don't know,' Mandala said eventually. 'So much that has lain at the back of my mind, not quite daring to come forward. Now, in this house where Maman grew up, like generations of Sorns before her, all those questions that have lurked for so long have come to the fore, and I want to know the answers.'

'Maybe you should have asked your mother,' Martha commented.

'How could I? I saw her so rarely, and only when she visited the school in which she had placed me. They were always such formal meetings, and always with a disapproving nun in attendance. What questions could I ask of a woman I scarcely knew, in a situation like that? Why, I didn't even know why the nuns so patently disapproved of Maman until after she died.'

Martha looked at her sympathetically. 'It must have been a great shock,' she said. 'Though you hid it well.'

She was startled to hear Mandala giggle. 'It was, of course, and poor Mr Leafield was so embarrassed about it. But once it had worn off—and I must confess, it did so very quickly—I really found it quite amusing.'

Martha snorted. 'You must be the only person who did.'

'Come, Martha, you must admit there is an entertaining incongruity in the daughter of an eminently respectable English family running away to France and establishing an extremely successful bawdy-house and then inheriting her family's English estates. I wonder what those respectable ancestors would think if they knew her illegitimate daughter now had control of it all?'

'Doubtless they'd turn in their graves,' Martha said with some asperity. 'Is this the sort of speculation you've been wasting your time with today?'

'No. It's the sort of speculation I had been wasting my time with until yesterday. There's something about this house which makes me think it wasn't quite like that. Am I right?'

Martha considered her answer carefully. 'It differs in certain respects,' she said cautiously. 'I'll not deny that.'

'You must know the truth,' Mandala told her. 'In fact, you are probably the only person left who does. Tell me, Martha. Tell me why Maman left a house she must have loved dearly—and a family, too, no doubt—to set up in such a profession in a foreign land.'

Martha hesitated. 'If your mother had wanted you to know, she'd have told you—or maybe left you a letter. She did neither, and I'm not sure I'm at liberty to do so.'

'It's too late to ask Maman,' Mandala pointed out reasonably. 'If you can tell me who else to ask, I'll gladly go to them, but I don't think you can. Besides, there must have been a lot of gossip, and no doubt oblique comments will be made now that I'm back. Surely I am best able to deal with them if I know the whole story —and as far as possible from Maman's point of view.'

The old woman considered the argument. 'There was gossip, all right,' she agreed. 'Most of it ill informed, no doubt. Yes, perhaps you should know more about your past; at the very least it may be a warning to you, if nothing else.'

'I know she ran away when she found she was with child,' Mandala said. 'Were her parents—my grand-parents—so very unkind to her?'

'They weren't unkind to her at all, and she didn't run away. When they learned of her condition, they arranged for her to go to some good people in Somerset. I went with her, and I can assure you that she had the very best of care. Once you were born and thriving, a decision had to be made about the future of both of you. Miss Purity knew she could go home, but she also knew it would make life very difficult indeed for her parents, as prominent Puritans, to have a daughter in the house with her bastard child—and there was never any question of her giving you up. In the end it was agreed to settle some money on her and she would go abroad. I elected to go with her. Your mother had expected France, with its licentious reputation, to be more tolerant of unfortunate women. She found it to be quite otherwise. No one would employ her in any even remotely respectable occupation and her money wouldn't last for ever. Finally she decided that if she were not to be allowed to be respectable, she might as well be *un*respectable—but do it with style. As you know, she was successful beyond her imaginings, but I can tell you this: she was never happy. You may have seen little of her. That was not because she didn't care. It was because she cared too much. She wanted you to have the sort of life she should have had, and she knew that too close an association between you would lead to you being tarred with the same brush.'

Mandala digested this for a few moments in silence. 'And what of my father?' she asked at last. 'Who was he? Why did Maman not marry him? Was he totally ineligible?'

'No man is ineligible in that situation,' Martha told her tartly. 'He refused, that's all. His parents were in favour —after all, your mother stood to inherit a fortune, and it wouldn't have been the first time an heiress had been brought to bed of a seven-month child—and your parents were naturally most anxious that a marriage should take place. But he was young and ambitious, and he thought a provincial wife, especially one firmly associated with the Puritan cause, would be a handicap.'

'He sounds most unpleasant,' Mandala exclaimed indignantly. 'What on earth induced Maman to allow herself to be seduced by him?'

Martha snorted. 'You've a lot to learn if you can ask a question like that,' she said. 'No woman "allows herself" to be seduced. Your mother loved him—or she thought she did. At all events, she certainly never loved anyone else. He was handsome, charming and clever, and he seemed very much a man of the world to the daughter of a country gentleman. I remember her telling me that he was the most handsome man she had ever seen—and I remember telling her that that was the least important consideration in the world. But, of course, she wasn't going to listen to an old maid like me, now was she?'

'How did she meet him, if he was so much a man of fashion?' Mandala asked.

'He was staying with Sir Dudley Courtenay—Sir Nuneham's father—so it was natural that visits should be made. Your grandparents were very much alive to the dangers of fortune-hunters and were very careful who might be allowed to push an interest with your mother, but this young man was entirely respectable, of a good family and with a promising future, even if he did not himself have an income that was much more than a competence. There was no reason to discourage him. Or so they thought.'

'Has he never made any attempt to contact my mother or to find out about me?'

'Not so far as I know; though, from something that was once said, I gathered that Miss Purity's parents informed his parents of the birth of a daughter. If so, I suppose they will have told him.'

'Did he realise those ambitions that were so much more important to him than my mother's well-being?' Mandala asked.

'As to that, who can tell the extent of a man's ambition?' Martha said warily. 'I did hear that he was doing quite well for himself, but that was a long time ago, and there's never been any point in enquiring further.'

'But you must know who he is,' Mandala persisted.

'I know his name, certainly. But if you think I'm going to tell you what it is, my girl, you can think again, for I shan't!'

'I can't think why you shouldn't. You've told me everything else.'

'Some sleeping dogs are best left lying—and that's certainly one of them,' her old nurse said in the categorical tone that Mandala knew was proof against any amount of wheedling. She dropped the subject of her father's identity.

'How much of Maman's history is known in Abbas St Antony?' she asked.

Martha shrugged. 'It's hard to say. The fact that she was with child must have become known, if only because even the most loyal servants gossip. I think we can assume that. Even if it hadn't become known, your arrival bearing the name Sorn will tell them all they need to know. If your mother had married, you would be otherwise called. It's what they know about your mother's activities in France that you need to worry about.'

'You've already said it would be strange if they hadn't heard rumour about that,' Mandala reminded her.

'That's right. If you take my advice, my girl, you'll behave with modesty, decorum and restraint. If you do, they may even come to believe the rumours are unfounded or at the very least be prepared to give you the benefit of the doubt.'

'How tedious!' Mandala exclaimed, and Martha was alarmed to see the glint of battle in her eye.

'Tedious it may be, but if you want to make your home here, you'll need to be on visiting terms with your neighbours—and you won't be, if you set out to shock them.'

'I wouldn't dream of setting out to shock anyone,' Mandala assured her.

'I don't suppose you would, miss, but you forget how well I know you. In some respects you are very like your mother. She could be very prettily behaved until someone made one ill-advised remark, and then she would respond with something quite outrageous while managing to look as if butter wouldn't melt in her mouth. You're just the same.'

'That doesn't sound much like the love-lorn girl you've been describing to me,' Mandala remarked.

Martha considered. 'No. She gradually changed, once she had to stand on her own feet. She was always an obstinate child, mind you—very sweet, but very stubborn. But those sharp retorts came later. I suppose at first they were designed to prove that unkind remarks —and there were plenty of those—failed to have the desired effect. Later on Madame de Rouen's acid wit became one of the hallmarks of her establishment, and she made no distinction between one recipient and another: Dauphin or divine, they all got the sharp end of Madame's tongue if she thought they deserved it.'

Mandala's eyes widened. 'Surely Maman didn't number divines among her clients?' she asked.

'Never you mind who patronised your mother's business,' Martha retorted sharply. 'Just you take care not to upset anyone.'

Mandala smiled. 'I'll try, Martha. I know you think I don't listen to you, but I do, and I know your advice makes sense, especially on this subject.'

'Hmm. I wish I could believe you'd remember it when the situation arises!'

CHAPTER TWO

THE EXCITING NEWS that the mistress of Abbas Manor had arrived entirely unannounced to take up her inheritance spread rapidly through the village and within twenty-four hours was winging its way through the county. Speculation throve. What sort of female could she be who, with such a history, had the gall to return to the home of her ancestors—such respectable people, too? The Manor servants were singularly uncommunicative. Yes, it was true Miss Sorn had arrived, and no, she had not been expected. She seemed well satisfied with what she found, and had made no unreasonable demands on her household—rather the reverse, if anything. Old Martha Rissington had returned with her. Perhaps they would like to ask *her* whether more servants were expected and when a baggage-train might arrive? Those who remembered Martha's way with presumptuous questioners decided it might be wiser to wait and see.

The handful of more prosperous families in the immediate vicinity were uncertain what to do. They lived on Manor land and should most assuredly pay their respects to the Lord of the Manor, but, if rumour was well founded, could they really be expected to visit —and be visited by—a woman with such a background? It was bad enough that her mother had not had the forethought to acquire a husband, but these things happened, and perhaps the passing of time blurred the edges of the mother's sin slightly, especially when one considered that she had at least had the grace to die. But if Purity Sorn really had earned her living in the way they said (and it had to be admitted that anything was possible in France), her daughter, brought up in that sinful atmosphere, was unlikely to be a fitting acquaintance for anyone with pretensions to gentility.

The village worthies, individually and under various

pretexts, took their concerns to the rector for his advice. The Reverend Leofric Southmoor understood, and was under no illusion as to where his duty lay. His living was in the gift of the Manor. As rector, he must pay his respects. As a Christian, he must give Miss Sorn the benefit of the doubt. He pointed out to more than one parishioner that it was perfectly possible either that the rumours were gross calumnies or that Mandala, appalled by her mother's way of life, had returned to Abbas St Antony to atone in some measure for her mother's sins. The parishioners, more cynical than the cleric, thought this unlikely, but agreed to reserve judgment until Mr Southmoor had found out for himself. All these consultations took place while Mandala was exploring her new home on her own, and it was the following day when the rector, who was not really looking forward to the interview, made his duty visit.

He was a tall, thin, ascetic man who might have been more at home in the celibate academic world of Oxford had he not married to please his family and found unexpected satisfaction in ministering to a rural community and appearing oblivious of the healthily boisterous activities of his innumerable—or so it sometimes seemed to him—progeny. His round and placid wife made sure he was comfortable and admired his sermons, and on the few occasions when he consorted with his fellow clerics, he realised he was a luckier man than most.

Mr Southmoor had never met Purity Sorn, but her reasons for leaving Abbas St Antony had become well known. It was a sad story of human weakness and one which emphasised how important it was for the parents of daughters to maintain perpetual vigilance. He did not blame Purity Sorn for a weakness for which she had paid a heavy price, but if rumour was true and she had earned her living in the manner described, that was a very different matter.

Of course, the notorious Purity was dead and answerable to a far more powerful judge than Leofric Southmoor, but what sort of daughter could she have raised? He could well understand the concern of his parishioners. Licence and immorality might well have flourished at the court of the late King Charles, but they met with little approval in rural Devon.

The rector was a charitable man. He had already told those of his parishioners who had consulted him that perhaps they should not at this stage judge the daughter by the mother. He had pointed out that the stories of a French bawdy-house were by no means established fact and might very well turn out to be nothing but malicious gossip. The more he considered the matter, the more certain he felt that Mandala would not have returned had she not been intending to live quietly and discreetly in this secluded valley. She could not fail to be aware of her invidious position, and he rather thought they could expect her to be a modest and retiring female, anxious to earn their approval.

He was therefore more than somewhat taken aback at the vision that swept into the little morning-room to greet him. A great many adjectives sprang to his mind. Modest and retiring were not two of them.

Miss Sorn's darkly gleaming copper hair was curled closely to her head with one long ringlet tastefully arranged in conscious artlessness over one creamy shoulder. Huge baroque pearls hung from her ears and a single strand of large, almost symmetrically round ones encircled her throat. Her bodice and matching overskirt were of dark green satin, the latter looped up over a bronze brocade petticoat to fall in a short train behind. Fine Honiton lace formed the bertha collar that edged the wide neckline; the same lace outlined the bottom of the pointed bodice and edged the bottom of the petticoat before continuing up its central panel to unite the eye with the point of the bodice. The two-tiered puffs of the fine lawn sleeves were bound in with the same lace, and it edged the cuffs. A massive pearl-encircled emerald with a pendent emerald drop broke the half-moon of the bertha collar, but Miss Sorn wore no rings, only a small gold watch which hung from a chain round her wrist.

The rector was momentarily bereft of words. Quite oblivious of the effect she had created, Mandala bestowed upon him her forthright smile and her hand.

'Mr Southmoor? Mrs Swinbrook tells me you are our rector, though I should have guessed so from your bands. How do you do? It is most kind of you to call.'

He bowed over her fingers, wondering as he did so whether this extremely fashionable young lady expected an equally fashionable flourish from him.

'We were not advised of your return, Miss Sorn, but I felt it incumbent on me not to delay in paying my respects to the owner of Abbas Manor.'

'No one was advised of my intention to come here—it was a sudden whim—and I appreciate your diligence. I look forward to hearing you preach. Mrs Swinbrook tells me you preach a good sermon.'

Mr Southmoor blushed with pleasure. 'I'm glad my efforts are attended to so carefully. I have heard that you lived in France. Were you able to follow our Protestant religion? They say it is no longer as easy as it used to be.'

'So I believe. I had no problems, however: immediately prior to Maman's death, I was assisting at a Huguenot school,' Mandala told him, judging it wiser not to mention the fact that Maman had first placed her in a Catholic seminary and that the bulk of her education had been in the hands of nuns.

The rector brightened considerably. Assisting at a Huguenot school was beyond reproach. 'Your mother sent you away to be educated, then? She did not keep you with her?'

Mandala looked suitably shocked, and the rector quite failed to spot the warning gleam in her eyes as she realised his drift. 'No. She could not believe that a brothel—even a high-class brothel—was quite the right place to bring up her daughter. I have to confess that I think she was right, don't you.'

'Well, yes . . . Yes, of course. Most inappropriate.' He hesitated. 'Miss Sorn, forgive me for asking, but does this mean . . . Are the rumours true?'

'Quite possibly,' Mandala told him cheerfully. 'It all depends on what the rumours are. Enlighten me.'

Mr Southmoor was flustered. He was totally unaccustomed to such forthrightness in a female: it indicated a

lack of modesty that verged on the brazen. Furthermore, in view of her own remarks, his question only
really required an apologetic assent: 'Alas, I fear so',
perhaps, or: 'Sadly, I'm afraid they are'. No more was
required, and she must have known that, for she did not
seem to be a stupid woman. Yet she insisted on being
told the precise nature of the county gossip concerning
her mother. He cleared his throat and chose his words
with care. Miss Sorn, might be indelicate. There was no
need for him to be as well.

'It is said—I don't know where the story originated
—that after you were born, your mother settled in
France and earned her living in . . . by owning, I *should*
say, a . . . a house of ill-repute.'

Mandala looked shocked. 'Then rumour lied, Mr
Southmoor. I assure you that Maman's bawdy-house
was of the *highest* repute! She numbered some of the
most exalted in the land among her clientèle. The house
was most sumptuously appointed, she served excellent
food and wine and—of course—always ensured that her
girls were *clean*, if you take my meaning.'

The reverend gentleman did, all too clearly. Had the
woman no shame? This was far, far worse than he had
expected! Such a female in a small community would be
undesirable at the best of times. To have her installed in
the Manor, owner of most of the parish and a good part
of the neighbouring ones, in a position from which she
could be expected to exert a great deal of influence—all
this created a situation which he could only deplore,
knowing that his power to do anything about it was
minimal. He clutched at the only straw he could
see.

'Will you be staying here long. Miss Sorn? It is natural
that you should want to see your inheritance, of
course, but I imagine this quiet corner has little to
keep you here. London, I feel sure, is more to your
taste.'

Mandala smiled. 'London, like Paris, has so much to
offer, but, you know, one can grow a little weary of a
perpetual round of pleasure. I was only too glad to be
able to come here to repair the ravages of the capital's

excitement. No, Mr Southmoor. This quiet corner has much to be said in its favour, and I have no plans to depart in the foreseeable future.'

The rector's dismay at this declaration was very evident but he disguised it manfully, if not entirely successfully, and managed to smile. 'Then we must hope it doesn't disappoint you, Miss Sorn. I look forward to seeing you in church. Good day, mistress.'

'Good day, Mr Southmoor.' Mandala opened the door and asked Martha, who was waiting outside for just this eventuality, to show him to his horse.

When the old servant returned to the morning-room, she found her mistress inelegantly sprawled in a chair, wiping tears of laughter from her eyes with a lace-edged kerchief.

'Oh, Martha, have you ever seen anything so ludicrous as that man's face?'

Martha pursed her lips. 'Well may you laugh, miss,' she said grimly. 'I fear you've done yourself a lot of harm this day.'

'Were you listening at the keyhole?' Mandala demanded.

'Of course I was, and I take leave to tell you you behaved abominably. Goodness only knows what he'll tell the county!'

'Within two hours, I guarantee you, everyone will know the village is harbouring a veritable Jezebel.' It was a prospect that seemed to leave Mandala unperturbed.

'And who can blame him if he came to that conclusion? Perhaps it was right not to lie about your mother, but why lie about London and Paris? Your only experience of either city has been linked to business, and I didn't observe you to regard that as a perpetual round of pleasure. In fact, for a woman of fortune and beauty, I thought you were always unnecessarily restrained in your sampling of what the capitals had to offer. Why did you give him such a false impression, miss? Tell me that.'

Mandala shifted uneasily. 'It was his face when he first saw me,' she said. 'He didn't expect to see a woman dressed in the height of fashion, though why I should eschew fine clothes just because I don't enjoy fashionable society is beyond comprehension. He so obviously expected me to be quiet and submissive and . . . and *ashamed* of Maman—and I won't be, Martha. No one can approve of the manner in which she supported us, but can you think of anything else she could have done in the circumstances?'

'No, I can't, since a respectable marriage was out of the question, but that isn't the point, and you know it. Do you think anyone will receive you when they have heard the rector's account of this visit?'

'You underestimate human nature, Martha. Do you really think so wealthy an unmarried heiress will be left to languish in solitude for long? I think not. Sooner or later people will find it expedient to seek excuses for me, and to visit. Especially those with sons needing an eligible *partie*.'

'Maybe so, but if you take my advice, miss, you won't forgo food while you wait for that day.'

The members of Mandala's household were agreeably surprised with their new mistress. She made no unreasonable demands on them but expected their work to be accomplished quickly and thoroughly. She always phrased her instructions as a request, which left everyone with the pleasant sensation that they were doing her a favour, and she never forgot to thank them when a task had been completed. In only one respect did her behaviour fall short of that expected of a well-brought-up, unmarried, gentlewoman. She insisted on riding alone. To be sure, she always took a Spanish Pointer with her, and, as often as not, a hawk, but no one could regard either of these as adequate chaperons. She rode well and often fast, and there was no horse in the stables that could keep up with Fatima when Mandala chose to give the little mare her head. Mandala saw little pleasure to be gained from being obliged to hold back because an accompanying groom on some phlegmatic cob could not keep up.

Mandala had ridden briefly the day after her arrival,

declining Jonah Swinbrook's escort. 'No, Mr Swinbrook,' she had insisted. 'I prefer to find out for myself.
Later, when I am more familiar with the estate, you can
take me out and draw my attention to the things I ought
to know.'

Jonah had therefore been obliged to content himself
with describing to his mistress the limits of her land, and
being quietly grateful that it was not the sort of place
where untoward events occurred.

Mandala had ridden out more extensively on the
morning of Mr Southmoor's visit and saw no reason to
change an agreeable way of spending a morning. She
ordered Fatima to be saddled as usual and set out once
more, her Pointer at Fatima's heels and a hooded merlin
on her gauntlet. She intended to go further today and in
a direction with which she was not yet familiar, towards
the junction of the three great estates of the area. There
was some open country here, Jonah had told her, ideal
for hawking, and Mandala felt it was about time Kit had
some exercise.

Mandala was not the only person out riding that
morning. Deveril York, too, enjoyed that particular
pastime, though there was almost invariably some
underlying purpose to his rides. On this occasion he had
ensured that his host was still in bed and had set off
early to avoid arousing Sir Nuneham's curiosity, saddling and bridling Teufel, the huge near-black horse he
had brought with him from Hanover, himself, there
being no one stirring in the stables yet. Deveril York
deplored a master whose grooms knew they could lie in
with impunity, but there was no denying that such
slackness had its advantages. He had an appointment in
Lyme, and the fewer people who knew about it, the
better.

The bracken and the densely wooded slopes of the
combes made rapid travel impossible, and he contented
himself with keeping Teufel at a steady trot, only rarely
increased to a canter when they found themselves with a
clearing to cross. He rather thought he was on Abbas
Manor land, and noticed with approval that there was
plenty of game. But apart from the deer and pheasants

and the unmistakable—and nowadays extremely rare
—rooting-place of a wild boar, he saw no sign of life. It
was a more promising landscape than he had yet discovered, and one well worth inspecting more thoroughly.

He was deep in such considerations, with only half his
attention on his horse, when Teufel threw his head in the
air and whickered. Deveril reined him in and listened.
The horse was right. Something was moving in the
woods ahead. It was too large and clumsy for a deer. A
horse? It was the most likely explanation and a most
unwelcome one. Deveril York had no desire to be
observed, but he doubted whether he could now melt
quietly and unnoticed into the surrounding woods. If he
stayed quite still, there was a good chance that whatever
it was might cross their path some way ahead and
proceed without seeing them. Chance, which had
favoured him so long, deserted him now.

A familiar dainty bay mare, her coat gleaming and her
head and tail-set betraying her North African origins,
turned into his path and halted, suddenly startled, in
front of him. He recognised the rider immediately and
observed with a horseman's appreciative eye that she
had no difficulty controlling the sidling, head-tossing
little mare with one hand, as the hooded merlin on her
other gauntlet obliged her to do. The Spanish Pointer in
attendance, as elegant as the horse she accompanied,
avoided the oiled hooves with the ease of much practice.

Deveril's eye approved both dog and horse. It
appreciated still more the rider. Mandala's military-
styled riding-coat was of her favourite dark green, a
colour that set off her copper ringlets to perfection. The
facings of the turned-back cuffs and the lining were of a
dull gold brocade that matched the skirt, and both
colours were picked up again in the plumes of her
flat-crowned, broad-brimmed man's hat. In contrast to
this opulence, the linen at her neck was plain and her
gauntlets were expensively well made but essentially
workmanlike. It was the dress of a woman who loved
clothes but did not let fashion interfere with her sporting
pleasures.

He swept off his hat in the same exaggerated gesture

he had used when they had met before. 'Madam,' he
began, and then, glancing behind her and seeing no
groom, he added, 'You ride alone?'

Mandala coloured. This was, she acknowledged
ruefully, precisely the reason a young woman should
have an escort. 'My groom will soon have caught me up.'

His eyes narrowed imperceptibly. Instinct, coupled
with much experience of women, told him she lied. 'I
think not,' he said.

The accuracy of his opinion, to say nothing of the
speed with which he reached it, disconcerted Mandala
and increased her unease. Her discomfiture transmitted
itself to the already restless mare and to the merlin, who
shifted its position and lowered and raised its hooded
head, setting its bell tinkling. 'You must be a stranger
here, or you would know you trespass, sir. These woods
are not common-land.'

'Look to your horse, madam,' he advised her, ignoring her comment completely. 'If you will ride alone, at
least make sure which of you is in command.'

She flushed again. 'It will take more than Fatima to
unseat me,' she snapped. 'As to my riding alone, I have
already told you my groom is somewhere behind me,
and it is scarcely gentlemanly to call me a liar.'

'Had I thought you a lady, I should not have done so.'

Mandala gasped. 'How dare you, sir!'

He smiled, and it crossed Mandala's mind that he
must have been an exceedingly handsome man before
the ravages of a dissolute life etched their mark on his
now harsh features. 'If I am in error, I plead forgiveness.
I had assumed you were Mandala Sorn. Is that not so?'

The insulting implications of this remark made
Mandala angrier than ever, an anger exacerbated by the
fact that she could think of no sharp set-down that might
be calculated to reduce him to embarrassed discomfiture
—a condition with which she strongly suspected he was
unfamiliar. She drew herself up haughtily and lifted her
chin. 'I am Mandala Sorn, sir—and you trespass. This is
my land.'

'Good. I am relieved to learn that I haven't missed my
way.'

Mandala controlled her fury with an effort, managing to keep her voice coldly impersonal. 'Pray what is your business, Mr York, that it brings you on my land?' She knew she had succeeded in startling him, and although it had been unintentional, it was none the less satisfying for that.

'You know my name?'

'Should I not? You know mine,' she pointed out reasonably.

'There is a difference: it's only to be expected that word of the arrival of one of the largest landowners should have circulated with some speed.'

'Together with a character reference, it would appear,' Mandala added bitterly.

This time, when he smiled, Mandala thought she saw something approaching sympathy in his eyes, though it was of fleeting duration. 'Not so,' he said. 'I knew who the owner of this land was and guessed you must be she. In general you bear little resemblance to your mother, but you share one unforgettable feature: your hair.'

Mandala's eyes searched his face with an eagerness he found uncomfortably touching. 'You knew Maman?' she asked. 'If you knew her name was Sorn, you must have been acquainted with her before—before she went abroad.'

Deveril shifted slightly in his saddle. 'I'm afraid that was a pleasure that was denied me. I knew her in Paris, as Madame de Rouen. I don't recall precisely how I came to know her true name, though I was not aware she had a daughter. You were a secret she kept well—in France, at least.'

'But not in Devon, it seems,' Mandala said ruefully.

He looked at her unsmilingly for a while before speaking. 'It seems that I may have done you less than justice,' he said at last. 'Perhaps you'll forgive me enough to permit me to visit you?'

There was a stiffness in his manner of speaking that made Mandala wonder at first whether he was much accustomed to the social niceties. Then she recalled that Mr Leafield had described him as moving in the most fashionable circles, so that could not be the explanation.

'I'm not at all sure about forgiving you,' she said lightly, 'but I shall be happy to receive you. At least,' she added in a sudden impulse to be frank, 'I shall if you're going to be pleasant.'

'You can always have me shown the door if I'm not,' he pointed out.

'I can, can't I? Except that I've a suspicion that you wouldn't go through it unless you wanted to.' She was suddenly serious again. 'Will you be able to tell me about Maman?' she asked.

He seemed startled. 'I'm sure you know more about her than I can ever tell you.'

'Not necessarily. She sent me away to school, and I rarely saw her. I really know very little about her, and most of that is what my old nurse—who used to be her nurse, too—has told me. I know some of the facts, but I don't really know what she was *like*.'

He smiled grimly. 'I hardly think the characteristics of a brothel-keeper are a fitting topic of conversation in a lady's household.'

Mandala laughed. 'But much more interesting than the weather, don't you think?'

'I take leave to tell you that you've inherited her wit as well as her hair, Miss Sorn. I suggest, however, that you polish your remarks on the weather. In a rural community, it is the only important topic for convese.' He reined Teufel back. 'Good day, Miss Sorn. I hope your groom can find his way home, for he has surely lost his mistress.'

Mandala declined to acknowledge this sally, but her lips twitched. 'Good day, Mr York,' she said in her most demure voice, and, gathering up her reins, she urged Fatima past the big Hanoverian and on along the riding.

Deveril York watched her thoughtfully, making no attempt to continue on his way until she was out of sight. He would have preferred to have met no one, but at least it had been an encounter he had turned to his advantage. In visiting Mandala Sorn, he had as good a reason as there was for being on her land, and if, as seemed likely, she enjoyed riding, perhaps she would be happy to have congenial company. He smiled cynically to himself.

Deveril York was past master at making himself congenial when it suited his purpose, and it would be no punishment to make himself agreeable in that quarter. She was beautiful and had a ready wit, though perhaps the less she knew about the other side of her mother's business—and his connection with it—the better.

Mandala rode on, her mind no longer contemplating the pleasures of hawking. Her encounter with Deveril York had given her much to think about. He had apparently revised his initial unflattering estimate of her character, and although there was something about him that made her inclined to keep a certain distance between them, nevertheless she suspected he could be an amusing companion, and that was certainly something she lacked. She was sure she would be able, sooner or later, to coax from him small pieces of information about Maman, though she had to admit that his reaction to the suggestion had been less than promising. All the same, she was inclined to look forward to his visit.

She continued through the woods until she reached the open area Jonah had recommended for flying Kit, and it was as the bird came back to the lure for the second time that it occurred to her that she was no wiser as to Deveril York's reason for being on her land—or, indeed, in Devon—despite her questions. He had somehow managed to avoid answering them altogether while at the same time establishing quite a lot about her. The realisation gave her an uneasy feeling, and she finally resolved that when he did pay his promised visit, she would rectify the position. She would not again allow him to slide away from her questions.

CHAPTER THREE

THE REVEREND MR SOUTHMOOR had been shocked by what he regarded as Mandala's brazenness but was not as uncharitable as she had assumed. He spoke to no one of his visit until he had had time to discuss it with his wife, who, while she lacked intellect and imagination, was by no means lacking in common-sense.

'It certainly sounds quite dreadful—and very worrying,' Mrs Southmoor agreed. 'She has displayed a degree of indelicacy one can hardly approve, but can one entirely blame her, brought up as she has been in a milieu where boldness is admired?'

'I would be inclined to think that myself, my dear, except that she has been educated by Huguenots, and I've never heard that they approve of loose behaviour.'

'Still, her mother's influence must count for something,' his wife insisted. 'Perhaps, when she sees how different things are here, she will mend her ways. In any case, we can hardly ignore her, can we? She is Lord of the Manor, and even if she were not, it would be your duty, as rector, to bring her to a realisation of the error of her ways.'

'The lordship of the Manor is precisely where the problem lies. If she were simply someone who had taken a house here, she could be totally ignored and then there would be a good chance she would remove to another locality. As it is, a certain amount of deference is due her by virtue of her rank, and, frankly, I doubt she intends to mend her ways. I don't think she was even aware how unacceptable her behaviour was. I fear she must be received, if only to a limited extent, but I do not like it.'

'To be sure, one would wish to keep the children away from her,' his wife agreed. 'Children have such a distressing predilection for undesirable acquaintants. All the same, we should give her the benefit of the doubt. I think we must be very circumspect in our comments on the subject to others.'

Unfortunately, too much circumspection creates its own speculation, and speculation is the mother of rumour and gossip. The rector was an honest man who was known for his truthfulness and his integrity. He could not tell an outright lie, but the words in which he told the truth were so carefully chosen that his hearers had no difficulty in putting their own conclusions to them, and, being less charitable than the rector, these were less kind.

It was noticed, too, that the tone of his sermons changed. No longer were his parishioners warned against the perils of Sodom and Gomorrah and exhorted to turn their backs on Babylon. Instead, the rector seemed preoccupied with the far less exciting texts of the Sermon on the Mount. Loving your enemy was all very well, at least in theory, but to give your cloak to a man who already had your coat—that was plain foolishness. If the rector had to go to such lengths not to offend the fashionable Miss Sorn, then she must have much to hide.

It was unthinkable, of course, that anyone should set their servants to find out more or to listen to any gossip that found its way into the kitchen, but nevertheless it was soon common knowledge that the Sorn household was reluctant to be drawn into commenting upon its new mistress. She lived well, but the Sorns always had, so that was not news. She dressed in the height of fashion, but anyone with half an eye could see that for himself. She took great pleasure in her horses and dogs, but that, too had been independently observed. She was a fair mistress, and so long as you got on with the tasks allotted to you, she did not interfere. This was very laudable, no doubt, but it was not what people wanted to learn. There was no news of any fine visitors from London and, if orgies were held, they must have been very restrained affairs, for the servants were obviously unaware of them.

This was all very disappointing, but there was enough reticence in the various accounts to suggest that there must be *something* going on to warrant a general verdict that Miss Sorn was not a respectable acquaintance and that, therefore, Lord of the Manor or not, she would not be received though she must be acknowledged. The decision was arrived at by the women over the chocolate cups that sustained them during their morning calls. Many husbands, observing Miss Sorn in her pew on Sundays, hoped that their wives would relax their condemnation of her and allow an exchange of visits. To their wives, this was a sure indication of the dangers of even the slightest association with a Jezebel.

But Mandala's greatest offence in the eyes of her neighbours, and the one which most surely earned their condemnation, was that she seemed oblivious of both their opinion and the social ostracism she endured. She appeared in church regularly, and her rank ensured that she left the building first. She was always affable, and if the Lord of the Manor bade you 'Good day'—as this one made a point of doing—the courtesy had to be returned. She gave no sign of being aware of their disapproval and even less sign that her social isolation might induce her to leave the neighbourhood. Anyone of such hardened insensitivity must be brazen indeed. No one could quite recall who had first had the wit to dub her a Scarlet Woman, but the term fitted their estimate of her sufficiently well to stick.

There was one person who regretted more than most that Miss Sorn was not received by the county's polite society, and that was Deveril York's host. Sir Nuneham Courtenay could not, as an unmarried man, visit her himself, and the general opinion of Miss Sorn prevented his permitting his young sister Isobel from making such a visit and therefore obliging him to accompany her. That Isobel would pay a visit if he told her to, he did not doubt, but he could not afford to have her associate with anyone whose acquaintance might lower her value in the marriage stakes.

The owner of Courtenay Place was twenty-eight and had inherited the baronetcy and its not inconsiderable wealth some dozen years before. Until he attained his majority, the stewardship of his estates had been impeccably discharged by his maternal uncle, and he came of age a wealthier young man than he had been at his father's death. At twenty-one, his fortune had seemed limitless. If ever there was a man destined to lead the fashionable world, it was he.

To start off as he meant to go on, he pulled down the old timbered house that had been home to generations of Courtenays and built in its place a baroque pile of Purbeck 'marble' which, while it was certainly impressive, was also cold, draughty and far too big to be comfortable. He was immensely proud of it, though Isobel, in common with most people who saw it, loathed it. Having built his house, it behoved him to furnish it appropriately, and the expense of these activities— added to the expense of his own wardrobe, his frequent visits to London and his marked lack of good fortune with cards, dice or horses—resulted in the limits of his fortune not only becoming rapidly apparent but also rapidly reached.

Isobel's dowry was beyond his reach—their late father had seen to that—but it was not huge. If she was to attract a husband sufficiently wealthy to please her brother, her reputation must be beyond the slightest vestige of reproach. He had initially thought that the arrival in Abbas St Antony of the unmarried heiress of the Sorn estates might offer another and more satisfactory solution to his problems. Sir Nuneham was sure that Mandala, could he but put it to her, would be the first to see the value of uniting their estates. So fashionable a wife would be a great asset: she would adorn Courtenay Place as few other women could do, and if he could but meet her in the usual way of paying and receiving calls, he knew she could not fail to admire his own virtues.

If Sir Nuneham had been asked to detail these virtues, the list would have surprised the rector. He considered himself handsome, and his collection of wigs must surely be the largest in Devon—and in Dorset, too, in all probability. He dressed to perfection and his small-linen was always well starched. He threw a very accomplished bow, showed to advantage in the dance and was no mean swordsman—or so his fencing-master assured him. What more could a woman ask? He was quite happy to overlook the unfortunate circumstances of Mandala's birth and her early life with a magnanimity that was more than compensated for by her fortune. In short, he had no difficulty in convincing himself that Mandala could count herself lucky if she had an offer from one such as he. It was very irksome to be obliged to reflect that there was a certain amount of difficulty attached to offering for a woman to whom one was unlikely to have the opportunity of saying more than 'Good day' as she entered or left the church.

Until he found a way of overcoming that slight problem, it remained a matter of some urgency to see his sister suitably settled. It bothered him not one whit that their opinions of what was suitable had nothing in common except Isobel's agreement that she would not be happy with a pauper. Sir Nuneham was unconcerned that her seventeen-year-old fancy was taken with young Mark Haddenham. She would soon outgrow that childish preference, and, besides, the family was Puritan and therefore quite unacceptable. The Haddenhams were warm enough, he supposed—Puritans often were—but he was looking for more than that. What Isobel needed was a husband with the breeding to be acceptable at Court and the income to support it. She was a biddable girl. If the right man could be pushed to the sticking-point, she would do as she was told and be perfectly happy. In his guest, Deveril York, he rather thought he had found that man.

Sir Nuneham looked out of his study window at the tall figure who was bending attentively towards his slight, fair-haired sister as they strolled along the terrace outside. Deveril York's wealth was reputedly vast, though you would not think so to look at him. The quality and cut of his clothes were always impeccable, even if he wore simple styles with few ribbons and the minimum of lace. He always wore his own hair and the red heels of his shoes were rarely more than an inch high. Not that he needed to enhance his height, Sir Nuneham thought enviously.

No one seemed to know how Deveril York had acquired his fortune, but he was accepted everywhere and was known to have been a close friend of the late King. It was a little strange that he was prepared to leave the fashionable scene for weeks on end—something Sir Nuneham would not have dreamed of doing. People came across him in France and the Low Countries, in Hanover, Hesse and Saxony, but friendly enquiries as to what he was doing there were turned off with a laugh and a joking comment, and the enquirer was home again before he realised he had been told nothing.

So much more exalted were the circles in which Deveril moved, that Sir Nuneham had been somewhat surprised when the older man had sought him out. The baronet knew himself to be very popular among the young fops of society. He had a genius second to none when it came to advising where to place a ribbon, but Deveril York was no fop and had always seemed to hold that section of society in small esteem. He had approached the younger man at a masque.

'They tell me you've built a fine baroque house, Courtenay,' he said. 'Almost a palace, I was told.'

Sir Nuneham demurred. 'Hardly that, though it's kind of people to say so. It pleases me, however, and many of my friends have expressed admiration of it.'

'It's a style I like myself,' Deveril said. 'Would you recommend your architect?'

Sir Nuneham blushed with pleasure. 'It is flattering of you to ask, but I can hardly do so—I designed it myself, you see.'

'A man of unexpected talents! I should hardly wish to do that myself, however.'

'It would be inadvisable unless you have made a study of the style. There is always Wren, of course. He might suit you. I had originally intended to employ him myself but we didn't altogether see eye to eye on some matters —his style is a little too restrained—and I must say that I've never regretted my decision.'

'I'm sure you haven't. Tell me about it.'

Sir Nuneham needed no further encouragement, and if Deveril York had not had an ulterior motive in furthering his acquaintance with the baronet, he would have been hard put to it to maintain his polite façade in the course of the younger man's barrage of cornices, columns and caryatids. His interest appeared undiminished, and Sir Nuneham's concluding flourish, which included an invitation to come down to Devon and see for himself, was accepted with as much alacrity as courtesy permitted, and not a little relief.

It was only later that it occurred to Sir Nuneham that he had been given a heaven-sent opportunity to further his sister's interests, and it was but a short step from that realisation to wonder whether perhaps York's unwontedly seeking him out like that might not betoken an interest on that gentleman's part in rather more than Courtenay Place. Deveril York was, after all, of an age when he must be considering acquiring a wife and producing legitimate heirs, and although his name had, from time to time, been linked with a succession of notable high-fliers, no sensible man would have considered any of them suitable for a more permanent contract. A discreetly reared, biddable girl of excellent breeding and comfortably dowered was a very different matter, and Sir Nuneham had no doubt that, once they were in each other's company, his guest would need no prompting to see this for himself if, indeed, it were not already in his mind. Nor did he doubt that so dashing a figure as Deveril York's would soon remove thoughts of Mark Haddenham from his sister's mind.

Deveril had not objected to being thrown discreetly together with his host's sister and had already extended his visit beyond the length warranted by a desire to see the house. This was a very hopeful sign, and Sir Nuneham was delighted to encourage his guest's readiness to walk with Isobel on the terrace, to ride with her (with Sir Nuneham as chaperon, naturally), even though Isobel disliked riding and was only barely competent, and to invite her participation in their conversation. Sir Nuneham had been somewhat disconcerted to learn that his guest was in the habit of riding alone at some unearthly hour in the morning and wondered if there might not be some implicit criticism of the quality of the company he and his sister could offer. It was not at all *comme il faut*, but extremely rich men were said to acquire and indulge such eccentricities and this one at least caused no one any inconvenience. So, beyond remarking upon it once or twice and receiving no explanation, he chose to ignore it. Less easy to ignore was the indisputable fact that Isobel disliked Deveril. Sir Nuneham deplored his sister's opinion and drew some comfort from the fact that at least she kept it hidden from their guest. He reminded himself that further acquaintance with York could only serve to change her mind, and did what he could to bring about that happy state of affairs.

In fact, Deveril frightened Isobel Courtenay. She was accustomed to the bluff straightforwardness of the Devon yeomen who formed the greater part of their acquaintance and with the elegant, superficial fops that were her brother's chosen friends. Deveril York came into neither category, and she wished he would go back to London or wherever else he came from. She had never met anyone quite like him, and was glad of it. Deveril was unfailingly courteous, but he made her feel like a child; there was often a sardonic glint in his eye which she neither liked nor trusted. She was reluctant to talk in his company because she always had the feeling she was saying something foolish, and, looking up at the harsh lines of his face, it occurred to her that she would not wish to see him angry. Nuneham had made it perfectly clear that he considered Deveril an ideal husband. Isobel could only hope that Mr York had no desire to take a wife who was a foolish child.

Having observed Deveril's behaviour towards his sister, Sir Nuneham felt the time was right to broach the subject. 'Devilish nice girl, m'sister,' he said casually one evening as they sat over a fine Armagnac.

'Devilish?' Deveril remarked. 'Hardly a felicitous word, surely?'

Sir Nuneham flushed. York had an unpleasant ability to make one feel *gauche*. 'Perhaps not, but what do you think of her?'

'Very prettily behaved,' Deveril said politely.

'So she should be. Very well brought up. Sticklers for

that, my parents were—and my uncle and aunt. She has a comfortable dowry, too.'

'So I should imagine. You must be very pleased.'

'It means I'll have no difficulty in getting her suitably settled.'

'I'm sure you won't.'

'Young enough to be biddable—and she's lived retired here. No fancy ideas. Of course, I may decide to take her to London, but I wouldn't be sorry to be able to accept an offer without that.'

'It's always a chancy business, exposing a pretty and well-dowered girl to the fashionable world,' Deveril agreed.

'Quite a responsibility, in fact.'

'Precisely.'

Deveril was disconcertingly unforthcoming, but Sir Nuneham had more sense than to push the issue. He diverted it to his own concerns instead.

'Thinking along those lines myself, as a matter of fact,' he confided.

'Indeed? It's certainly something every man has to consider.'

'I'd like an heir to the title—and a mistress to adorn Courtenay Place.'

'It's certainly the only adornment that's lacking,' Deveril said, in a tone from which he managed to expunge every trace of sarcasm.

'It is, isn't it?' Sir Nuneham replied happily. 'The finishing touch, the crowning glory, that's what Lady Courtenay needs to be.'

'You have someone in mind?'

Sir Nuneham hesitated. 'I have and I haven't. That's to say, I have my eye on someone, but meeting her —that's the problem.'

'For a man of your address? Surely not!'

'You'd think so, wouldn't you?' Sir Nuneham took the compliment at face value. 'Thing is, she has a somewhat . . . murky past.'

'Intriguing.'

'Very beautiful, of course. Mother came from a good local family. Purity Sorn. Won't mean anything to you.'

Sir Nuneham paused and glanced at his guest, but he saw nothing in Deveril's expressionless face to disabuse him of his assumption. 'Omitted to marry the father, whoever he was, but that's not the problem—our late monarch made that sort of thing almost respectable. Mother supported herself by running a brothel—a very high-class brothel. In France, they say, but in this remote spot that might well signify Cornwall.'

'Not if it was high class,' Deveril pointed out. 'The fashionable world doesn't go to Cornwall.'

'True. It's not too willing to come to Devon,' Sir Nuneham agreed a trifle bitterly. 'Wherever it was, I don't hold it against the daughter, but she's not received, and I certainly can't ask Isobel to call.'

'Hardly,' Deveril agreed. 'Beautiful, you said?'

'Ravishingly.'

'And wealthy, no doubt?'

Sir Nuneham twisted uneasily. It was hardly in his own interest to let Deveril York know how necessary a wealthy wife—or brother-in-law—had become. Nor, since rich men were never averse to increasing their wealth, did he want to put ideas into his guest's mind of marriage to anyone but his sister. 'As to that, I couldn't say. Comfortable, I suppose, but she seems to live quietly. Dresses well,' he added hastily, in case he had conjured up a picture of a retiring dowd. It was perhaps just as well that York had never yet returned from one of those early morning rides in time to attend the parish church. At least he had not seen Mandala Sorn for himself.

Deveril York was not deceived, but he was considerably amused. He had a very fair idea of the considerations flitting through his host's mind, and he knew how annoyed Sir Nuneham would be if he knew that he had already made Mandala's acquaintance and, moreover, had received permission to visit. He had not done so yet, though he had every intention of it, and he rather thought it might prove amusing to cut the ground from under his host's feet. Deveril had not come to this God-forsaken corner of the kingdom to find a wife any more than he had the slightest interest in Baroque

architecture, and he had every intention of keeping his
true purpose to himself. If he ever did marry, money
would not be his criterion—and neither, for that matter,
would beauty. In his experience, beautiful women were
invariably mercenary. In so far as he had given the
matter of a wife much thought, he was looking for
something else, something more, though he would have
been hard put to it to define it.

Whatever it might be, he certainly had not found it in
Isobel Courtenay. A pretty child, but a child, and one
who was far too easily persuaded to agree to whatever
point of view one put forward. It had not taken Deveril
long to realise that Sir Nuneham had had an ulterior
motive in inviting him. The knowledge perturbed him
not at all, it served to put them on a level footing, but he
soon suspected that Isobel feared him and he had toyed
briefly with the idea of charming her out of her dislike.
He had rejected the idea almost as soon as it had
occurred to him. He had not the slightest intention of
offering for the sister in order to relieve the brother of
his financial embarrassments, and he had never been
one to break hearts just for the fun of it. Far better if she
continued to fear him. He had other fish to fry, and all he
was sure of at the moment was that the Courtenay estate
was no place to do it.

The biggest set-back he had experienced since coming
here had been to learn that Sir Nuneham and his admit-
tedly rather distant neighbour, Nathaniel Haddenham,
were not on visiting terms. Since the latter was a well-
known Puritan who had been reported as having been
critical of King James, it was hardly likely that the two
men should have had much in common, but Deveril had
hoped, even assumed, that at least visits would be
exchanged. That this was not so had been confirmed by
Isobel, whose increased restraint when he had once
dropped the name into the conversation was enough to
tell him that distance was not the only reason for the
breach between the families.

Be that as it may, it was imperative he should have
converse with Nathaniel Haddenham—and soon, as his
recent visit to Lyme had established. So, if there were to

be no visits by the Courtenays which he might reasonably have been expected to accompany, he would have to make his own. It was because he had foreseen the possible need to move about the county without his host's knowledge that he had established the practice of riding alone before his host came down. Nothing could have pleased Deveril more than the discovery, on his first morning at Courtenay Place, that Sir Nuneham considered mid-day a good time to emerge from his room, even though, when he did so, it was evident that he must have awoken at a reasonable hour: an appearance such as Sir Nuneham presented was not achieved in anything under an hour and a half. The Courtenay household had therefore become quite used to seeing their guest ride out at an early hour, and by the end of a week he knew the estate as well as its owner and was fairly familiar with much of the adjoining land.

A visit to Haddenham Hall, urgent as it might be, required a certain amount of careful planning: it was desirable that no one should know where he was going, and the distance involved made it as necessary for him to leave as early as on his recent visit to Lyme. He had been fortunate to have been unobserved—at least by anyone from Courtenay Place—on that occasion, but Deveril York was not a man to pin the result he wanted on the whim of luck. He was fortunate in that Sir Nuneham, having broached successfully—as he thought—the matter of his sister's suitability as a wife, was in an expansive mood that evening and was very happy to extend the usual post-prandial entertainment of brandy and cards sufficiently far into the following morning to guarantee that the baronet would sleep later than usual. Sir Nuneham would be unaware of the precise time of his guest's departure, and, although there was always the chance that one of the grooms might be up and about, it was so slight that Deveril felt it was worth taking. On his previous occasion he had been up before even his own man. Today Denham was already hard at work.

'Saddle him up,' Deveril said. 'He'll do as he is.'

The groom shook his head and flicked a piece of dust from the horse's rump as if to indicate his disapproval, but he fetched the heavy saddle none the less. It was wiser not to argue with Deveril York. 'Do I need to fence questions?' he asked.

'You may: I've a long ride ahead, and I doubt I'll be back this side of noon. Best to say you think I've gone to see a horse I'd heard of that might suit—but don't say anything unless you have to.'

The man nodded, and then permitted himself the ghost of a grin. 'Would that be a Puritan horse, Mr York?'

Deveril smiled grimly. 'Let's just say it's a dark one, Denham. I only hope it suits my purpose.'

Nathaniel Haddenham received his visitor with courtesy but little pleasure. His arrival was not entirely unexpected. The name of Deveril York was well known in some circles though rarely uttered, and his presence at Courtenay Place—apparently to cast his eye over its owner's sister—was no secret. When he had heard of it, Mr Haddenham had suspected that Isobel Courtenay might be the excuse rather than the reason. He rather thought this call would reinforce that view.

'You are welcome, sir,' he said, a shade stiffly. 'Does your host know of this visit?'

Deveril smiled blandly. 'Sir Nuneham is a late riser, and I ride out alone most mornings. My departure today will have occasioned no comment, and no one is aware of my destination.'

'A tattle-monger who links my name to that of Deveril York is something I can well do without,' the older man told him bluntly.

'You live quietly here, and few people outside the county know of you,' Deveril commented.

'And those few who do are the very ones I should prefer to remain in ignorance,' Haddenham retorted. 'I was brought up a Puritan, and a Puritan I remain at heart. The restoration of the monarchy was inevitable and I accepted it as such, though I deplore the laxity of much of modern life that has followed it. I make no secret of my opposition to the Papist cause. Consequently, whenever some hothead devises a plot, my name is mentioned. Now we have a Catholic king and he is—inevitably, I suppose—easing the position of his co-religionists. I cannot like this and I fear what it may lead to. If his Portuguese wife should produce a son, we stand to have Catholicism re-established on these shores. It is no secret that I should prefer to see the Protestant daughters by his first wife succeed him, and that is the view of many in this area.'

Deveril inclined his head in acknowledgment of the accuracy of this. 'To what extent does your support of the Princesses go?' he asked.

Nathaniel Haddenham looked at him, carefully schooling his expression so that it revealed nothing. 'I stop short at treason,' he said.

'And if there were another, legitimate, claimant to the throne who was also a Protestant?'

'In place of James? Or his daughters?'

'James.'

'You refer to Monmouth, of course. He cannot prove that his mother married the late King, and Charles himself denied it, though he never denied he sired the boy. How, then, can Monmouth have a legitimate claim?'

'Charles had little choice but to deny a marriage to Lucy Walters—he needed the political union that Catherine of Braganza offered, and it could hardly take place if there had been an existing arrangement. You can't gainsay that, apart from that denial, young Monmouth has been treated exactly as his heir.'

'And has plans above his station as a result,' Haddenham said flatly. 'Learn the lessons of history, York. Usurpers in this country do not usually succeed.'

'So your objection is largely on the grounds of expedience, and you might feel differently were he assured of success?' Deveril asked.

Nathaniel Haddenham paced his hall in silence for some moments. 'No, I think not,' he said at last. 'He's handsome and charming, by all accounts, but ill advised and easily persuaded—not good traits in a monarch. The Princess Mary, on the other hand, is married to a strong Protestant ruler. Stadtholder William is an able man. He's made his United Provinces a force to be reckoned with in the Low Countries.'

'You would support their claim to the succession?'

'After James, yes,' Haddenham said cautiously. 'I'll not support anything that could lead to another civil war. I was only a child during the last one, but I remember it vividly.'

'Thank you for your frankness, Mr Haddenham. I see no reason why you need become embroiled in political events, but I'm sure your future support will be very welcome, perhaps when Nature has run its course.'

'You may tell your master that I'll support him on the throne, but I'll not support a rebellion to put him there.'

Deveril did not let his annoyance show. Nathaniel Haddenham might live retired in Devon, but he had far too shrewd a grasp of what was going on. How much of it was intelligent guesswork and how much he was the quiet recipient of things that should not be known, Deveril did not know. It would be easy to underestimate the old man, and he would do well to remember that. He must take care to give him no hint of the extent of William's deviousness.

His thoughts were interrupted by the appearance of Mark Haddenham, a slightly-built young man of twenty-three or four with a pleasant, fresh face and clothes that, while workmanlike, carried indications that he did not take his Puritanism quite as far as his father.

'I heard we had a visitor from Courtenay Place,' he said, though his face had clouded when he saw Deveril as if he had expected someone else.

'Mr York was riding this way and, having strayed on to our land, felt he should introduce himself. Mr York —my son, Mark.'

Deveril smiled. 'I have heard of you. Miss Courtenay has more than once referred to you. Always with approbation,' he added hastily.

The younger man flushed.

'Iso—Miss Courtenay is very kind. We have known each other since childhood, you understand.'

'I imagined that to be the case.'

'It is said you are come to Courtenay Place to offer for

her.' There was a defensiveness in the young man's tone
that Deveril entirely understood.

'Gossip should never be entirely believed! A charming girl, but very young, and a trifle . . . restrained.'

'She has not been about in the world very much,'
Mark said, springing to her defence.

So that was how the wind lay, Deveril thought. They
would suit well, though he doubted whether the parent
of the one and the brother of the other would agree.
'That would account for it,' he said smoothly. A glance
at Nathaniel's face told him his guess had not been far
out, and gave him an excellent opportunity to change the
subject.

'There is one thing on which you can enlighten me,' he
said mendaciously. 'The other day, when I was riding, I
encountered a most striking young woman on an almost
equally striking little mare. Dressed in the very height of
fashion, but unattended, and with only a merlin and a
Pointer for company.'

'Mandala Sorn!' Mark exclaimed, a mischievous gleam
in his eye. 'Devon's Scarlet Woman, I'd have you know.
Isn't she a beauty? Rich, too. Such a pity she's not
received!'

'That's enough, Mark,' his father said repressively,
frowning. 'Don't condemn a lady's reputation so freely.'

'Oh, come, Father. She's already been condemned by
every tabby in the county! I've said nothing that Mr
York won't be told elsewhere.'

'Sadly, that's true,' the older man reflected. 'The girl
has had no opportunity to be taken for herself. She has
been judged entirely by her mother.'

'Is that quite fair, Father? She's given no indication of
feeling a need to atone for her mother, and as a result she
has antagonised people who might have been willing to
overlook the past.'

'You make me curious,' Deveril said. 'You can't drop
the subject now, you know. What's this woman's story?'

'She is the bastard daughter of Purity Sorn, who
inherited Abbas Manor and its estates several years
ago,' Nathaniel told him.

'Sorn,' Deveril interrupted him. 'Don't I know that

name? A Puritan family, I believe?'

'Very much so, but there's nothing of the Puritan about this Sorn. I doubt if she has a political thought in her head, and if she does, it is unlikely to favour anything that might lead to a return of Protestant zeal.'

There was an irony in Haddenham's voice that intimated to Deveril that he had known very well what lay behind his visitor's question. He chose to ignore it and to continue as if his sole interest were in Miss Sorn herself. 'Is it known who her father was?' he asked.

'No, but her mother was sent away, and left the country shortly after her daughter's birth. That much is undisputed fact. The rumour has always been that she set herself up as the madam of a brothel in France and made her fortune. Be that as it may, she certainly doesn't seem to have married, and she equally certainly made a fortune far in excess of that which she inherited with the Manor. It almost makes one wonder whether she had another string to her bow in Paris. At all events, she had the decency never to appear here herself, leaving the estates to the stewardship of Jonah Swinbrook, who was overseen by the family's London attorneys. She died recently, and the daughter, having apparently put her affairs in order in France, has descended upon the Manor and taken up residence there.'

'As she has every right to do,' Deveril commented.

'Quite. The problem that has arisen is two-fold. First, she gave no prior warning of her intent to come here. Had she done so, people would have had time to adjust to the idea. Second, as Mark has indicated, there has been nothing in her bearing or her manner calculated to soothe ruffled feathers. She dresses in the height of fashion, as you have yourself observed; she carries herself with a self-assurance unusual in unmarried females; and at no time has she intimated that her mother's actions were in any way reprehensible, let alone sinful. The rector called on her in the spirit of a Christian extending a welcome, and was thunderstruck by the brazen way in which she not only admitted that her mother *had* run a bawdy-house but proceeded to expand upon the high quality of its clientèle and the care her mother took to ensure the continued good health of her customers.' To Deveril's surprise, Nathaniel Haddenham chuckled. 'I must confess I should very much like to have been a fly on the wall when that little morsel was conveyed to Southmoor's ears. His face would have been an entertainment in itself.'

'Was she being deliberately provocative?'

'Quite possibly. It has resulted in her almost total ostracism, though I'm bound to say that it doesn't seem to worry her at all.'

Deveril was thoughtful for a few moments. He wondered just how much was known about Purity Sorn's bawdy-house in this remote valley, and hoped it would prove to be only as much as her daughter had revealed. 'I don't suppose you know any more about this bawdy-house?' he said. 'Whereabouts it was, for instance?'

Nathaniel hesitated. 'A little. The ill-feeling was such that I have been able to instigate a few rapid enquiries. Miss Sorn's claims seem to be entirely true. It was in Paris, in the rue des Flandres, and the clientèle could scarcely have been more exalted.'

Deveril frowned. Haddenham's enquiries had been to some effect, and in a remarkably short time, too. For a man who lived in a backwater, he maintained a highly efficient source of information. Deveril almost envied him. 'It sounds as if she must have been Madame de Rouen,' he suggested.

Nathaniel permitted himself the ghost of a smile. 'I rather thought you would know it,' he said. 'I gather she was very discreet.'

'I imagine, in that business, she would need to be, wouldn't you?' Mark butted in, surprised that his father should think such a thing merited comment.

Deveril smiled. 'In Madame de Rouen's line of business, discretion would be essential.' He stood up. 'And now I shall take my leave. It would never do to allow Sir Nuneham to send out a search-party. Mr Haddenham, Mark: your servant.'

Deveril York had far more to occupy his mind on the return journey than he had expected to have when he set out that morning. He had been led to understand that

Nathaniel Haddenham was an elderly Puritan who could easily be persuaded to lend his land to the support of any cause that would dislodge a Catholic monarch. Well, he was certainly an elderly Puritan, but he was not only fully aware that there were two ways of achieving the desired end, but also which of them was the more likely to be successful, and why. There was no question of his becoming embroiled in any scheme, and certainly not in this one of Stadtholder William. Nathaniel Haddenham's comments seemed almost to suggest that he himself had a highly efficient, if perhaps informal, system of gathering information.

He had obviously got wind of Monmouth's plans, though not of the part William was playing in furthering them. The rebellion planned by Monmouth and Argyll was doomed to failure, but its failure would achieve two ends: it would remove a claimant to the throne while at the same time providing the first ripples of Protestant agitation that could, with careful manipulation, become the flood that would bring William and his wife to power. Deveril's visit was ostensibly on Monmouth's behalf. Certainly that was what the Duke himself believed. He played a dangerous game. No one must guess that in promoting an uprising that would be initially successful, he was also promoting the Stadtholder's long-term interest. Proven complicity with either side would see him hanged by the King.

That Haddenham had his own sources of information was further borne out by the amount he had gleaned concerning Mandala Sorn. She had been in Devon a relatively short time, and it had taken more than one or two idle questions to find out as much as Haddenham had done. He kept sheep, he traded in wool. He must have contacts through the Staple. Whatever the explanation, his contacts were efficient and accurate. It reinforced Deveril's belief that he should not be underestimated.

And what about Mandala Sorn? Deveril smiled. He had intended to pursue the acquaintance, partly to annoy Sir Nuneham, partly because it might prove useful. Now he was determined to. He had little choice.

Haddenham had made it perfectly clear that he would play no part in forthcoming events, and time was getting short. Deveril needed to form an opinion of Mandala Sorn's loyalties—or lack of them, which was sometimes far more useful. She might prove to be as willing to help as her mother, but if not, or if he judged it inadvisable to let her know what was in the wind, her help would have to be involuntary. So far as he could judge from what he had seen of Abbas Manor so far, it was ideally suited for his purpose. Better acquaintance with its owner would confirm that opinion—or not, as the case might be. It would certainly be no penance to find out. Mandala was unquestionably beautiful, and he had formed the impression she was also intelligent. She must certainly be feeling the lack of congenial company. Who better to remedy that lack than Deveril York, who knew very well how to make himself congenial?

He shortened the reins and pressed his calves into his horse's sides. Teufel broke into a canter. The visit to Haddenham Hall had not been the success he had hoped, but neither had it been a disaster. He had once heard a seaman declare that when things went wrong on board ship, the thing to do was to tie a knot and go on. Mandala Sorn was going to be Deveril's knot.

CHAPTER FOUR

MANDALA RECEIVED THE neatly folded slip of paper with some surprise. 'A gentleman, you say?'

The serving-girl bobbed a curtsy. 'Yes, miss. He says as how you knows him, and he's come to pay his respects.' Her eyes shone. This was the first courtesy call Miss Sorn had received since the rector departed with a very red face. Such a distinguished-looking gentleman, too. The one who was said to be staying at Courtenay Place, unless Joan was very much mistaken. Not that she had ever seen him before but she had heard him described, and there could not be two such, not in Abbas St Antony. She could not wait to get back to the kitchen to tell them. Perhaps it meant that Miss Sorn was going to be accepted, after all.

With a curiosity as great as the servant's but with a far greater talent for hiding it, Mandala unfolded the paper. There were just two words inscribed on it. 'Deveril York.' So his request for permission to visit had not been mere civility. Her spirits rose, because, no doubt, of the prospect of conversing with someone whose horizons were not limited to the laundry, the dairy or the stables.

'Show him into the morning-room, Joan.'

'I've done so, Miss Sorn.'

'Good. Send Martha to me, please.'

'She's gone down to the village. Won't be back yet awhile, I don't reckon.'

'Mrs Swinbrook, then.'

'She's busy in the dairy. The new dairymaid needs watching all the time—don't seem able to remember the simplest thing.'

Mandala hesitated. She rather thought Deveril York had begun to revise his original impression of her. If she entertained him without a chaperon, he might well revert to his original opinon, and she did not want that. Nor had she any desire to send him away. The people of

Abbas St Antony might have assumed that Mandala
Sorn did not care whether she was received or not, but
the truth was, she did care. Depending upon one's own
company could lead to a very lonely existence. If
she sent her visitor away now, he might not return.
Besides, he had known Maman, so there was no need to
dissemble, quite apart from the fact that her short
acquaintance with him suggested that he might be an
entertaining visitor. There were other servants, of
course, but Mandala could place no dependence on their
ability not to gossip about what they heard, and she had
no desire to learn that anything she was told about her
mother had become common knowledge.

'Very well,' she said at last. 'Ask whichever of them is
first able to do so, to come to the morning-room.'

'I could come, miss,' Joan said helpfully and
hopefully.

'Thank you, but it won't be necessary. You have your
own tasks. Mr York is an old acquaintance, and I don't
think he will be too deeply offended if his reception is a
little lacking in ceremony.' Mandala reflected that, if the
first statement was an exaggeration, the second was
almost certainly true and that, taken together, they
should satisfy Joan. If the maid had any further doubts,
they should be assuaged when Mandala immediately left
the room to welcome her visitor, clearly in no doubt
herself.

As she swept into the morning-room, carefully leaving
the door open, Deveril turned from the window through
which he had been surveying the knot-garden, removed
his hat, and swept her his customary exaggerated
bow.

'Miss Sorn—unattended again, I see.'

'My household is busy. We don't expect morning
calls, so everyone is occupied. The open door is all the
protection I need.'

'You're perfectly safe without an attendant, Miss
Sorn. I haven't the slightest intention of seducing
you—not at this hour of the day.'

'You reserve that activity for the afternoon, I dare
say.'

He laughed. 'I was right. You're no tedious simpering miss!'

'Did you expect one?'

'I was more than half afraid you might choose to play the conventional unmarried maiden.'

'If that had been my intention, I should hardly have entered the room without my maid,' Mandala pointed out.

'Very true, though I observe you are not sufficiently inclined to throw convention to the winds to close the door.'

'A degree of unconventionality is one thing, Mr York. Foolhardiness is quite another.'

'I stand rebuked. Miss Sorn, when we previously met, I was remiss. I was aware that your mother was quite recently dead and failed to offer my condolences. Please accept them now—belated but sincere.'

'Thank you, sir. I suspect you were better acquainted with Maman than I, but I cannot forget how much I owe her. There are many, no doubt, who deplore the way she chose to support us, but at least she ensured that we were never destitute.'

He looked round him. 'You are very far from destitute now,' he said.

'Thank God—and Maman.' She looked at him curiously. 'Were you one of her more regular visitors?'

With something of a shock, Deveril realised that she had assumed him to be one of Madame de Rouen's customers. It was a natural assumption to make in the circumstances, and even though it was not the case, this was hardly the time to explain the true connection. 'Alas, no. Your mother ran an excellent house, where one met interesting and useful people, but my work took me away so often that I was but rarely able to enjoy the delights of the rue des Flandres.'

'Your work?' Mandala was surprised. He behaved with the assured arrogance of one who commissioned others to labour on his behalf. There was something about Deveril York that drew her to him, while at the same time something made her feel uneasy, as if things were not quite as they appeared, but she had never taken him for anything but a gentleman.

'A turn of phrase—my affairs would have been a better word,' he said smoothly, glad that she did not seem to see anything strange in the amendment. 'What brought you to Devon? I should have thought London would have been more to your taste.' He cast an appreciative eye over the dull gold of her gown.

'So did I, but I found it palled very quickly. Of course, I had no acquaintance there and no entrée. Things might have been different if I had. So I came here, and I find I like country life.'

'Even though you have no acquaintance here and—from what I hear—no entrée either?'

She flushed, but lifted her chin in a gesture of defiant stubbornness that he was surprised to find touching. 'They assume I am the same as Maman, for whom they have no understanding and make no allowances.'

'I had heard that you went to some pains to give the rector precisely that impression.'

Mandala sighed and had the grace to look a little shamefaced. 'Your enquiries have been to some effect, I see. It was very wrong of me, but, I assure you, quite irresistible. All the same, it was probably a mistake.'

He smiled, and Mandala was suddenly aware of the extent to which a warm smile could transform his harsh features. 'Succumbing to an irresistible urge is frequently a mistake,' he told her. 'Is it something you do often?'

'I assume you speak with the voice of experience,' Mandala replied, thinking it wiser to ignore the question.

'A hazy recollection of the errors of my youth, no more than that,' he said. He had noticed her omission but did not comment upon it. Instead, he returned to the window and looked out. 'Tell me, Miss Sorn, is all your land like this?'

She joined him, puzzled. 'Like what? It's not all knot-gardens, of course.'

'I referred to the woods. It seems to be extensively wooded and with an abundance of these deep valleys.'

'The combes, you mean? It is beautiful, isn't it? So far

as I have been able to explore, most of it is exactly like that. There is a small amount of more open land to the east, near the Dorset border, and as you go north the hills are still there but the woods are much less dense. You must have observed that yourself. Indeed, it wouldn't surprise me if you were far more familiar with my land than I am myself: you were riding across it, as I recall, the day I arrived.'

'I had not been long in the locality at that time,' he said stiffly and with a reasonable degree of truth. 'I had strayed.'

'To some effect, if you thought you were still on Courtenay land,' Mandala remarked without animosity. 'The landscape continues like this until it drops sharply down into Lyme Bay. I wish I had grown up here,' she added wistfully. 'These woods would have been the perfect place to play hide-and-go-seek.'

'The same thought occurred to me,' he said, and Mandala looked at him quickly, for whereas she had spoken truthfully but not seriously, he was entirely serious.

'Joan said you wanted me,' said Martha's voice from the door, and they both turned to look at her. The old maidservant had no difficulty in recognising their visitor. 'It's our friend the trespasser, if I mistake me not.'

'It's all right, Martha,' Mandala assured her. 'Mr York is aware that he erred. It appears that he was also acquainted with Maman and has come to offer his condolences.'

Martha looked at their visitor with sharpened interest and narrowed eyes. She sniffed. 'Thought there was something familiar about you,' she said. 'Then I told myself all cats are grey at night and it was just a chance resemblance. I don't recall that the name was York, though. And what may your true reason be for being here, sir? That's what I'd like to know.'

Deveril raised a haughty eyebrow, clearly indicating that he did not have to answer to a servant and cursing himself for not having recognised someone who had evidently seen him in the rue des Flandres. He had his own reasons for antagonising nobody at Abbas Manor.

'Your suspicions do you credit. They may be misplaced, but they indicate you have your mistress's interests at heart. I can only assure you that the reasons for my visit are precisely as Miss Sorn has explained.'

'Hmm. She's young enough to be easily bamboozled! I don't suppose this sudden recollection of an acquaintance with her mother had anything to do with discovering that the daughter is a very rich woman?'

'A discovery which has not yet proved a strong enough lure for the young men of Devon, has it? Make your own enquiries, good woman, and you will find that I have no need of a rich wife.'

'When did that ever stop a man?' Martha retorted.

Deveril turned to Mandala, carefully hiding his annoyance and speaking with a blandness that had deceived many who were not well acquainted with him. 'I am clearly unwelcome in your maid's eyes, if not in yours, Miss Sorn. I shall therefore relieve you both of my company, but I should like your permission to visit again. With respect, Miss Sorn, you must feel the lack of acquaintance.'

Mandala could feel Martha's disapproval, but Deveril's assessment of her situation was all too accurate. Apart from the rector, there had been no visitors, and there was no one with whom she could converse on equal terms. Deveril York certainly came into that category, and any hesitation she had was entirely because she quite simply was not sure what to make of him. He was easy to talk to and difficult to shock. He had a quick wit and appreciated a similar attribute in others. But Mandala sensed, though she could not define, that there was something more to Deveril York. Martha thought he was making up to her because of her wealth. Mandala suspected that Martha was wrong, but she had no idea of his ulterior motive in seeking her out. It was just that her instinct told her there was one. It was a lowering thought: she would infinitely have preferred him to seek her company for its own sake. Still, she was not going to refuse the offer of his company on such flimsy grounds, because, all other considerations apart, she enjoyed it. She smiled up at him. 'You may visit, Mr

York, but you will appreciate that I shall be happier in future if there is a chaperon present.'

He bowed, and cast a fleeting glance at Martha. 'I would not expect it to be otherwise,' he said, and paused. When he continued there was a glint in his eye. 'Does it have be a shrew who dominates the conversation?'

'It will depend upon which servant can most easily be spared,' Mandala told him, repressing a little smile with some difficulty.

He noticed the half-concealed smile but did not comment. Instead, he lifted her hand to his lips and kissed it. The smile in his eyes caught hers, and her lashes fluttered as she sought to avoid the embarrassment of so direct and warm a gaze. His strong fingers held her hand a shade too long and pressed them a shade too much, and Mandala knew he would return. It would be most immodest to let him suspect how pleased that realisation made her!

'Good day, Mr York,' she said demurely.

'It has been, indeed,' he replied.

He allowed Martha to escort him to the door, and rode away knowing the old nurse watched his progress until a curve in the drive hid him from sight. But he did not then follow the most direct route back to Courtenay Place, preferring, on the excuse of this legitimate visit, to range rather more widely over Mandala's land than might have been expected of a visitor. So far as he could tell, it confirmed his expectations. It was just the sort of landscape he had been looking for, and, whereas Sir Nuneham's land had only pockets of dense woodland, Abbas Manor seemed to have little else. As Mandala had said, it was a perfect place to play hide-and-go-seek, a judgment reinforced by the presence, in unexpected places, of unattended barns. These were not of a size to compare with the huge buildings attached to the Manor House itself, but they could offer shelter to a game-keeper or storage for the coppicing tools so much used in this sort of landscape, as well as for the hazel wands they produced. Their great merit lay not in their smallness but in their position, nestling in the little valleys in a way that meant they were almost completely concealed. The Manor of Abbas St Antony would suit his purpose very well indeed. Its mistress must be cultivated. Deveril smiled to himself. That task at least should be no penance.

When he returned to Courtenay Place, he sent for Denham and despatched him to Poole on the cob, attending to the big Hanoverian himself. If Sir Nuneham thought it eccentrically generous to allow a man leave to attend his mother's funeral at such short notice, he forbore to say so. Perhaps if his visitor had to saddle up his horse for himself he would ride less often, and that would leave him more time to pay court to Isobel.

Unlike Sir Nuneham, who would not have dreamed of saddling his own horse though he was perfectly capable of doing so, Deveril thought nothing of it, and the very next morning he was once more on his way to Abbas Manor. Time was beginning to press, and he still had at best a superficial knowledge of the topography. He needed to be a great deal more familiar with it, and he needed to form some estimation of Mandala's views on one or two matters of some political importance. Discretion would have dictated an interval of two or three days before his next visit, but Deveril knew he did not have time for such a luxury.

Mandala herself was very surprised that he should repeat his call so soon, and also a little vexed. She always took care with her appearance, but if she had expected him, she would have selected a gown which was rather more sober. She did not possess any that were truly Puritan, and perhaps that was something she should remedy. Deveril York dressed with a restraint that more than hinted at Puritan leanings, and she did not want him to conclude that she was a shallow-brained flibbertigibbet.

Deveril saw nothing to cavil at in the green velvet overskirt looped back over an ivory slipper-satin petticoat trimmed with horizontal rows of braid. The wide scoop of her neckline was deeper than he had hitherto seen her wear, revealing the first alluring promise of her breasts. There was a maturity in her figure and an unconscious sensuality in her movement that made him wish fleetingly that so much did not depend upon his skill in dealing with the mistress of Abbas Manor. He looked at Joan, who had followed her mistress into the room and remained standing, her hands demurely clasped in front of her apron, just inside the door. It was perhaps as well she was there, he thought ruefully. More than anything else, he needed *carte blanche* to visit Abbas Manor, and must do nothing that might risk Mandala's taking him in dislike. Perhaps later, if all went well and he remained in England, it might be interesting to pursue the acquaintance on a more personal level. For the time being, such considerations must wait.

His bow was neither effusive nor cursory. 'Miss Sorn, as you see, I avail myself of your permission to call.'

The curtsy with which she responded was as carefully calculated as his bow, he noticed appreciatively. 'You are welcome, Mr York, though I confess I had not anticipated so prompt a repetition of yesterday's visit.'

'Drawn by the lure of your fine eyes, mistress.'

She laughed. Such pleasantries were customary and meant nothing, flattering as they might be to receive. She gestured to a chair. 'Pray be seated, Mr York,' she said, setting the example.

They exchanged brief observations on the weather, which they agreed was pleasant though still with a nip in the air when the sun had gone down, and speculated upon the probabilities of a good harvest, which, they both agreed, was difficult to forecast so soon though the hay looked good enough. Deveril asked if he might be shown the knot-garden. 'I admired it yesterday, but one seldom sees so fine an example in England nowadays.'

Mandala rose to her feet. 'I shall be happy to do so,' she said. 'My steward tells me my grandparents refused to remove it during the Protectorate, and, in fact, were so angered by the disapproval of so innocent a pleasure that they extended it, and this was continued during the late King's reign. There is a topiary garden, too, which is said to be noteworthy, but I can offer you no avenues, no canals.'

Joan fetched her mistress's cloak, which their visitor

placed carefully round her shoulders, and they left the house, the maid several discreet steps behind. The low box-hedges of the knot-garden set off the pink, red and white of the roses within, while further from the terrace they enclosed the herbs so essential to any good house-wife, not only to flavour the food and disguise any putrefaction, but also to provide the household's medi-cines. The terrace itself was edged with lavender and the whole area bordered by high, clipped yews, leading to a gradually sloping expanse of scythed lawn in which were dotted, with no apparent design, thirteen yew columns wired and trained into cones. One, smaller than the rest, stood slightly apart. Another, taller, stood in the centre of the lawn.

'Jonah Swinbrook, my steward, tells me that they represent Christ and the twelve apostles,' Mandala told him. 'The smaller one, the outcast, being Judas. But when I mentioned this to Martha, she scoffed, and said in *her* day they had been King Arthur and the knights of the Round Table, so you may please yourself whom you believe.'

'I imagine the change of identity prevented their being cut down under Cromwell's rule,' Deveril commented.

'What a simple explanation!' Mandala exclaimed. 'I should have thought of it myself. We have *Mort d'Arthur* in the library. I must read it, and find out who the little outcast is.'

Deveril laughed. 'A most unfitting book for a delicately nurtured female!'

'Really? In that case I shall undoubtedly enjoy it.'

They both laughed at that, and Deveril felt the time was appropriate to venture a sounding on another mat-ter. 'I had heard your grandparents were Puritans,' he said. 'They do not appear to have held too rigidly to the tenets of that faith.'

'They don't, do they? I fancy it was not in their religious beliefs that they differed from the general view, but in certain practical aspects of its interpretation.'

'You mean that their religion was Puritan but not their politics?' Deveril remarked.

'Do I?' Mandala said doubtfully. 'To be truthful, I

understand little of politics. They seem to bring nothing but trouble to those who become involved, and they complicate life unnecessarily. For my part, I have no interest and no desire to participate. I leave politics to those with nothing better to do.'

'Very wise,' Deveril said, smiling, and judged it to be a good time to drop the topic. It would be unwise to let it appear too important. 'Shall we return to the house?'

They made their way back across the lawns to the terrace, easier in each other's company than when they had left it. Deveril was well pleased with the outcome of his visit, and Mandala bade him farewell with a feeling almost akin to regret. He hesitated before actually departing, however, and broached another matter in a manner that suggested it was something of an after-thought.

'I have twice encountered you riding, Miss Sorn,' he said. 'From the type of horse you choose and your ability to handle her, I deduce it's a pastime that gives you great pleasure.'

'Indeed it is,' she agreed warmly. 'My daily rides are something I would be very loath to forgo.'

'Then perhaps you will permit me to accompany you—with your groom, of course. I, too, enjoy riding, and the addition of congenial company would enhance that enjoyment. Tomorrow, perhaps?'

Mandala inclined her head. 'I shall look forward to that.'

When he had gone, Mandala went about her day's tasks with an unaccountably light heart. She had en-joyed Deveril York's company, and there was no denying that there would be a great deal more pleasure to be gained from having someone like him to converse with than in riding alone. She was beginning to appreci-ate how very isolated her existence had become and although she thought she had managed to convince herself that she did not mind, that she positively pre-ferred it, the few hours of Deveril's company she had so far enjoyed had shown her that she was deluding herself. No company might be better than poor company, but it was no substitute for a companion who laughed at the same sorts of things, who recognised allusions and who saw no virtue in the convention that decreed that a gentleman must never correct a lady, no matter how mistaken she might be.

She looked forward to the next day's ride, and was not disappointed. The nature of the terrain obliged them to ride in single file quite frequently, which made conversation difficult, and meant that the groom was trailing behind. Similarly, when they came to a riding in the woods or a clear stretch of pasture, their horses invariably out-distanced their escort's, and they were obliged to wait for the poor man to catch up. They rode widely over Mandala's estates and she enjoyed showing Deveril land he was not familiar with, for it made her feel less of a stranger herself and she was pleased that his interest was clearly not feigned. His questions frequently went beyond her own knowledge: When was this last coppiced? How often did Swinbrook tour the estate? On such occasions they referred to the groom for the answers. It was hardly surprising that the groom came to the conclusions he did.

'You mark my words,' he said in the kitchen. 'He's got a good eye for a piece of prime property, be it female or agricultural. There'll be an offer from that quarter before the year's out, just you see if there isn't.'

Mandala tried not to think about such things, but there were times, in the quiet seclusion of her bed-chamber, when they crossed her mind and she was obliged to remind herself that Deveril York neither did nor said anything that might lead her to think that his mind was working along those lines. She would content herself with his company and enjoy it while it was available—had he not already made one or two inconsequential remarks that suggested that his stay here might not be long extended?

She was therefore disproportionately downcast when the groom sent a message to the house to say that the cob seemed to have strained a tendon. The Manor did not maintain a large stable: there was Mandala's little Barb, the general-purpose cob, and some plough-horses which could, if need arose, be put to the old-fashioned, ungainly carriage. They were certainly no substitute for a groom's mount. When Deveril arrived, he found Mandala dressed for riding but pacing up and down in impotent anger.

When he heard the reason, he frowned. He enjoyed Mandala's company but it would be no penance to substitute for the ride a stroll on the terrace. His displeasure had another cause. He dared not stay in Devon much longer. He had one more piece to fit into his carefully constructed plan, and he rather thought he might have caught a glimpse of it the previous day. A horse with a strained tendon would be out of commission for some time. There was a solution, but would Mandala accept it or would she throw up her hands in decorous horror?

'You were clearly looking forward to the ride,' he said hesitantly.

'Yes, I was,' she replied. 'It is particularly annoying to have it brought to one's attention at the last minute like this. Why, I wasn't even able to let you know that we would have to change our plans.'

Deveril forbore to point out that, without the cob, she could hardly have let him know, even if she had learnt of the animal's condition the previous evening. 'If I may make a suggestion . . .' he went on doubtfully.

'Anything—if it will allow us to ride,' she assured him.

He appeared to hesitate once more. 'If you would consider riding without a groom, we need delay no longer than it takes to throw the saddle on Fatima.'

Mandala paused in her pacing and stared at him, and he noticed a glint of pure mischief in her eyes. He was taken aback. He had thought he had her measure. He knew she would not really be unduly concerned at the idea of having no chaperon, but he had expected her to make the conventional expressions of demurral before finding some plausible justification for doing what she wanted. That glint told him that he had underestimated her.

'An excellent suggestion,' she declared. 'I should have thought of it myself!' She turned to Martha, who had also noticed the mischievous expression of which she had long ago learnt to beware. 'Will you ask someone to bring Fatima round, Martha?'

Only the presence of Deveril York prevented the maid from telling her mistress that, if she wanted to pursue so indecorous a course, she could run her own errands. She pursed her lips. 'You shouldn't even be considering such a thing,' she said flatly.

'I know I shouldn't, but it seems to me this is one occasion when being called the Scarlet Woman can be turned to advantage: I'm sure it's exactly what such a one would do! Besides, I am sufficiently well acquainted with Mr York now to know that I stand in no danger from him.'

Martha sniffed, and looked the visitor up and down. 'If that's the case, then it's only because it suits his purpose. He dresses decorously enough, I'll allow, but—with all due respect, sir—that's not a face any parent would leave a daughter alone with, and that's a fact.'

Deveril grinned appreciatively. 'If that's your idea of respect, Mistress Rissington, I'll take good care not to rouse your bad opinion! Miss Sorn will come to no harm in my company. You have my word on it.'

'And even if I did, no one would know, would they?' Mandala concluded cheerfully, thus destroying the effect of his carefully chosen words.

Since Mandala was the mistress and Martha only her old nurse, there was nothing the latter could do beyond make her protest. She therefore contented herself with a final sniff before going into the kitchens to send a boy out with a message for the stables.

'I fancy you'll not hear the end of this from your maid for many days,' Deveril said, as they rode away from the house.

'You misjudge her,' Mandala told him. 'Martha's a realist. Once I've gone, the harm—if there is any—is done, and she'll not harp on it. She calls it not crying over spilt milk, and it's something I've come to respect her for: she'll rail at me before I do something she considers foolish, but once it's done, she drops the matter. If subsequent events proved her right, she'd help me to pick up the pieces and never once would she say "I told you so". That's just not her way. I think that was why Maman had such a high regard for her.'

'Do you often do foolish things?'

'I don't think so. It's more a matter of doing them without what Martha calls "due consideration"—this ride being just such an impulse.' She looked up at him, and he thought there was just a hint of anxiety in her eyes. 'I *am* quite safe with you, am I not?' she asked.

'You are today: I've given your maid my word.'

Mandala laughed. 'Where would you like to go?'

Deveril directed her towards the spot where he thought he had glimpsed a barn standing in splendid isolation and which had looked to be considerably larger than most such buildings that were not close to farms. It had appeared to be nestling at the bottom of a combe, and he confessed to a curiosity about it.

'You mean the Tilnorth Barn,' she told him. 'It's a fascinating place. I rode there once in the evening, and it was most uncanny.' She shivered. 'I don't think I would want to go there alone again, but in broad daylight and with an escort, it should be unexceptionable, don't you think?'

'A barn is a barn,' Deveril said matter-of-factly. 'You must have allowed the evening light to affect your imagination.'

'Not so,' Mandala insisted. 'It's well known hereabouts that the Tilnorth Barn is . . . well, not exactly haunted—that would be too unbelievable—but not entirely *right*. People are very reluctant to go there, you know.'

'I didn't,' Deveril said. 'Tell me about it.' The Tilnorth Barn was beginning to sound increasingly perfect.

'It's rather sad, really.' Mandala told him. 'Abbas St Antony wasn't always where it is now, but where the Tilnorth Barn is. It's believed to have been the great tithe-barn attached to the church, and certainly all around it are peculiar little humpy hills which Jonah told me are the remains of the old village houses, now overgrown with grass and brambles. When the Black

Death swept inland from Weymouth three hundred years ago, they say, nearly everyone in the village died. The Lord of the Manor—it belonged to Sorns even then—and his son survived, and so did some of the peasants, and they decided to leave such a dreadful place to rot and crumble and founded a new Abbas St Antony here. Jonah told me that it is well documented in the family records, but I'm ashamed to say I haven't felt inclined to go through them. I suppose I should, some day.'

'Then why did they leave the barn standing?' Deveril asked.

'It's a very good barn,' Mandala said. 'Jonah thinks they kept it to start with so that they had a storehouse and could build their dwellings first. It remained useful, so they kept it in good repair when everything else was crumbling. Of course, it was made of stone and the cottages weren't—they would very soon have disappeared, though the church and the Manor House must have taken longer.'

'Hence its reputation of eeriness,' Deveril commented.

'I suppose so,' Mandala replied. 'All those poor souls who died must be buried near by, for they could hardly be in the present churchyard.'

'A lowering thought,' Deveril agreed. 'It sounds as if it may not be a very popular spot.'

'The barn is still used, of course, but Jonah admits that villagers are reluctant to visit it, and he says he's the only person who's prepared to go there alone.' She chuckled. 'I don't suppose anyone would go there at night, not even Jonah. I certainly wouldn't.'

'I should hope not,' Deveril said severely. 'It would be *most* indecorous.'

For the second time that day, he saw the imp of mischief in Mandala's eyes. 'Yes, wouldn't it?' she said, and he reflected that it might be wise to take more care with his utterances. The last thing he wanted was for Mandala, in the foreseeable future, to throw propriety to the winds where the Tilnorth Barn was concerned.

When they reached the old building, Deveril realised it was precisely what he had been looking for. It proved to be unexpectedly large, and almost completely concealed now that high summer was fast approaching and the trees and undergrowth were heavy with the varying shades of foliage. He dismounted, and handed Teufel's reins to Mandala.

'Hold him,' he said. 'I'd like to look inside. I shan't be long.'

'Certainly not!' Mandala declared. 'We can tie them both up. Help me down, Mr York: I've never been inside, either.'

Deveril hesitated briefly, as much on the grounds of propriety as any desire to inspect the interior alone, but he said nothing and held up his arms so that she could slide down from the saddle into them with no fear of stumbling. A groom would have done as much, and, although he was suddenly very conscious of the body beneath the riding-dress, he lifted her down as impersonally as any groom would have done, and it did not cross Mandala's mind to regard his assistance in any other light.

'It is massive, isn't it?' she remarked, as they stood before the huge stone structure.

'It's certainly big enough to have been a tithe-barn,' he agreed. 'I see your steward doesn't bother to keep the doors locked.' He swung open one of the massive central doors as he spoke.

'I don't suppose he needs to, if people are afraid to come here,' Mandala commented, peering into an interior rendered the more dim by the bright sunshine outside. She stepped over the threshold and gazed about her, her eyes soon becoming accustomed to the light. Even so, the roof seemed to soar into gloomy space, the definition of its oak beams blurred by the cobwebs of centuries. At one end, under the gable, the sunlight through the pigeon-holes cast a chequered pattern on the dirt floor, a pattern whose regularity was interrupted by the occasional accumulation of straw, twigs and feathers in which birds, not all of them doves, had raised their chicks over the years.

'I had not realised it was so vast,' she remarked. 'It could almost be the church.'

'Some tithe-barns are like that,' Deveril said, following her in and looking around him approvingly. This really was a most promising building, and nearly empty, too. There was a pile of long-stemmed roofing straw at one end, some hurdles and a pile of hazel wands. That was all.

Mandala shivered. 'There is something strange about it,' she said. 'It isn't exactly a—a *welcoming* place.'

'That's your imagination at work,' he told her. 'If you hadn't been told the history of the place, it wouldn't have occurred to you.'

'It isn't just the barn that feels like that. The whole area is the same—and I had that feeling before Jonah told me, so it can't be fancy. I can't say I blame anyone who doesn't want to come here.'

'Then perhaps it's just as well that it's so far from the house: you'll be less tempted to wander out here,' Deveril said.

Mandala looked suddenly guilty. 'It is a long way, isn't it?' she said. 'Perhaps we should return before tongues start to wag.' She turned to leave the barn, and stumbled on a stone hidden among some loose straw. Deveril's hand caught her arm in a surprisingly vice-like grip that kept her from falling. Mandala turned to thank him and found herself, tall as she was, looking up into eyes that were neither grey nor blue but somewhere in between, in a face suddenly wiped clean of cynicism. He still held her arm, though his grip had slackened, but she was almost unaware of it and made no attempt to detach herself. She was hypnotised by those eyes, drawn to them as though an invisible silken thread were being slowly tightened.

Deveril felt it, too, and in one swift, co-ordinated movement he had swept her into his arms, at the same time tossing aside his own hat and then gently removing Mandala's. His lips sought her upturned mouth, and there was such a lingering tenderness in his kiss that she was conscious only of a desire to be ever closer to the strength she sensed in the body that held her so close.

Her arms found their way somehow to his shoulders, as her lips responded with a fervour she had not known she possessed, and Deveril's own response was to hold her even closer until their bodies touched in an eager sensuality that left neither of them in any doubt that they both sought the same ultimate fulfilment.

It was Deveril who first recognised the danger of the path they both trod. He raised his head and kissed her forehead, as one kisses a child's.

'Enough,' he whispered, slackening his hold, sensing her reluctance to be released. 'This should not have happened. I gave my word.'

Mandala was puzzled at what seemed so abrupt a change of mood. She was hurt, too, that he could so easily withdraw from her, for, although he held her still, she felt as if the desire she had known he had for her had gone. 'What is it?' she asked. 'What's wrong?'

Deveril smiled bitterly. Another time, another place, he thought, and there would be nothing wrong. 'You have ridden with me on the assurance that I would behave with perfect propriety. I have betrayed that trust. Come, let me throw you back into the saddle and we shall go back. Will you accept my assurance that nothing like this will ever happen again?'

The hint of a smile touched her lips, and she looked up at him from under her lashes. 'I would far rather not,' she said.

Deveril was decidedly taken aback. He had said what convention dictated in the circumstances and had expected the conventional reply. He was not often disconcerted, and it was not an entirely welcome sensation when it occurred. 'I don't think you mean that,' he said stiffly.

'I'm not disputing that we should go home now,' Mandala told him. 'Nor that you have behaved abominably—I'm quite sure that is precisely the sort of behaviour that makes a chaperon so necessary. All I said was that I do not want an assurance that nothing like it will ever happen again.'

Deveril had by now had time to recover himself. He bent down and picked up the two hats, dusted Mandala's off and placed it carefully on her red curls, arranging it as closely as possible at the angle it had assumed before.

'I suspect this is not the first time that you have helped a lady to dress,' Mandala said shrewdly.

He laughed. 'Far from it! Though such an opinion should not even occur to a lady, much less find expression.' He guided her out into the sunlight and untied Fatima's reins from the dog-rose that held them. 'Your horse, madam,' he said.

Mandala put her foot into his cupped hands, and he tossed her up into the saddle. She settled the reins in her gloved hands and smiled demurely down at him. 'Thank you, Mr York,' she said.

'I take leave to tell you, Miss Sorn, that you're a minx.'

Mandala sighed. 'I expect that's all part of being a Scarlet Woman, don't you?'

Deveril swung himself up into Teufel's saddle. 'I'm beginning to think it might be,' he said. 'Shall we go?'

CHAPTER FIVE

It was not to be expected that the visits of the wealthy Mr York to the beautiful Miss Sorn could continue for very long without word of them slipping out, and it was even less surprising that sooner or later Sir Nuneham's valet should happen to mention to his master the destination of his guest's daily rides. Sir Nuneham made no comment: one did not gossip with one's servants. His master's silence neither discomposed nor deterred the valet, who, like everyone else at Courtenay Place, knew perfectly well what Sir Nuneham hoped for from his guest.

'Far be it from me to listen to gossip, Sir Nuneham,' he went on, 'much less to repeat it, but I gather the Manor servants are in daily expectation of a declaration.'

'The brown full-bottomed wig with this, I think, Charles,' was Sir Nuneham's only comment.

The lack of apparent interest with which he received the valet's story served to cover the seething indignation he felt. He did not doubt its essential accuracy. He doubted that matters between his guest and his neighbour had reached a level at which a declaration might be imminently expected, but not that they were moving in that direction. And this was the man to whom he had opened his doors and into whose company he had thrust his sister! Isobel was attractive enough in the normal way, but she paled into insignificance beside Mandala Sorn's beauty, just as her respectable dowry paled beside Mandala's fortune. Were these things sufficient to overcome the disadvantages of the heiress's perfectly scandalous upbringing? Possibly—after all, he was himself perfectly willing to overlook them, should the opportunity arise. But there was a difference: he, Sir Nuneham Courtenay, had a pedigree that permitted him to be less than rigid about these things when occasion demanded. Deveril York, so far as he knew, had none.

His wealth was undeniable, and no one could pretend that he was not a gentleman, but neither could anyone ascertain any details about his family. Had it not been for the late King's friendship—and His Late Majesty had had a regrettable tendency to an indiscriminate choice of cronies—no one would have received Deveril York. It behoved him to make a respectable marriage, and Isobel was nothing if not respectable. Her brother had seen to that. For Deveril to pursue his interest elsewhere was nothing short of an abuse of hospitality —and if Sir Nuneham had not had too much delicacy to pay visits of his own to Mandala Sorn, it might be a very different declaration the servants would be gossiping about.

It was therefore a very angry Sir Nuneham who entered the elegant library of beautifully arranged but largely unread books to find his guest with a hitherto unopened volume on his knee, a comfortable robe replacing the coat he had worn earlier in the day.

'You have returned from your ride, I see,' Sir Nuneham began.

Resisting the temptation to advise his host to refrain from stating the obvious, Deveril agreed that it was so.

'Allow me to express the hope that these indefatigable rides are proving useful to you.'

A slight frown crossed Deveril's face. His host was very angry about something. He cast his mind quickly back. No, he had been nowhere, said nothing, met nobody who could possibly arouse suspicions as to his real purpose here. 'Useful?' he countered. 'I enjoy the exercise, and this is beautiful countryside.'

'Enhanced, no doubt, by the addition to the landscape of an heiress who combines her wealth with beauty.'

The last vestige of his frown cleared. So that was what was upsetting his host! 'Such an asset would enhance any landscape, don't you think?' Deveril said.

'So it is true. You have met the beautiful Miss Sorn?'

'We are old acquaintances.'

Sir Nuneham frowned. 'You made no mention of it when I told you about her.'

'Why should I? I could not be sure that she and I

had ever met: I had not at that time been formally introduced, you see.'

Sir Nuneham coloured angrily as a number of explanations for this tantalisingly incomplete statement occurred to him. 'Explain yourself, sir. What precisely do you mean?'

Deveril smiled. 'Sadly, I don't have the lady's permission to tell anyone how we met— it never crossed my mind that I might need it.'

Sir Nuneham snorted. 'In her mother's house, I don't doubt! Yet you have visited her daily—unless gossip lies.'

'On this occasion, gossip tells no more than the truth. She is an interesting companion.'

'I'm sure she is! Nevertheless, she is not received locally, and your visiting her puts me in a difficult position since you are staying here.'

'Nonsense! What you really mean is that I've had an opportunity to fix my interest with her, thus possibly undermining your own chances—chances you have so far failed to avail yourself of because you were afraid of what the gossips would say.'

Since this was precisely what was in Sir Nuneham's mind, though only half admitted, even to himself, the open acceptance of it by his guest and the amused tolerance of his tone made him angrier still, and with his anger came a childish petulance.

'It's not as though you have any need of her fortune,' he said bitterly. 'I would be less angry if you weren't a guest in my own house.'

'You delude yourself, Courtenay. You'd be equally annoyed, no matter who I was.'

'I've more than half a mind to tell her what you really are. To tell her your interest is her land and her money, not her person.'

Deveril smiled cynically. 'On the contrary, I find her person infinitely interesting. The rest is the gilt on the gingerbread. Indeed, she has much to interest me just at present,' he added truthfully.

At about this moment, Isobel chanced to enter the adjacent room and, hearing her brother's voice raised, most reprehensibly tiptoed across the floor and put her ear to the door.

'Tell me this, York. Do you or do you not intend to offer for her?'

Deveril had no such intention, but he saw no reason to tell Sir Nuneham so, and, in any case, he had found out all that he needed. An excuse to leave the area with a minimum of delay had much to recommend it. He closed the book and carefully replaced it on its shelf, observing that the delay in answering stoked the fires of Sir Nuneham's anger still further.

'As to that, I'm not entirely sure that I've made up my mind.'

'Not made up your mind? Do you mean to tell me you've been merely trifling with her?'

Deveril considered. 'No, I wouldn't go so far as to say that. The fortune doesn't matter—I've plenty for both of us, and I also have the entrée to circles that will be happy to accept her if she comes as my wife. I have to ask myself if I can turn her into the sort of wife I need. After all, I don't want to appear at Court with a gauche schoolgirl at my side.'

'No fear of that,' Sir Nuneham retorted. 'She'll learn fast enough! I'd wager a considerable sum on that!'

Deveril appeared to reflect. 'Do you know, Courtenay, I think you're probably right? I owe you my thanks for helping me to make up my mind. I'll offer for the girl—and I'll waste no time going about it.'

Outside the door, the colour fled from Isobel's cheeks. Deveril's recent absences from Courtenay Place had convinced her that he had lost any interest he might have had in her, and was only prolonging his stay so that his departure should not follow so hard upon the heels of his arrival as to give rise to talk. Of all the men in England, Deveril York was the last she wished to marry. How could she move from relative penury to the extremes of wealth that he possessed? How could she change from a provincial miss to the assured and self-possessed wife of a wealthy courtier? She shuddered. She could imagine all too clearly what life would be like,

married to this harsh, unfeeling man who had determined to 'turn her into' the sort of wife he needed. How
could Nuneham push him into making an offer like that?
Had he no care for his sister's happiness? All these
thoughts and more tumbled through her head during the
pause that followed Deveril's announcement, and then,
pressing a handkerchief to her lips to stifle any sobs, she
lifted her skirts and fled in a most unladylike manner to
her room.

In the library, the silence was broken by Sir Nuneham.
'Very well, sir. Give me leave to say that, if that is your
intent, you have abused my hospitality and trifled with
my sister, to whom you were earlier most attentive.'

'I don't think you'll find her suffering from a broken
heart,' Deveril told him. 'In fact, she doesn't even like
me above half. It's my belief she'll be quite relieved.'

'I know my sister better than you,' Sir Nuneham
retorted. 'She cannot be expected to remain under the
same roof with one who has trifled with her feelings, her
expectations.'

'And since you can hardly ask her to leave, you'd like
me to do so, is that it?' Deveril said cheerfully. 'Very
well. I'll be gone before dinner. Will that suit you?'

Sir Nuneham could only agree that it would, and left
the room with some semblance of dignity. He returned
to his own, his emotions seething. At one blow, Deveril
York had frustrated all his plans. The man had no
intention of bestowing his name—and, more importantly, his wealth—upon Isobel and was determined
to annexe Mandala Sorn's fortune, a fortune he had
admitted he did not need, and which Sir Nuneham had
become accustomed to thinking of as his own rightful
expectation, even though he had not—so far—done
anything to establish a claim to its present owner.

That, he thought savagely, looking at his reflection in
the glass, was something he might still have time to
remedy. He sent for his valet, and ordered him to set out
his riding-clothes and to instruct the stables to send a
horse round in fifteen minutes.

His valet was considerably taken aback to learn that
his master had decided to ride at this unearthly hour

—why, he had left his room barely a half-hour before! The news that the horse was to be ready in fifteen minutes was a blow that struck deep.

'Fifteen minutes, Sir Nuneham?' he asked incredulously.

'Fifteen minutes,' his master confirmed.

'Forgive my impertinence, Sir Nuneham—but *fifteen minutes*? Have you thought what that means? The implications, Sir Nuneham!'

'I regret it as much as you, Charles. The fact remains that time is of the essence. We shall both of us have to be content with something a little short of perfection. Fifteen minutes. I mean it, Charles, and I shall leave the house half dressed if I have to.'

Charles hastened to assure his master that it need not come to that, but added that he hoped Sir Nuneham would not be taking his less-than-perfect appearance anywhere that mattered.

'Oh, no, nothing like that,' Sir Nuneham promised, and with that the valet had to be content.

Sir Nuneham's appearance might have its shortcomings on this occasion, but they were not apparent to Mandala Sorn, who was so overcome with amazement at receiving a visit from that quarter that she quite failed to notice any imperfections in his Steinkirk cravat or his lace-edged gloves.

Since she knew precisely where she stood in the eyes of her neighbours, she realised that it must be a most pressing matter that had brought Sir Nuneham here. She was about to dismiss Joan, when her visitor said, 'Miss Sorn, I realise the impropriety of the suggestion, but I come here on a most . . . a most *delicate* matter. Dare I ask to speak to you in private?'

She inclined her head. 'Certainly, sir. Joan, wait outside, but first, send to the kitchen. I feel sure Sir Nuneham will partake of tea after his ride.'

'You are most kind, Miss Sorn. Some refreshment would indeed be welcome.'

When Joan returned with the tea-tray containing the locked caddy and the kettle as well as the thin porcelain cups and the teapot, Sir Nuneham was sitting opposite Mandala commenting upon the continued good weather. Mandala lit the oil-soaked wick under the kettle, and dismissed her maid.

'Now, Sir Nuneham,' she said, when they were alone once more and safe from interruption. 'To what do I owe the honour—the entirely unexpected honour—of this visit? A delicate matter, I think you said?'

'Indeed, and it concerns yourself. I have done you a grave disservice, Miss Sorn. I have harboured a serpent in my bosom, and you have been its victim.'

'Dear me,' Mandala remarked, struggling to conceal a smile. 'This is most intriguing. Do explain yourself, Sir Nuneham, for I tell you plainly, I haven't the slightest idea what you mean.'

'How should you have?' he asked, and since the question was clearly rhetorical, Mandala made no attempt to answer it but hoped that an expectant look would elicit clarification.

'I have had a visitor this last little while. You know him, I believe. Deveril York.' He paused, awaiting Mandala's confirming nod. 'Miss Sorn, I was shocked —nay, appalled—to learn that he had foisted himself upon you unbeknown to me.'

'Hardly that, Sir Nuneham. His company was not unwelcome. I have not, after all, had much opportunity to get to know my neighbours.'

If Sir Nuneham was aware of the implied criticism, he gave no sign of it. 'York can make himself charming enough, I don't doubt,' he said. 'I fear he has been taking advantage of you, however, and I feel it is my duty to warn you.'

'Taking advantage?' Mandala echoed. 'In what way?'

'He has heard—forgive my lack of delicacy, Miss Sorn, but it is necessary—he has heard of your reputation, or, to be more accurate, your mother's. He is a very rich man, but do not fall into the trap of taking his advances too seriously. He plans only to seduce you.'

She spoke with a cold dignity that surprised her visitor. 'Indeed? Then he went about it in a very strange way. A maid or a groom was always present and at no time during his visits here was his behaviour anything but that of a gentleman.'

'That's the cleverness of the man,' Sir Nuneham assured her hastily. 'He seeks to lull you into complete confidence. He may even seek to seduce you by first offering you his hand, but do not be deceived, Miss Sorn. Such an offer is worthless. He has already spoken for my sister, and been accepted.'

Mandala raised her eyebrows. 'You surprise me, Sir Nuneham! You would allow your sister to be allied to a man such as you have just described?'

Sir Nuneham shifted uneasily on his chair. 'As to that, it is an arrangement of some standing.' He sought a suitably impressive phrase. 'An arrangement of dynastic importance to the two families. They will deal well enough together, I don't doubt. I fear he will lead you astray as your mother—do forgive me, Miss Sorn—was once led astray. He claims an acquaintance of long standing, and sees that as justification enough. Deveril York is a devious man, Miss Sorn, and, I fear, plays a double game.'

Mandala had little time and no respect for a man who was by his own admission—though less bluntly worded —willing to sell his sister as a brood mare. There was, however, sufficient truth in what he said and un-answered questions in her mind as to the true purpose of Deveril's visits to make her disinclined to dismiss his accusations out of hand.

'If what you say is true, then I am grateful to you for warning me. If it eases your conscience at all,' she went on, privately doubting that he was aware of even owning a conscience, 'I have found Mr York a pleasant companion—a very pleasant companion—but I have no immediate thoughts of marriage. If he were to offer for me, the offer would be declined. I assure you that, once that situation had arisen his visits here would be discouraged.'

Sir Nuneham smiled with relief and seized the opportunity she had just given him. 'I take leave to tell you, Miss Sorn, that I believe local opinion has sorely misjudged you. You speak like a woman of sense and character. Perhaps you will allow me to make amends by visiting you more formally?'

'With your sister, perhaps,' Mandala suggested wryly, and was amused to note the infinitesimal hesitation before he replied.

'I'm sure Isobel will be happy to agree with me that we should,' he said.

Poor Isobel! Mandala thought. First she is betrothed to a man for no other reason than to give him heirs, and now she is to be obliged to visit the local heiress because her brother is prepared to sacrifice propriety for a fortune. Mandala had few illusions about a man of Sir Nuneham's sort. He had given himself grounds for arguing that the Scarlet Woman was not as red as she had been painted, and those grounds would enable him to justify visiting her. She doubted whether he would have bothered had she not been a rich woman.

When he had left, promising to bring his sister to visit her very shortly, Mandala's spirits were downcast. She was unsure how to account for this. She supposed it was bound to have a lowering effect to discover that the man whose company had proved very agreeable was already bespoken, and that he should certainly not have been visiting another unmarried woman. She did not doubt that Sir Nuneham spoke the truth. Servants' gossip—to which, of course, she never listened—said that the rebuilding of Courtenay Place had drained his fortune. It followed that he had every reason to want to attract so wealthy a husband for his sister. Mandala thought none the worse of him for that, nor could she censure him for his interest in her own fortune. Neither, apart from the possible impropriety of his visiting her at all, could she level much criticism at Deveril. Only once had he overstepped convention's bounds, and she was obliged to admit that it had not been precisely unwelcome. Had Deveril himself not put an end to it, who knew where it might not have led? He seemed to value her company, but at no time had he given her cause to expect a declaration. But neither had he given any hint of an arrangement with Miss Courtenay, and Mandala was bound to acknowledge that that indicated an element of duplicity in his character that she could not entirely approve. Perhaps this was what she found so lowering.

She knew of only one cure for such a depression of the spirits, and ordered Fatima to be saddled. As she turned the little mare into one of her favourite rides, she regretted that the terrain around Abbas Manor precluded galloping flat out, for she knew that the exhilaration of such a pace would raise the lowest spirit. Still, even a restricted canter had a beneficial effect, and she was in a more sanguine frame of mind when Fatima shied away from a figure coming through the trees in front of them.

Mandala had no difficulty in recognising the slight form of Isobel Courtenay, who invariably accompanied her brother to church. Small ringlets of fair hair escaped from the soft brown worsted chaperon, the hood that exactly matched the cloak covering her from the neck to the ground. Not, Mandala observed, a very flattering colour for a girl whose fairness teetered on the edge of mousiness and whose bearing proclaimed a temperament to match. She also observed that the girl clutched a band-box in either hand.

'Miss Courtenay? It *is* Miss Courtenay, is it not?'

Isobel cast her a scared yet timidly appealing glance from her rather pale blue eyes. 'Yes,' she whispered. 'And you are Miss Sorn. I've seen you in church.'

'As I have seen you.' Mandala looked beyond her visitor. 'Do you have no maid with you, Miss Courtenay?'

The girl flushed slightly and shook her head. 'I had no time . . . I thought it best not.'

Mandala made no attempt to follow these unconnected statements. 'Does Sir Nuneham know you are here?' she asked.

'Oh, no! He knows nothing of it, and must not,' Isobel added urgently.

'Forgive my curiosity, Miss Courtenay, but to what do I owe this visit?'

'I'm not visiting you,' Isobel said hastily, and then, realising that this was not entirely courteous, 'I mean, that was not my intention. I am going to Exeter.'

'To Exeter!' Mandala exclaimed. 'On foot and un-accompanied? You must be mad! Or desperate,' she added, seeing the girl's stricken face. She slid from her saddle and lifted the reins over the horse's head. 'Come,' she said more gently. 'Why don't you come back to the Manor with me and tell me about it?' She saw Isobel's hesitation, and smiled. 'I'm not really as depraved as everyone says, you know.'

'Oh, no, I'm sure you're not. You couldn't be, could you? I mean . . .' Isobel's voice faded away in confusion.

'I promise you there will not be even so much as a hint of impropriety and not an orgy in sight,' Mandala assured her, and was rewarded with a shy smile. 'You will be perfectly safe, and if you still fear for your reputation, I undertake not to breathe a word to a soul about your visit.'

Isobel thanked her, and Mandala thought it wisest not to mention the servants, for whom no such undertaking could be given.

By the time they reached the Manor, Isobel was clearly exhausted. Mandala suspected she had never done anything more strenuous than stroll in the gardens, and preferred not to speculate upon the girl's probable condition had she ever reached Exeter. Mandala led her to the small sitting-room where she liked to sit and sew, and persuaded her to put her band-boxes safely on the window-seat and to allow Mandala to take her cloak and her chaperon from her. Isobel sank gratefully into a chair by the fire and agreed that a cup of chocolate would indeed be welcome and, yes, some macaroons would not be declined. The hem of her pale blue satin petticoat was wet and muddied and her matching satin slippers quite soaked through. Why it had apparently failed to occur to her guest that pattens might have been a wise precaution for one planning a long walk, Mandala could not imagine. She supposed it was some consolation that neither the petticoat nor the matching striped overskirt had a train to hinder the wearer's progress. She waited until the comforting warmth of the fire and the chocolate were having their effect, and then said, 'Now perhaps you'd like to tell me about it.'

Isobel longed to pour out her troubles to someone else, even to so notorious a female as Miss Mandala Sorn, but she was unaccustomed to the luxury of being able to unburden herself and found it difficult to begin.

'My brother spends a great deal of time in London,' she ventured.

'Fashionable men often do, I believe,' Mandala commented.

'He is very fashionable, isn't he? I wish I were only half so modish.'

'It only requires confidence,' Mandala said. 'Tell me about his visits.'

Isobel looked surprised. 'I can't. I know nothing about them except that, on the last one, a man called Deveril York—a very rich man indeed—said he wanted to see the new Courtenay Place. Nuneham thinks his reason was just an excuse, that he had heard Nuneham had a sister of marriageable age and wanted to look her over. Anyway, an invitation was extended and accepted, and he has been staying with us. I don't suppose you know him—he hasn't been to church while he's been here.'

'As a matter of fact I have met him,' Mandala said cautiously.

Isobel heaved a sigh of relief. 'Then you know what a perfectly dreadful man he is!' she exclaimed with a vehemence that surprised her hostess.

Mandala was puzzled. There was much about Deveril York that made her disinclined to take him entirely at face value, but she could not imagine that he would have comported himself in anything other than a thoroughly decorous manner towards his host's sister, the woman he wished to marry. 'He is not immediately likeable,' she conceded, reflecting that this statement was certainly true. 'But what has he done to give you so extreme a dislike of him?'

Tears welled up in Isobel's eyes. 'Everything!' she said, and then realised that this was perhaps a shade too excessive to be entirely believable. 'Oh, he's polite enough, I grant you, and has never overstepped the bounds of propriety. I didn't think he was at all impressed with me and I had every hope he would decide to look elsewhere for a wife. He is so *old*, Miss Sorn! Nuneham says he's at least thirty-five. Miss Sorn, I'm just a schoolgirl compared with that—and he makes me feel like one.'

Looking at her, Mandala was not surprised. She could not be more than four years older than Isobel herself, yet she was forced to admit that she felt closer to Deveril's advanced years than to Isobel's youth. 'So his age is your only complaint? I believe many men have proved positively doting husbands of child brides.'

Isobel looked sceptical. 'I can't quite envisage Mr York as a doting husband, can you?' she said, and Mandala was obliged to agree. 'He always seems so severe, so unfeeling,' Isobel went on. 'At the same time, I have a feeling I can't quite explain: it sometimes seems to me as if he is holding himself in check.' She shuddered. 'I shouldn't want to anger him, and I'm sure I should do, sooner or later.'

Mandala was startled to realise that, sheltered and naïve as Isobel was, she had read quite clearly into Deveril's character something that Mandala had sensed but never analysed. There was a disturbing underlying force to Deveril York, a sense of power leashed, a feeling not dissimilar to that sensed from the saddle of a spirited, high-bred horse before one dropped one's hands and gave him his head. She shared Isobel's certainty that the girl would, sooner or later, anger him. A little of Isobel's vapid character would soon cease to charm him, and she doubted whether Deveril had much patience. The more she saw of Isobel, the more convinced she was that Sir Nuneham was doing his sister no service by forcing this marriage on her.

'If you feel so strongly about Mr York, why did you agree to marry him?' Mandala asked.

Isobel stared at her. 'But I haven't!' she exclaimed. 'That's why I've run away! I know Nuneham will make me accept, but I can't, I can't!'

Mandala was thoroughly confused. 'Hasn't he offered for you, then? Or has he given you time to consider?'

'I don't need any time,' Isobel assured her. 'He hasn't

offered yet, so I ran away. I thought I might find
employment in Exeter or even Bristol. Anything would
be preferable to Deveril York.'

Mandala could not agree with those sentiments, but
this was not the time to say so. 'If he hasn't declared
himself, Miss Courtenay, don't you think you're being
rather precipitate? You have just said yourself that you
didn't think he was impressed by you. That suggests
that, while he may have come to Abbas St Antony to
"look you over" as you put it, he has decided you won't
suit after all.'

Isobel shook her head and the tears welled anew. 'I
thought that until today and then . . . They say that
listeners hear no good of themselves and I know it's
wrong to listen at doors, but I heard Nuneham's voice in
the library. He was obviously annoyed about something,
so I listened.'

'Go on.'

'Nuneham was arguing with Mr York. He asked him if
he intended to offer for me or whether he was just trifling
with me. Mr York said he hadn't made up his mind. He
didn't know if he could turn me into the sort of wife he
needed, that he didn't want to appear at Court with a
gauche schoolgirl beside him. That's what he called
me—a gauche schoolgirl—and it's all the more mortify-
ing because it's true.'

Mandala was silent. She turned Isobel's words over in
her mind. There seemed to be little room for misunderstanding there. It was a cold-blooded approach to marriage and not one which would suit Mandala, but it was
not uncommon. The only incongruity she could spot was
that Deveril had never struck her as a man who would
want so malleable a wife as the reported exchange
suggested. She did not doubt the truth of Isobel's claim
that no offer had yet been made, and that in itself
raised a number of interesting questions. Why had Sir
Nuneham told her a lie?

This was a matter she could ponder later in the
solitude of her own room. For the present, it was more
important to decide what to do with Isobel. In no
circumstances could she be allowed to proceed with her

plan to go to Exeter, much less to Bristol. The right thing to do, of course, was to persuade her to go home, but Mandala doubted her ability to get her to agree. She detected a hint of the stubbornness that often accompanies rather undecisive characters, and in this particular instance she could not bring herself to blame Isobel. She glanced down at the girl's blue satin slippers.

'You certainly can't walk to Exeter in those,' she said, 'and I don't have a horse in my stable that would suit; nor, if I did, do I have a manservant or a maid I could spare to go with you. It seems to me that the best thing would be to stay here. You will be perfectly safe—no debauches, no orgies, upon my honour!'

Isobel smiled perfunctorily. 'The more I see of you, the less inclined I am to believe all those tales,' she said. 'The thing that does worry me is that you will feel you have to tell Nuneham where I am.'

'I ought to do so, I know, but the circumstances are rather peculiar. I see no reason why you shouldn't stay here for a few days. I will concoct some story that will satisfy the servants and ensure they hold their tongues for the time being. Fortunately, I have no visitors, so you can safely walk in the immediate gardens without risk of discovery. How will that arrangement suit you?'

Isobel heaved a sigh of relief. 'Just so long as Nuneham—or Mr York—can't find me,' she said. 'I was already beginning to wonder if I would ever be able to reach Exeter when you found me, and, besides, I am not too far from Haddenham Hall, am I?'

'No,' Mandala agreed, bewildered by the sudden introduction of her other near neighbour. 'Is that important?'

'Not really,' Isobel assured her. 'Only, if Mark Haddenham should hear of my disappearance, he might be quite worried, mightn't he? If I am fairly close, it will be easier to reassure him.'

Quite a number of things dropped quietly into place with those naive words. So that was the way the wind blew! Mandala cast her mind over the congregation until it conjured up the pleasant, fresh-faced young man who shared Nathaniel Haddenham's pew. No wonder Isobel

considered Deveril York to be old. Mark Haddenham
certainly seemed a more natural choice for a young girl
than the rake, reformed or otherwise, that Deveril
undoubtedly was. Her understanding was that the
Haddenhams were no paupers, though their Puritan
leanings meant they were regarded with caution by
many. She doubted very much whether Sir Nuneham
would consider they had enough to offer his sister for
him to approve a match between the families, and she
doubted even more whether a Puritan like Nathaniel
Haddenham would be willing to relieve any financial
embarrassments experienced by the likes of Sir
Nuneham Courtenay. No, neither side would welcome
the match, even if Mark Haddenham felt as strongly
about Isobel as she did for him. There was always the
chance that it was an entirely one-sided fancy on Isobel's
part.

Mandala made no comment on the insight she had just
been given, but instead suggested that they see Mrs
Swinbrook and ask her to prepare a room for Isobel.
Sooner or later, Mandala would have to devise a story to
account satisfactorily for Isobel's presence, but for the
time being it would be enough to say only that she would
be staying for a few days.

As she lay in her large four-poster bed that night,
Mandala found she had much to occupy her mind. She
had a shrewd suspicion that, had Isobel's affections not
already been captured, wittingly or not, by Mark Haddenham, she could have been quite easily persuaded
that the worldly-wise Deveril York was a suitable husband. He was the sort of man with whom it would be
very easy to fancy oneself in love. It was perfectly
possible that a biddable, impressionable young wife
might suit him very well—and when the novelty of her
innocence wore off, as it undoubtedly would, he would
simply absent himself from home and find his pleasures
elsewhere. There were plenty of establishments similar
to that of Madame de Rouen, and no shortage of men,
married or otherwise, to patronise them. It was more
difficult to decide why Deveril, having come to Devon to
pay court to Isobel, should have spent so much time with

Mandala. He had claimed he had come initially to offer his condolences on Maman's death, and such a reason might account for one visit, but not for several. He had made no advances to her of any seriousness, and had treated her with no particular concern or tenderness. She had found his company agreeable, enjoying his occasional ascerbity of tongue. He had seemed to regard her in a similar light, but was that enough to account for his visits? She did not think he had sought her out to shock the people of Abbas St Antony, since she could not imagine his caring a fig for their opinion. Of course, there was always the possibility that he was delighted to escape from Sir Nuneham. Having now met the baronet, that would not surprise Mandala at all.

None of these considerations accounted for Sir Nuneham's behaviour. Why had he been so anxious to warn Mandala against his guest? Why had he lied about Deveril's position with regard to Isobel? Perhaps, having heard of his visits to Abbas Manor, Sir Nuneham assumed that Mandala might entice Deveril and thus thwart Sir Nuneham's plans for his sister. Perhaps he feared that his guest had sensed Isobel's dislike, and was looking further afield. It was equally possible that he simply sought an excuse to pay a first visit to Mandala before fixing his own interest in that direction. He certainly had good cause to need her fortune, if gossip was to be believed.

Whatever the explanation in each case, one thing was abundantly clear: neither man had behaved in an entirely straightforward way, and both must therefore be regarded with considerable caution. Having reached this eminently depressing conclusion, Mandala finally stopped tossing and turning and fell asleep.

CHAPTER SIX

'COME IN!' Deveril called, thinking that perhaps his host had sent a man to see if he could be of assistance in speeding the no-longer-welcome guest on his way. He looked up in surprise to see his host himself enter his bed-chamber. 'Courtenay! An unexpected pleasure!'

Sir Nuneham was oblivious of the irony. 'Have you seen Isobel?' he asked.

Deveril glanced at him quickly through narrowed eyes. What game was his host playing now? 'No. It seemed hardly appropriate. Why?'

'You're sure? You haven't spoken to her? You haven't caught a glimpse of her out walking, perhaps?'

Deveril put down the small pile of linen cravats he had been folding and looked carefully at Sir Nuneham. The baronet's face was devoid of all the affected suavity it normally displayed. He was clearly a worried man.

'I haven't spoken to her, and I haven't caught a glimpse of her from this window,' he said. 'You left the house shortly after our recent . . . discussion. I went down to the stables to tell my man what we were doing. I came back here for some luncheon, and since then I have been getting ready to leave. I shall spend the night at the inn in Abbas St Antony and go on in the morning. None of these activities has brought me any contact, however slight, with Miss Courtenay. Does that satisfy you?'

Sir Nuneham's worried frown deepened. He had no desire to say anything that might jeopardise his sister's good name and hitherto unblemished reputation, but, on the other hand, Deveril was exactly the sort of person who might know what to do.

'She is nowhere to be found,' he said at last. 'She is certainly not in the house or pleasure gardens, and I very much fear she has run away.'

'Why should she do that? Might she not have gone riding?'

Sir Nuneham shook his head. 'She rarely rides, as you may have noticed, and when she does, she always takes a groom. Besides, I have already enquired in the stables.'

'But why should she run away?' Deveril persisted. 'What makes you think she has?'

'I've no idea—it's a complete mystery. Her maid says she has taken her winter cloak and hood and two band-boxes crammed with whatever they would hold, which isn't a great deal, of course. A clean night-smock is missing, a brush and comb, some kerchiefs and a shawl. It looked as if she had tried to squash in a change of gown and discarded it on the floor when she failed.'

It was Deveril's turn to frown. 'It certainly sounds as if she has run away,' he agreed. 'I presume she took overshoes or pattens—and also that she has changed into something more practical than her dress this morning.'

'Meg says not. She says she is still wearing that blue—and the blue satin slippers that match it.'

'She won't get far in those!' Deveril exclaimed. 'Has no one any idea in which direction she went?'

'None at all. She hasn't been seen.' He hesitated. 'There is one possibility that occurs to me.'

'And that is?'

'I wondered if she might go to Haddenham Hall.'

'Why should she do that?'

Sir Nuneham's continued hesitation was tinged with embarrassment. 'The thing is, she imagines she has a—a . . . fondness for young Mark Haddenham. Most unsuitable, of course, and so I've told her, but there it is. She might have had some hen-witted idea of fleeing there.'

'Except that we have no idea why she should be fleeing at all,' Deveril pointed out. 'Does young Haddenham return this fondness?'

Sir Nuneham looked surprised. 'How should I know? I've never asked him. Wouldn't do to put ideas into his head that might not be there already.'

Deveril forbore to comment on this aspect of his host's brotherly concern for his sister's happiness. 'With your permission, Courtenay, I'll delay my departure. It seems to me you'll need as many reliable and discreet people for this hunt as you can find. We need to find your sister and get her back here as soon as we can, preferably before the servants have anything more to gossip about. Whatever we find, you may rest assured of my discretion.'

'Thank you, York,' Sir Nuneham said gratefully. 'Your help will be very welcome. Where do you think we had better begin? Shall I get keepers to search the woods?'

'Not yet. Not if you want to avoid gossip. I suggest we both ride over to Haddenham Hall as if nothing had happened. If you are right, the matter is quickly resolved and I'll wager Nathaniel Haddenham will be no more pleased to find her on his doorstep than you.'

During the ride over to Haddenham Hall, Deveril's mind was at least as occupied as her brother's with Isobel's disappearance, but with a different emphasis. He was naturally concerned, as anyone must be, at the possible loss of reputation a well-bred girl could suffer as a result of such an ill-judged action. He was far more concerned that her flight must, unless she was speedily found, result in a country-wide search. It did not suit Deveril's plans at all to have the woods between Lyme and Taunton beaten by keepers and landowners in the search for one silly female. The more he could do to ensure that they found her—and quickly—the better. There was a great deal at stake.

A degree of wariness accompanied Nathaniel Haddenham's greeting to his unexpected visitors, but a glance at their faces told him this was no social call. He showed them into a small room created by the walling-off of part of the Great Hall that gave this medieval house its name, and closed the door behind them. He listened in silence while Sir Nuneham told his story.

'You have my commiserations, Sir Nuneham,' he said. 'I shall be happy to do all I can to help you to find Miss Courtenay, but she is not here, and I'm not at all sure why you should expect her to be.'

Sir Nuneham reddened. 'She's a sensible girl on the whole, but she's only young, and has these girlish fancies,' he said. 'She imagines she has a fondness for your son. I dare say it's entirely her imagination, and I don't suppose he has done anything to encourage it, but it's there for all that and she might very well have thought this was the best place to be.'

Mr Haddenham said nothing, but went into the Hall to send a servant in search of his son. When Mark arrived shortly afterwards, his father said, 'Have you seen Isobel Courtenay today?'

'Isobel? No, Father, I haven't seen her for some time.'

'She hasn't been here?'

'Good heavens, no! Why should she do that?'

'Is there any reason why she might think you would offer her sanctuary here?'

'None at all! It would be a most improper thing to do!'

'Quite. Where else might she be?'

Mark looked from his father to their visitors, and some of the colour left his cheeks. 'I assume she's disappeared?'

'So it would seem.'

'Father, we must waste no time! We must get the keepers out, have them beat the woods. She could be anywhere. Anything might have happened to her.'

'If we act precipitately,' Deveril broke in, his voice deliberately calm, 'we spread word of her disappearance throughout this county and the neighbouring one. Before we send out search-parties, we must consider whether there is an alternative.'

Mark shook his head. 'If a cottager had found her, he would have sent word back to Courtenay Place or told the rector. She might be on Manor land, of course, but she wouldn't have gone to the Manor House itself.'

'How can you be so sure?' Deveril asked.

'She asked me once what it was Miss Sorn or her mother had done that was so terrible, and when I said I couldn't tell her, she said it must be very dreadful indeed and that she hoped she would never have to meet her. That was before Miss Sorn came here. When she did, Isobel said how glad she was Miss Sorn was not to be received because she didn't think she *could* visit her, no matter what. No, it won't have occurred to her to go there.'

It seemed to Deveril's dispassionately amused ear that this speech indicated a frequency of association and a degree of familiarity between Isobel and Mark that far exceeded any Sir Nuneham had imagined. It looked as if Isobel's brother had still not assimilated the inference of Mark's words, though Nathaniel Haddenham, who was not under the same strain as Sir Nuneham, could not have failed to notice. He did not seem at all surprised, an observation from which Deveril drew his own conclusions. All four men were unanimously of the opinion that they must do all in their power to minimise the risk to Miss Courtenay's reputation that would ensue if she were still missing once darkness fell, an eventuality that became increasingly likely as time passed. There was nothing for it but to spread the net wider, to have every inch of land searched—and to do this would need the services of every able-bodied man on both estates. It was decided that the reason for the search that would be given was the return of Miss Courtenay's horse to its stable without its rider. The servants at Courtenay Place would know this was untrue, of course, but their loyalty to the family should be enough to ensure their silence.

Over the next two days, it became clear, even to the preoccupied baronet, that Mark Haddenham's increasing distress at Isobel's continued absence must be attributable to more than neighbourly concern. Sir Nuneham was genuinely unable to suggest any reason for Isobel's disappearance, and Mark found this hard to accept.

'I know what it was,' the younger man insisted. 'You intended to force her to marry York. I mean no disrespect, sir,' he added, turning to Deveril, 'but she was frightened of you. She was terrified of being made to marry you.'

'Indeed? Then she was the victim of an overactive imagination,' Deveril said stiffly. 'I certainly gave her no cause for fear. Whatever may have been Sir Nuneham's aspirations, I can assure you I had no thought of marrying her, and I did nothing to lead her to believe that that was my intention.'

When Courtenay and Haddenham lands had been

meticulously and fruitlessly explored, the search was extended to Abbas Manor. While the keepers and farm workers of the other two estates worked gradually inwards from the boundaries, Deveril volunteered to advise Miss Sorn of their activities and request the help of some of her own people. His own anxieties were increasing hourly. The woods were saturated with searchers. The only hope for his own scheme was to find Isobel quickly. Not only would that result in the instant withdrawal of the search-parties, but it would mean that those who had spent so much time in the woods these last two days would turn their entire attention to their other tasks which had been temporarily set aside. There was even the probability that keepers would be expected to do a few days' farm work to enable the accumulation of tasks to be cleared. This would mean that the woods and combes would be quite empty—a perfect situation, if it could be brought about. It was dependent upon finding Isobel, and Deveril wondered when Sir Nuneham would be prepared to consider abandoning the present search and send messengers instead to Dorchester and Exeter and Taunton, perhaps as far afield as Salisbury, Bristol and even London, since, if there were no trace of her dead or alive in the countryside around her home, it must mean she had somehow—despite her satin slippers and unsuitable gown—gone further.

He approached Abbas Manor as he always preferred to do: down the gently sloping combe that gave him a sudden view of the topiary lawn with the knot-garden and then the house beyond. To avoid cutting up the closely scythed turf of the lawn, it then became necessary to make a détour to reach the front of the house, but that was no great inconvenience. Deveril found an inexplicable satisfaction in the thirteen neatly clipped yews set with eccentric disharmony in the neatly clipped grass. There was something gratifyingly anarchical about the contrast between order and disorder, and he wondered what a garden would be like that did not depend upon symmetry for its effects.

As he pondered these thoughts, his eye was taken by a blue-clad figure in the knot-garden who was walking towards the gap in the yew hedge that led to the topiary. His first thought was that it must be Mandala, and he was about to hail her when it occurred to him that this figure was of too slight a build to be the mistress of the Manor. He backed his horse quietly into the trees and watched through narrowed eyes. No, it was not Mandala. This woman was too short as well as too slight, and as far as he could tell from the few curls that escaped the lace kerchief over her head, her hair was fair and quite different from Mandala's deep copper. The dress, too, was blue, and that was not a colour associated with Mandala. It was, however, the colour Isobel Courtenay had apparently been wearing when she disappeared. Whoever she was, she seemed to know her way: there was nothing indecisive in her manner of walking. Had she been here all the time? Was Mark Haddenham so bad a judge of a woman's mind? Quite probably he was, Deveril thought cynically. It would take a greater experience of life than young Haddenham possessed to judge a woman's mind accurately. What was more puzzling was why Mandala had not sent word to Sir Nuneham to tell him his sister was safe. She must have known he would be worried. Whatever the explanation, it was from Mandala he must seek it, not from Isobel.

His arrival caused no surprise and little comment, Joan merely remarking that it had been a day or two since they had seen him—much as she might have remarked upon the weather—as she opened the door of Mandala's sitting-room and showed him in.

Mandala had been working on the household accounts and had given instructions that she was not to be disturbed, so that it was a look of mild annoyance that greeted Deveril as he entered. It cleared at once, however, and she threw down her quill and smiled.

'You catch me adding and subtracting, sir, and I am proficient at neither. Thank you for the respite!' Then she noticed that there was no answering smile on his lips, and she frowned. 'What brings you here, Mr York? Your face tells me it was not to pass the time of day.'

Instead of answering her, Deveril turned to the maid who was standing, as she knew she should, just inside the door. 'Leave us, Joan,' he said curtly. 'I have words to say to your mistress that are best said in private.'

Joan was young and, unlike Martha, disinclined to answer a gentleman back. She hesitated, looking at Mandala.

'Yes, go, Joan. And I think on this occasion you had better not wait outside the door. Go back to the kitchen —you must have plenty to do.'

'I have that, mistress. If you're sure . . .' she added doubtfully, and then, on Mandala's assurance that she was, she left the room, closing the door carefully.

'Will you not be seated, sir?' Mandala asked. 'The sooner you unburden yourself, the better, I fancy.'

'Thank you, but I prefer to stand. I do not imagine I shall take up much of your time. Tell me, was it Isobel Courtenay I saw in your knot-garden as I arrived?'

'I imagine it may well have been.'

'Are you aware that she has been missing from home for more than two days and nights?' he went on.

'I can hardly fail to be, since she has been here during that time.' Mandala forced herself to appear unconcerned in the face of his evident anger.

'Did it not occur to you that Sir Nuneham might be very worried?'

'Of course it did! However, Isobel has been perfectly safe here under my chaperonage. Would Sir Nuneham have preferred me to let her continue with her plan to walk to Exeter?'

'He would have preferred you to let him know she was safe!'

'So that he might rest easy in his bed? He should have anticipated the consequences when he started laying plans for her future that didn't coincide with her own!'

'Since when has a schoolgirl expected to plan her own future?' Deveril demanded. 'Any caring guardian would expect to make the best possible arrangements for his ward.'

'To the point of alarming her into running away?' Mandala retorted. 'What do you think would have happened to her in Exeter—or sooner? She even had plans to go on to Bristol if there was no work for her in Exeter.'

Deveril stared at her briefly in silence. 'Work? What work could Isobel Courtenay do?'

'I haven't the slightest idea what she thought she could do, but I have a shrewd idea what she would end up doing—particularly if she reached Bristol! And I would have thought that a man of your sort might be able to appreciate how little choice in the matter she would be given!'

Deveril's mouth tightened and the harsh lines of his face deepened still further. If Isobel had been treated to that expression, Mandala thought, it was no wonder she had been so frightened. She was herself finding it difficult to appear unconcerned, but she lifted her chin a fraction and determined not to let him suspect that her heart was quaking.

'I still don't understand why you didn't let Sir Nuneham know,' Deveril went on. 'Your failure to do so has caused distress and inconvenience to a number of people, as well as putting well-laid plans in jeopardy.'

'Now we're beginning to hear the truth at last!' Mandala exclaimed. 'The real reason for all this anger is because poor Isobel so dreaded the thought of marrying you that she fled the house to escape your declaration. Your pride has been hurt. Your plan to acquire a gently-born wife has been rendered untenable—even you won't drag an unwilling bride to the altar!'

Deveril frowned. 'Why was she so sure I should offer?' he asked.

'She tells me she was listening outside a door when you expressed your intention to her brother. I don't know what you've done or said, but she's terrified of you. Also, she believes her affections are engaged elsewhere, and that makes it worse.'

'Young Haddenham.' Deveril nodded.

'You knew—and you still intended to offer? How callous can you be?' Mandala exclaimed.

'Quite a lot more callous than that,' he said grimly. 'As it happens, I did not know. It's something I've discovered since her disappearance.'

'Do you still intend to go ahead with your plans?'

Deveril smiled sardonically. 'The discovery of Isobel Courtenay means that my plans can continue without hindrance.'

Mandala stared at him, aware of a sinking feeling somewhere inside that she could not explain. 'You really intend this to make no difference?'

'Why should it? It has been satisfactorily resolved.'

'I doubt if Isobel would see it in that light.'

'Fortunately, it has nothing to do with Isobel.'

'The fact that you can say so underlines the total unsuitability of such a match!' Mandala exclaimed. 'Isobel is timid and shy. She will be in her element running a country household because she knows precisely how to do so, but she would be quite lost in a grand London house where she was expected to play the hostess to the brittle, gossip-mongering high-fliers of London society. Surely you can see that?'

'You have a flattering notion of my life away from here,' Deveril remarked.

Mandala flushed. 'I know very little of it, but I have a shrewd idea of how you can behave when you're not being the gentleman. Isobel's nature and her sheltered background both leave her unfitted to be your wife.'

He took a pace towards her with an expression on his face that made Mandala step involuntarily backwards against the edge of the table at which she had been writing. His face was hard, his eyes unsmiling, and when he reached out and grasped her upper arms in a grip of such intensity that she could almost feel the bruises develop, she knew fear. It took a considerable effort of will not to let him see how much he had alarmed her.

'Let me go, sir,' she said in a commendably calm voice.

He ignored her request. 'No one could accuse you of having either a timid nature or a sheltered background,' he said. 'Are you offering yourself in Isobel's place?'

'Of course I'm not! Do you expect me to submit to a lifetime of being bullied and brow-beaten? You much mistake me if you do!'

'Is that how you see marriage?'

'No, sir, it's not. It's how I see marriage to *you*! No wonder poor Isobel was terrified! But I am not so easily frightened—and neither have I a brother to plan my future for me, for which I am eternally grateful!'

'Your brother's problem would be to find a man willing to take on such a virago as you,' Deveril commented. 'It had occurred to me that it would be amusing to seduce you. Now I think my pleasure would be in bringing you to heel.'

As her mouth opened to retort, his own descended on it, hard and unyielding, forcing her head back as his hands pulled her roughly towards him. His arms slid round her body in a grip that lost none of its strength in the change, and she was disconcertingly aware of the power of his body against hers.

When he lifted his head from that harsh, unsought kiss, she shook her head and whispered, 'No,' but he silenced that objection with another kiss, less cruel and demanding this time, but lacking none of its predecessor's strength. The instinct to resist melted under the questing insistence of his lips, and an unfulfilled desire swept through Mandala's veins. Of her own volition she sought to be ever closer to the source of power that radiated from this man. Her unexpected and sensual compliance aroused Deveril's own desire, and the nature of their embrace subtly changed as each vied with the other to express the emotions that had overtaken them. As Mandala's mouth opened again under the entirely pleasurable demands of his own and his tongue sought hers within, she gave a little groan of expectant pleasure, and Deveril knew that the desire he felt to possess her was total and immediate. He knew, too, that there would be no naïve schoolgirl's last-minute pulling back for the woman who responded with such sensuality to this caress. Time seemed suspended as they clung together in urgent embrace, and then, suddenly, the mood was broken.

A voice at the door said apologetically, 'I am so sorry, Mandala, I had no idea . . . Mr York!'

Startled, they both turned to face Isobel, who coloured with confusion. 'I didn't know you were expecting a visitor,' she went on.

'I was not,' Mandala assured her, moving unobtrusively away from Deveril's embrace, and vitally aware that, while his hold had slackened at the sound of Isobel's voice, his hand did not finally drop from her waist until she was sufficiently far from him to leave no choice. 'Mr York's arrival was entirely unexpected.'

'But not unwelcome,' Isobel observed. 'You told me that you had met him. I had no idea you were on terms of such—such intimacy.'

Mandala flushed. 'We are not, I assure you,' she said, realising, as she uttered the words, how unconvincing they must seem.

Deveril glanced from one woman to the other, a cynical smile on his harsh features and a glitter in his eyes that neither woman understood or trusted. He bowed ironically towards Isobel. 'You cannot be unaware of Miss Sorn's reputation,' he said. 'We are old friends. Your brother will tell you that I have been an almost daily visitor here—until your disappearance. He wasn't very happy about it,' he concluded in an almost reminiscent tone and smiled blandly, ignoring Mandala's gasp of outrage.

'Nuneham knows about your visits?' Isobel echoed.

'Oh, yes,' Deveril said cheerfully. 'Took me to task about them only the other day. He seemed concerned that I might no longer wish to offer for you.'

Mild, timid Isobel reddened with shame and anger and exhibited an unexpected streak of iron. 'Indeed? These things may not seem so very dreadful among men, whom I do not pretend to understand, but I take leave to tell you, Mr York, that I was not entirely overjoyed at the idea of marrying you before, and after today, I have no intention whatever of doing so. Why, you don't even have the grace to look ashamed of yourself!'

'Perhaps that's because I've never learned to be ashamed of enjoying myself.'

Furious at the implication of this remark, Mandala raised her hand to strike him, and found it caught in mid-air in the grip she knew so well. 'Don't interfere, Mandala,' he said curtly. 'This discussion is with Miss Courtenay.' He turned to Isobel. 'Be careful what you say, Miss Courtenay. If you persist in this refusal, you will be rejecting not only me but my not inconsiderable fortune, and your brother won't like that.'

'I no longer care what Nuneham likes!' Isobel declared. 'If this is how you behave before you've even made a formal offer, what can I expect when we're married? No, Nuneham will have to find another way to restore his fortunes.'

Deveril refrained from pointing out that, since he had never intended making an offer, his behaviour was his own business. If Isobel could be driven further into her present stated position, even Sir Nuneham would have to abandon any last faint hope that his guest would change his mind. 'Then I suggest that you return home without delay, and tell him so. You may rest assured that I shall inform him that I have no desire to acquire a reluctant bride. We must hope his relief at your safe return will be sufficient to overcome his natural annoyance at seeing a fortune slip through his fingers.'

Isobel regarded him in scornful silence for a few moments before turning to her hostess. 'I must thank you, Mandala, for opening my eyes further to the true nature of a man I had already taken in dislike. I must thank you, too, for your kind hospitality. I realise now how very impractical my original scheme was, and you saved me from the disastrous results it would have had. May I impose upon your generosity in one more thing? Could you ask one of your servants to escort me back to Courtenay Place?'

'Certainly not!' Mandala exclaimed. 'I shall take you home myself. Oh, I know I am not received,' she added with a hint of bitterness, 'but nevertheless, assurances from me that you have been in no way compromised will bear greater weight than those of a servant. Mr York,' she went on, turning to Deveril, 'you are very much *de trop*. You have made it clear to Isobel that there is no future together for the two of you, and you have made clear to both of us your estimation of me. I see no point in your remaining in this house and very little in your ever returning to it. Please go.'

Deveril bowed, and somehow succeeded in turning the gesture into one of mockery. 'I'll go, Miss Sorn, and with alacrity. You seem almost to have acquired the arts of a skilful tease. Did your mother teach you? If so, she had an apt pupil. It is not a characteristic of women that I particularly admire, but, happily, I am unlikely to encounter it again.'

Mandala flushed, and her green eyes flashed with anger at the calculated insult. 'I, for my part, hope never to see you again! Perhaps you would be kind enough to seek out Sir Nuneham before you leave the vicinity, and tell him that his sister is on her way home.'

'I had naturally intended to do so,' he said stiffly, and then his voice softened. 'Good day, Mandala.'

'Goodbye, Mr York,' Mandala replied, annoyed that he should still choose to insult her with a form of address he had no justification for using.

'Goodbye? Not yet, I fancy—not just yet,' he said cryptically, and left the room before she had time to retort.

Since Isobel did not enjoy riding and this was an occasion when a degree of style might be appropriate, Mandala sent word to the stables that she would have the horses put to the carriage. This was a great, lumbering vehicle built by some long-dead Sorn for show rather than style or comfort. An immensely long vehicle, the almost square body was slung between high wheels at the back and small ones at the front so that it looked like some monstrous dusty beetle spread-eagled in front of the house. It looked as if it was a very long time indeed since it had last left the coach-house, and Mandala hoped it would not fall apart on the rough tracks between Abbas Manor and Courtenay Place. In this, she underestimated the zeal of her steward. Jonah Swinbrook had never seen the coach put to before, but his job was to see to it that, like everything else on the estate, it was well maintained and ran smoothly. This he had done. A coach so rarely used did not warrant the keeping of a team of carriage-horses, but the plough-horses, though perhaps less elegant, were perfectly capable of drawing it on the slow, painful journey.

When they drew up at Sir Nuneham's ornate portico, Mandala's muscles felt as though they had endured a hundred miles of jolting instead of just ten, and she groaned inwardly at the thought that she would have to endure it again on the return journey.

Sir Nuneham came to the door himself, and Mandala was pleased to observe that he was genuinely relieved to see his sister again, quite unharmed. He showed them into a large saloon which managed without difficulty to combine elegance with discomfort. No one had thought to light the fire, so the room had no welcoming cheer about it, and so oppressive to the spirits was the whole effect that Mandala was almost surprised to be offered a cup of chocolate and a dish of sweetmeats, all of which were beyond criticism.

'Mr York tells me that you offered Isobel shelter and deterred her from a course of action that could only have been disastrous,' Sir Nuneham said to Mandala. 'I owe you my gratitude.'

'Not at all,' Mandala said politely. 'I am sure any neighbour would have done the same.' She hesitated infinitesimally. 'Is Mr York still here?'

'York? Why, no! He could hardly remain after Isobel had given him so unambiguous a statement of her feelings towards him.' Sir Nuneham could see no useful purpose in letting either woman know the essence of his earlier conversation with Deveril York. Isobel was timid enough as it was. Better by far that she should believe she had sent York away than that she should learn he had never intended to offer for her. As for Mandala, Sir Nuneham had his own plans in that direction, and it could only work to his advantage to let her believe his recent visitor to be a philanderer.

Mandala nodded, an inexplicable disappointment creeping into her spirits even though she had not really expected any other answer. She returned to the more immediate matter that had brought her here. 'Your sister has been entirely safe in my care, Sir Nuneham,' she assured him. 'I am aware that my reputation might not lead one to expect it, but Isobel has been as carefully looked after as any guardian could wish.'

'Mandala's ideas are even stricter than yours, Nuneham,' his sister broke in. 'At least, where I was concerned,' she added, recollecting that the standards Mandala allowed herself differed very considerably in some respects from those she had allowed her guest.

'I don't doubt that Miss Sorn did everything that was right,' Sir Nuneham replied. 'You were very fortunate that she found you.'

'I see that now,' Isobel admitted. 'I shall *try* not to give you cause for concern again, Nuneham, but I shall be much obliged if you will stop trying to find a husband for me that suits you. It will not be you that has to live with him.'

Sir Nuneham would not allow that to pass unchallenged. 'Perhaps the choice of Deveril York was a trifle ill advised, but a fortune such as his is inclined to blunt the shrewdest judgment. You can't expect me to play no part in planning your future, though. I am your guardian, after all, and can be expected to have your best interests at heart.'

Abashed, Isobel agreed, and Mandala reminded herself that, as a visitor, she could hardly draw their attention to the fact that the judgment of anyone who could persuade himself that Deveril York and Isobel Courtenay were suitable marriage partners must be very suspect. So she replaced her cup on the silver tray and stood up. 'If my slight intervention has cleared up any misunderstanding between you two, it has been worth while. Perhaps you would escort me to my coach, Sir Nuneham. I really should delay my return no longer.'

The baronet hastened to her bidding, assuring her as he handed her into the antiquated vehicle that, so far as he was concerned, her reputation was entirely retrieved and he would say as much to anyone who asked.

Since Mandala did not think it very probable that people who thought they knew his mind on the subject, and had already made up their own, would suddenly start asking him if he now held a different opinion, she merely smiled politely and bade him farewell before leaning back against the squabs and resigning herself to another ten bone-shattering miles.

Sir Nuneham Courtenay was not one to miss pressing home any conceivable advantage he felt he might have, and the very next day found him paying a courtesy call on the mistress of Abbas Manor. He was shown into a pleasant room at the rear of the house, and made a quick appraisal while Mandala was informed of his arrival. It was all very old-fashioned, of course, but that did not really matter because he had no intention of removing from the far more impressive Courtenay Place, even if marriage to Mandala would make him Lord of the Manor. He was unsure whether to keep the Manor and its lands. If, as he hoped, Mandala had sufficient wealth for his purposes, there would be no need, and it would always be excellent collateral, old-fashioned or not.

These happy thoughts were interrupted by the present owner of Sir Nuneham's future wealth, and he greeted her with a warmth that was enhanced by the fact that she was wearing the informal undress-gown that was now so fashionable for receiving morning callers. 'I have come, not only to pay my respects, but also to convey my thanks for your care of my sister,' he said, eyeing Martha, who clearly intended to stay, with some displeasure. Mandala Sorn need not play propriety quite so rigorously—after all, had he not only yesterday intimated to her that he considered her reputation to be all that one could wish? This business of Isobel's foolish escapade had made them friends, and a chaperon among friends was surely superfluous.

Mandala smiled, and indicated that he might like to be seated, following the gesture by sitting down herself. 'Not at all, Sir Nuneham. I'm sure any neighbour would have done the same. Martha,' she continued, turning to the old servant, 'I think we would both like some refreshment.'

Any hope Sir Nuneham might have had that this request would send Martha to the kitchen was short lived, the maid simply going to the door and conveying the instruction to the servant outside, and when the tray appeared with Madeira and glasses in acknowledgment of the fact that their visitor was a gentleman, it was Martha who poured it out and handed each of them a glass before retiring to her seat by the door.

'I hope Isobel is happier now that she is not in daily expectation of a declaration from Mr York,' Mandala said. 'She really had taken an aversion to him, you know.'

Sir Nuneham sniffed. 'Foolish child. She tells me now that she was frightened of him! I promise you, he behaved with perfect propriety.'

'He would hardly have behaved otherwise in your house,' Mandala pointed out. 'I don't think it was a question of his doing anything to frighten her, but he has a very . . . forceful personality, and Isobel is young and rather timid. I fancy her fear was in reality a fear of being swamped by his stronger character, though I doubt if she would put it quite like that.'

Sir Nuneham looked doubtful. 'Perhaps you're right, Miss Sorn. It was none the less a great disappointment to me. I had hoped . . .'

The door was flung unceremoniously open, and Joan, harassed and red-faced, burst in, only just remembering to bob a curtsy. 'Oh, mistress, there's been the most awful to-do, you'd not believe! I'm surprised you didn't hear the uproar! Cook's belabouring it with a ladle and the poor thing's more confused than ever, and if we don't do something soon, every pie in the kitchen will be trodden into the floor, and that's a fact!'

'What on earth are you talking about?' Mandala demanded.

'The little Dexter cow—the one Jonah Swinbrook bought at Taunton market for the house. We all told him it would be a mistake, and now look where we are!'

'Calm down, girl, do!' Martha interjected. 'We're none of us the wiser. Count up to five and tell us what's happened.'

'She's a sight too tame, and that's the truth,' Joan said. 'She got out of her field—don't ask me how, for I don't know—and wandered up to the house. There's steps

down into the kitchen, mistress, as you very well know,
which you'd think would make any cow stop and think,
like, wouldn't you? Not her! Oh, no! Down she comes,
dainty as a lady, wreaks havoc and then can't get up
them again. When I left the kitchen, she was running
round and round waving her horns, and cook was beating her with a ladle. Everyone else was running around
screaming.'

'Has no one thought to fetch a man in from the fields?'
Mandala demanded.

'Why, no, Miss Sorn. I thought you should be told
first,' Joan said, surprised.

'I'll go, mistress,' Martha suggested. 'She's a sweet
enough thing when she's not surrounded by half-wits. If
she got down those steps, she can be coaxed up them
again. With your permission, of course,' she added
doubtfully, looking at Sir Nuneham.

'Yes, of course—you must go. Joan, you will do
exactly as Martha tells you, and so will everyone else
there. Do you understand?'

Joan assured her that she did and followed Martha
out, only just remembering to close the door behind her.

Sir Nuneham could not believe his luck. He knew
perfectly well that a gentleman would now take his
leave, thus allowing his hostess to attend to her domestic
crisis and relieve her of the embarrassment of being
alone with him.

Not that Mandala seemed the least bit embarrassed,
he noted with satisfaction. This did not at all surprise
him, considering her background, but it was none the
less reassuring. He must hope that the little Dexter cow
would take a long time to be pacified and even longer to
be coaxed back to her field. He had no intention of
forgoing this opportunity to be alone with the heiress.
He resumed the conversation as though there had been
no interruption.

'As I was saying, Miss Sorn, I had hoped to make an
advantageous match for Isobel, and I am by no means
convinced that, with a little effort on her part, she
couldn't have overcome her initial dislike.'

'Oh, come, Sir Nuneham! You must know that she has

a fondness for Mark Haddenham. Even were Deveril York twice as accomplished a rake as he is, he would be hard put to it to excite the interst of a girl who fancies her heart is already bespoken.'

'Mark Haddenham!' he said bitterly. 'A provincial Puritan—no fit match for the sister of Sir Nuneham Courtenay!'

'Perhaps not, but if you thought of Isobel as someone on her own account and not just as your sister, perhaps you could realise that she's ideally suited to be the wife of a provincial gentleman. I have no idea what Mr Haddenham's feelings for her may be, but she will make a happier match with someone like him than with a Deveril York.'

'Happier!' he said scornfully. 'You've picked up some odd ideas in France, Miss Sorn! Marriage is not a question of happiness, it's a matter of property— property and breeding.'

'Isobel's fancy has not been engaged by some impoverished younger son with his living to earn,' Mandala pointed out. 'Most people would regard Mark Haddenham as a very pretty catch. I can see no reason why a woman shouldn't try to make a happy marriage as well as a prudent one—or a man, either.'

'The ideal situation,' Sir Nuneham agreed. 'I fancy it is rarely encountered, however.' He paused, not quite sure how to broach what was in his mind, and then decided that ingratiation was a good way to start. 'You are yourself a woman well equipped to make any man happy,' he said.

Mandala fixed him with a glare that would have frozen a more sensitive man. 'Indeed?' she said repressively. 'I think that is not a matter which need concern us.'

'It pains me to disagree with a lady, but I must do so in this instance,' Sir Nuneham told her, smiling indulgently. 'Mandala—I feel your friendship with my sister entitles us to eschew the formalities—it can't be denied that your wealth is a powerful lure, but your beauty is such that men would desire you had you not a penny to your name.'

'Quite possibly,' Mandala said drily. 'Whether they

would wish to marry me as well is quite another matter.'

'Not at all!' Sir Nuneham reached over and seized her hand. 'Such beauty in the mistress of his house would enhance any man's position.' He pressed her hand to his lips and kissed it ardently.

Mandala got to her feet and Sir Nuneham was obliged to do so too, since he was not prepared to relinquish her hand. 'I think you had better leave, Sir Nuneham, before you overstep the mark and regret it.'

'Come, Mandala, there need be no coyness between us. I am offering for this delicate hand,' he said, raising its fingers to his lips and kissing them one by one. 'I can give you a position in society that you can achieve by no other means.'

'A position made possible by my fortune, no doubt,' she said sarcastically.

'I won't deny that it would play its part, because you wouldn't believe me if I did, but that isn't the only reason for my interest in you. Mandala, your background, your unique upbringing, make you infinitely desirable as a wife. Once the door is closed on friends and acquaintances and we are on our own . . .' He left the sentence unfinished, and his hand slipped round her waist, revelling in the sensuality of the unconstrained body beneath the informal satin gown.

'Sir Nuneham, you forget yourself,' Mandala said icily, trying to slide unobtrusively from his grasp, and failing. 'Let me go, and take your leave. I shall try to behave in future as if this hasn't happened.'

'Come, come! You play your part well, but you don't deceive me. Why, you must have learned tricks other women don't even dream of! And, I promise, you won't find me lacking in appreciation of them!' He had undone the single button that fastened the bodice of the undress-gown as he spoke, and his hand was fumbling under the smock beneath, which now, the loosened gown no longer keeping it in place, began to slip down her shoulders. As the smooth white curve of her breasts was exposed, he sighed and sank his mouth into the valley between, intending to progress by seductive degrees to the tips that thrust, rosy and tempting, towards him.

The time had passed when he would listen to reason, and Mandala knew from faint cries still emanating from the kitchen regions that she could not count on release from that quarter. She could only thank goodness that he lacked Deveril York's strength, and she reached for the large and handsome Delft vase that stood on the court cupboard close by. Her movements were necessarily restricted by Sir Nuneham's clasp; she had only one free hand, and the vase was heavy and difficult to grasp from this angle. She managed to clutch it by the rim, however, and raised it as high as she could, intending to bring it crashing down on the baronet's skull. Her efforts served only to upset her balance, and as she swayed in the attempt to right herself, her leg found itself hooked behind one of Sir Nuneham's, and his balance, too, was overset.

He cried out with surprise, and loosed his hold of her as he went down. His head hit the ornate cupboard upon which the vase had so recently been standing, but the sound of that impact was deadened by that of the vase fragmenting on the wooden floor. Sir Nuneham slid to his knees and then into a crumpled heap among the shards of blue and white pottery.

Mandala clutched her gown around her and stared at him in dismay. Was he dead? Had she killed him with the vase? She could not even recall having felt the vase make contact with his head, though that had certainly been her intention. From his position, it seemed probable that he had also hit himself on the cupboard. Would that have been enough to kill him? Whatever the cause, he lay there unmoving. If she had killed him, she would have to fetch the servants to do whatever it was one did in these circumstances, and she would rather they did not see her in her present state of disarray. She noticed now that the single button of her gown was missing. Perhaps, if she ran upstairs and found a brooch with which to fasten it, they might not notice. She had no desire to have her servants tell the magistrate of the state she was in—that would simply confirm the local opinion of her morals.

She slipped out of the room and down the corridor towards the hall. Matters still seemed to be unsettled in the kitchen, though the fact that no sound was now filtering into the room where Sir Nuneham lay must mean that the problem was slightly abated. She frowned to see the front door not completely closed, and quickly fastened it. The sound of the catch clicking into its mortice brought someone to the door of the small room where she more usually received visitors.

'So there is someone there,' a familiar voice said, and Mandala spun round to find herself face to face with Deveril York.

He looked her up and down with the irony of familiarity that missed nothing, and she instinctively clutched the bodice of her gown more closely over her bosom.

'I appear to intrude,' he added drily.

Mandala flushed. 'I cannot imagine what you are doing here or how you got in! The servants are all busy.'

'So I gather. The door was open, and since I have little time at my disposal, I let myself in. I assumed that a servant would soon come to fasten it. I came to see you, but I am clearly *de trop.*'

Mandala was fast retrieving the wits that his unexpected appearance had scattered. 'Not at all,' she said. 'In fact, your arrival is most opportune. I think I've killed Sir Nuneham Courtenay.'

'Indeed? I'm not surprised that someone should do so, but I would not have expected it to be you. Why?'

'I don't doubt that you now hold the same view of me that everyone else seems to do, but I do *not* customarily welcome men's advances—and certainly not those of men like Sir Nuneham.'

'Thus at least proving your good taste, if not your high moral standards,' he remarked dispassionately. 'Now I understand your . . .' he hesitated as if seeking the right word, but surveying her in such a way that Mandala almost felt as if she was wearing nothing at all ' . . . your dishevelled appearance. May one enquire just how you murdered Sir Nuneham?'

'I don't know that I have,' Mandala reminded him, 'but he *is* very still. I hit him with a vase—or perhaps his head hit the cupboard. I'm not sure which.'

'Not that rather large one depicting Adam and Eve?'

'Yes, that's the one,' Mandala told him uneasily.

'Did it break?'

'Of course it broke! There must be a thousand fragments on the floor!'

Deveril shook his head sadly. 'A pity. That was a superb piece: far too good to waste on Courtenay! You'd better take me to him.'

There was no denying that it was a relief to shift some of the responsibility for action to someone else's shoulders, and Mandala gratefully led Deveril to the room where her victim lay. Mandala half hoped they would find him sitting up and rubbing his head, but he was exactly where she had left him. Afraid of what she might find if she went too close, she stayed by the door while Deveril stepped quickly over and dropped to one knee by the inert body. It was a few seconds before he lifted his head towards her, the trace of a smile on his lips.

'Would you be relieved to learn that he still lives?' he asked.

'Of course I would! I didn't *intend* to kill him! Are you sure?' she added doubtfully.

Deveril rose and came over to her. 'Quite sure,' he said. 'Will you follow my advice?' Mandala nodded. 'Good girl. Go to your room and make yourself look less like someone who has been tumbling in the hay. No, I know you haven't been: it may surprise you, but it so happens that I believe you. If others see you like that, they will arrive at quite another conclusion, I promise you. Make yourself decent, and then come back. Don't be in too much of a hurry: I want Courtenay gone before you get here. Do you understand?'

Mandala assured him that she did, and hurried from the room before the servants began to return to their tasks. Deveril's advice was sound, and she had no hesitation in following it.

When the door had closed behind her, Deveril wasted no time. A smaller vase held some wild flowers and these he removed, dashing the water in Sir Nuneham's face. The baronet stirred and groaned. He put up his hand to his face and brought it away wet, and he stared at it as though to try to understand why it should be so. His eye fell upon two black leather riding-boots facing him. He followed them up to their owner.

'York?' he said. 'Where am I?' and then, remembering at least that much, 'What are you doing here?'

'Extricating you from potential embarrassment,' Deveril told him grimly. 'Pull yourself together, and be off! If the servants see you, the story of how Miss Sorn protected her virtue will be round the county in a matter of hours, and it will lose nothing in the telling. You'll be a figure of ridicule from Dorchester to Bristol, and probably as far as London.'

Sir Nuneham had by this time located the bump on his head caused by the blow, and it was difficult to tell whether his sudden flinching was because of Deveril's words or the pain.

'She hit me, the vicious hell-cat!' he said.

'She thought she'd killed you,' Deveril replied. 'Count yourself fortunate you're no more than bruised. Bear in mind another time that if you insist on behaving like any back-street tom, you must expect occasionally to meet a recipient of your favours who retaliates in kind.'

Sir Nuneham struggled to his feet, knowing he must look as foolish as he felt. It did nothing to improve his temper. 'And what in God's name are you doing here? I thought you'd left the county.'

'Only Courtenay Place. My reason for visiting Miss Sorn need not concern you, Courtenay. It is, however, unlikely to provoke the same reaction as yours has done.'

Sir Nuneham flushed. 'You take a damned sight too much upon yourself, York!' he said, casting his still befuddled mind back over the conversation. 'This is Miss Sorn's house. What right have you to tell me to go? When Miss Sorn tells me to do so, perhaps I shall.'

Any hint of tolerant amusement disappeared from Deveril's face. 'When I saw Miss Sorn she was very distressed and in a state of considerable *déshabillé*, for which I gather you were responsible. I told her to make herself look respectable again, and undertook to get you off the premises by the time she had done so.'

'Why you? Why should you issue such orders and give such undertakings?'

'Simply because I was there. Any gentleman would have done the same, but perhaps that is beyond the comprehension of one who loses no opportunity to seduce an unattended female.'

'I'll have you know I offered my hand—and my title—to Miss Sorn,' Sir Nuneham answered indignantly.

'I take it that she declined,' was the bland reply.

Sir Nuneham shifted uneasily. 'As to that, when she has had time to consider all the advantages, I'm sure she will come round to my view.'

'I don't advise you to bet on it,' Deveril told him. 'Not until your luck has shown signs of changing, at all events. Now go. I think Miss Sorn has had quite enough of your company for one day.' He picked Sir Nuneham's hat up from the floor, and handed it to him.

'I'm damned if I see why you should order me from a house that isn't yours,' Sir Nuneham grumbled as he put it back on his head. 'You're up to something, and I don't like it. I'll get even with you, York, even if the attempt kills me.'

'As it may very well do,' Deveril said dispassionately. 'Now go. Miss Sorn has no desire to meet you on the way out.'

Sir Nuneham was sure there must be some devastating put-down by which, could he but think of it, he could reverse their present positions, but his head hurt so much that it eluded him. He made his exit with an outward show of dignity that he was far from feeling, and when Martha opened the door a few moments later, she saw only Deveril York picking up pieces of china from the floor.

'You!' she said. 'Where's Sir Nuneham? And Miss Sorn?'

'Sir Nuneham? Has he been here?' Deveril looked mildly surprised. 'I believe Miss Sorn will be with me in a moment. Do you think she will be very angry when she sees I have foolishly knocked over this vase?'

'Furious, I should think,' Martha told him cheerfully.

'She had a particular fondness for it.'

They both turned as Mandala came into the room now formally dressed in a plain gown of modest cut. The neck was wide, as fashion demanded, but shallow and edged with an upstanding lace frill that added to its modesty. The sleeves were tight to the elbow with turned-back cuffs revealing the puffed linen sleeves of the shift, and the overskirt was parted in the front and looped back to show an absolutely plain pleated petticoat in precisely the same shade of amber satin. There was no train, and her only other adornment was a single strand of pearls. Her gleaming copper hair was parted in the middle, and one long ringlet fell carefully over her right shoulder. Deveril thought he had never seen so complete a transformation achieved in so short a time.

Martha was less complimentary. 'Humph!' she said. 'Quite the little Puritan, aren't we?'

Mandala seemed to have regained her composure, and ignored this sally. 'Have you got the little Dexter out of the kitchen, Martha?'

'Back in her field as if nothing had happened. Best you don't go near the kitchen yet awhile. She wrought havoc there, and no mistake, though it's my belief the fault lies mostly with the cook and the spit-boy, who frightened her half to death with their shouting and beating. I see Sir Nuneham's gone.'

'I think he felt it advisable,' Mandala equivocated a little apprehensively, but Martha seemed to detect nothing amiss.

'This one's broken the Creation vase,' the maid went on, pointing to the débris on the floor.

'I deeply regret it, Miss Sorn,' Deveril interjected quickly. 'I fear my elbow caught it. Your maid tells me it was a favourite piece, which makes my apologies the more necessary.'

Mandala coloured slightly, and hoped Martha would not speculate on the reasons. 'I was fond of it, but not to the extent that I wouldn't sacrifice it if I felt I had to,' she said.

'That's not what you said when one of the girls nearly knocked it the other day,' Martha reminded her. 'Still, I dare say it makes a difference when a man's the cause.'

'All the difference in the world,' Mandala told her. 'You have no need to remain here, Martha. I'm sure you've work to get on with.'

'Have you ever known me not to have? But I'll not leave you here with Mr York, begging your pardon, sir. It wouldn't be seemly.'

'Martha, it will be perfectly seemly. Mr York won't be here for long. Leave the door open, if it makes you feel happier.'

Martha sniffed her disapproval but closed the door behind her. Mandala looked gratefully at Deveril.

'Thank you, Mr York. You seem to have accounted satisfactorily for all the irregularities that have beset me this morning.'

'Courtenay says he offered for you and was rejected. He seems to think you will change your mind later, when you've had time to consider the advantages.'

Mandala smiled weakly. 'He deludes himself. It has never crossed my mind to see him as a possible husband, and after his behaviour today it is quite out of the question. I could never marry a man who was prepared to take that sort of advantage of me.'

'I see.'

Mandala wondered if it were her imagination that there seemed suddenly to be a distance between them. Perhaps she should change the subject. 'What brought you here, Mr York?'

Uncharacteristically, he hesitated. 'I have no desire to justify Sir Nuneham's actions,' he said at last, 'but you should remember that your mother's profession is common knowledge—and you have done nothing to minimise the gossip that knowledge has aroused. It is only to be expected that people will assume you have the same standards as she. You should strive to be doubly circumspect in your speech, your actions—even your dress. The gown you were wearing when I arrived—or half wearing!—is very fashionable, but you cannot deny that it is not one in which to receive a man, unless you wish to confirm his preconceived ideas about you. The one you are wearing now is much more suitable.'

'I didn't know he was coming,' Mandala protested. 'Nor was I expecting you, and, while I will accept with hindsight that you may be right, I feel bound to say that it is quite wrong to base assumptions on anything so trivial as dress!'

'Nevertheless, human nature is such that people do. In your position, you need to be more careful than most.

'Are you then to be arbiter of my wardrobe? I seem to recall that you have behaved on occasion as if you were under precisely the same misconception as Sir Nuneham!'

'Not precisely the same,' he said drily. 'I have so far escaped such violent rejection. A fact which almost makes me wonder whether I might not press home that advantage,' he added, as if considering a course of action for the first time.

Mandala backed against the door. 'Don't dare,' she began.

He laughed. 'I don't have time—but if I did, your lack of tactics would be my greatest ally. You are blocking the only means through which help can arrive or you may escape.'

Mandala stepped hastily away from the door, her colour heightened as much by his bluntness as by her own stupidity. Once more she sought to redirect the conversation. 'Why did you come here?' she asked.

'I came to tell you that I'm leaving Devon. The last time we met, you told me you wished never to see me again, but I was vain enough to hope that you did not entirely mean it.'

She flushed. 'I meant it, though I feel bound to say that today's events have made me profoundly grateful that you came. When will you return?'

'I haven't the slightest idea. Perhaps never.' He glanced down at her. 'Would that upset you?'

'Not at all. Why should it? You have a gift that amounts to genius for always making me seem in the wrong. It will be pleasant to be relieved of that chastening sensation.'

He looked surprised. 'I thought at one time that we were on relatively good terms.'

'Did you? It suited me to have some company.'

'Is that all? I had thought—even hoped, perhaps —that you might feel rather more than that. Will you at least wish me good luck?'

'Will you need it?'

'Quite possibly. It's always a useful ally.'

'Then you have my best wishes. Good day, Mr York.'

He took her hand and raised it to his lips. 'I very much fear it may well be "Goodbye", Mandala,' he said, and even as she opened her mouth to ask why, he was gone.

CHAPTER SEVEN

ON THE 11TH OF JUNE, three ships hove to off Lyme Regis. In the late afternoon seven boats put ashore from them, and James Scott, the thirty-six-year-old Duke of Monmouth, landed with eighty-two friends. A declaration was read out by one Joseph Taylor rejecting the right of King James II to sit on the throne of the three kingdoms of England, Scotland and Ireland on the grounds that he was a traitor who had not only started the Great Fire of London but had also murdered his brother, the late King Charles. It exhorted all good Protestants to rally to the side of the man who would rid them of a Catholic king and restore Parliamentary government. By next morning, eight hundred west-countrymen had flocked to the green and gold banner.

In the days since Deveril York's departure, Mandala had resumed her custom of riding unattended across her lands; often, to the dismay of her servants, not returning home until dusk. But whereas before she had ridden as much to fill her time as for a pleasure in the activity itself, now there was a restlessness to her excursions as if only in continuous movement could she hope to assuage the energy imprisoned within her.

Deveril York was never far from her thoughts, no matter how hard she tried to push him away, and his presence in her mind did nothing to ease her unquiet spirit. There had been a period of several days when he had seemed to be the ideal friend: when they had ridden and talked together in the perfect amity of old acquaintances. His behaviour had done much to make her revise her first unfavourable impression, but she now knew him to be a devious man with little sense of honour where women were concerned. Had he not come to Devon to pay court to Isobel Courtenay? Yet, while in daily expectation that he would make an offer, he had visited

Mandala. He had been to some pains to reveal to her a different side to his nature, but this had been nothing more than a trick to lull her into precisely the revised opinion of him that she had formed. Then he had tried to seduce her.

Mandala chose to overlook the fact that his advances had been far from unwelcome—that merely served to illustrate his skill. If Isobel had not come in, who knew what might have happened? That was when they had both learned that he had deceived them: Mandala had been quite unaware of his intentions towards the younger woman, and Isobel had clearly been shocked to see, in the arms of another, the man from whom she expected a declaration. The fact that Isobel had no desire to receive a declaration from that source in no way mitigated the offence.

Yet with evidence before her of such undoubted duplicity, what was Mandala to make of his entirely honourable behaviour following Sir Nuneham's visit? He had made it clear that he thought she had to some extent encouraged—albeit unwittingly—the baronet's behaviour, but he had helped her by getting rid of her unwanted guest. He had, moreover, by taking the blame for the vase, prevented any kitchen-gossip from arising. That was the action of an honourable man. How could she balance these two conflicting faces of Deveril York?

It was with unanswerable questions like these that Mandala found her mind occupied on her daily rides, and perhaps it was her failure to arrive at an answer that increased her restlessness and her sense of frustration. It certainly accounted for her failure to observe as closely as she might the wooded landscape around her, so that, when she entered the clearing in which stood the Tilnorth Barn, she was totally unprepared for the two men who grabbed Fatima's bridle and ordered her to dismount.

Their voices told her they were Dorset men, and their clothes proclaimed their rural occupations. One was armed with a pitchfork, the other held a crudely made but undoubtedly efficient pike. She had never seen either of them before.

'Who are you?' Mandala asked, ignoring their order to dismount.

'Never you mind that, mistress,' replied the one with the pitchfork. 'Just you do as you're told and get down.'

'Certainly not,' Mandala said with a force that she hoped disguised her dismay. 'This is my land and that's my barn, and you're no tenants of mine, so what are you doing here?'

'We're putting England back on the right road,' the pikeman said virtuously.

'Well, whatever that may mean, the road doesn't run through Abbas Manor,' she retorted. 'Are there any more of you?'

They both laughed. 'You could say that, I reckon,' the pikeman told her.

As he spoke, a figure appeared from the far side of the barn where the doors were. His luxuriantly curled wig and the heavy lace of his cravat proclaimed him to be no bumpkin, an impression endorsed by his affected drawl. 'Whom have we here?' he asked, and his eyes under slightly hooded lids looked Mandala up and down in a calculating way that quite belied the languor of his voice.

'A woman, my lord,' the pikeman said, stating the obvious.

'Is that what it is? Ah, yes, I see you are right. Not, I fancy, some serving-wench, either.'

'I am Mandala Sorn. This is my land—and my barn. I do not recall giving you permission to be here.'

'Your memory is correct, Miss Sorn. Your permission was not sought.'

'Then what . . .?'

He stepped forward and threw her an effusive bow. 'Ford Grey, at your service. Allow me to help you to dismount.'

Mandala stayed where she was. 'Ford Grey?' she queried. 'This man called you "my lord".'

'Lord Grey of Warke, if you prefer, but I do not insist on such ceremony from a beautiful woman. I pray you, dismount.'

By this time a considerable number of men had

assembled to watch the exchange, and Mandala realised
for the first time that her woods must be full of them.
Most were countrymen or tradesmen—miners, some of
them, she guessed from their clothes. There was also a
sprinkling of gentlemen, who had apparently been inside the barn. Nothing she saw inspired her to answer
Lord Grey's prayer. She calculated her chances of getting away altogether by suddenly setting her spur and
her whip to Fatima's side. They were slim: the man with
the pitchfork did not look as if he would give up the reins
without a struggle, and if he did, there were plenty to
replace him.

'Thank you, my lord. I prefer to remain.'

Another figure advanced through the crowd, which
parted at the touch of his fingers, and Mandala found
herself looking down into a handsome face marred only
by a hint of weakness in the full-lipped, almost petulant,
mouth. He must have been of an age with Deveril York,
but whereas the latter's face bore the harsh lines of
cynicism, this one showed signs of the softness of dissipation. His most striking features were dark eyebrows
which extended far beyond the outside edges of his eyes
until they disappeared under the dark curls of a heavy
wig. A simply knotted lace cravat, no longer as fresh as
when it had been tied that morning, none the less lay
white against his purple coat—a coat, Mandala noted
without immediately perceiving its significance, of the
colour more usually worn by kings. He rested a hand on
Fatima's neck, the gesture of one who was both at home
with horses and liked them, and when he smiled up at
Mandala, his face was entirely transformed. The petulance vanished, and a most persuasive charm took its
place.

'You must be Miss Sorn,' he said. 'I had heard you had
taken up your inheritance. I knew your mother.'

Mandala stiffened. 'That will hardly be a recom-
mendation, sir, if you imagine that I accept the same
standards as Maman.'

'My information is that you do not. I am James Scott,
Miss Sorn. Duke of Monmouth and Buccleuch. Can I
not persuade you to dismount? There is something I

should like to discuss with you, and I think you would be happier if there were not quite so many listeners.'

Mandala looked about her. She had no idea what they might have to discuss, but she could see no advantage in doing so in front of all these curious bystanders. She gave her reins to the man who already held Fatima's bridle and unhooked her leg from its horn, sliding down gracefully into Monmouth's assisting arms. He placed her arm on his and led her to the barn, requesting most of those followers who might have expected to follow them to remain outside. Lord Grey accompanied them, together with three or four other close friends of the Duke, and these threw a cloak over a neat stack of hazel rods to form a makeshift seat for their visitor.

She looked at the Duke with a frankly curious eye. 'So you're the Duke of Monmouth,' she commented. 'Your father's favourite son, they say. I live remote from the world here and, in any case, have little interest in politics, but in the last few days word has penetrated even here that you have landed to rid the country of its Catholic king. I had assumed you would be on your way to London by now. What has happened?'

'Tactics need not concern you, Miss Sorn, but it was never my intention to march straight on the capital.'

'You would need a rather larger army than I see outside to have any hopes of success in that direction, I think,' Mandala suggested.

Monmouth flushed. 'They are rising all over the West Country, where disaffection is very great. As we march, they join us. We shall remove the usurping Duke of York.'

'And who will you place on the throne in his stead? Yourself? Or do you see a return to Parliamentary government in another Protectorate?'

'A king is needed, naturally, and, as you said, I was King Charles's favourite son. He declared me his heir. I am the rightful King of England.'

'No, Your Grace. You cannot be: a king has no power to bequeath his kingdom to his bastard.'

'That's very true, but I am no bastard, Miss Sorn. My parents were married in France long before my father

Open your heart to love with 4 Best Seller Romances FREE

Can you resist the promise of wild, passionate romance...the shy glances, the stolen kisses, the laughter - and the tears? If, deep within your heart, you're a true romantic, then these are love stories for you. Stories that comprise a unique library of books from Mills & Boon - we call them Best Seller Romances. From the very first page you'll understand why these books have enthralled thousands of readers and now rank among our Best Sellers.

As your special introduction to our most popular library, we'll send you 4 Best Sellers, an exclusive Digital Quartz Clock and a surprise mystery gift absolutely FREE when you complete and return this card.

Now, if you decide to become a subscriber, you can receive four Best Seller Romances delivered directly to your door, every two months. If this sounds tempting, read on; because you'll also enjoy a whole range of special benefits that are exclusive to Mills & Boon. For example, a free bi-monthly newsletter packed with recipes, competitions, exclusive book offers and much more – plus extra bargain offers and big cash savings.

Remember, there's absolutely no obligation or commitment – you can cancel your subscription at any time. So don't delay any longer...complete, detach and post this card today. The romance of your dreams is beckoning – don't keep it waiting!

PLUS A QUARTZ CLOCK and a Mystery Gift

FREE BOOKS CERTIFICATE

Dear Susan,

Your special Introductory Offer of 4 Free books is too good to miss. I understand they are mine to keep with the Free Clock and mystery gift. Please also reserve a Reader Service Subscription for me. If I decide to subscribe I shall receive 4 new books every two months for £7.80 post and packing free. If I decide not to subscribe, I shall write to you within 10 days. The free books and gifts will be mine to keep, in any case.

I understand that I may cancel or suspend my subscription at any time simply by writing to you. I am over 18 years of age.

2A8B

Name _____ Signature _____
(BLOCK CAPITALS PLEASE)

Address _____

_____ Postcode _____

NO STAMP NEEDED

To Susan Welland
Mills & Boon Reader Service
FREE POST
P.O. Box 236
CROYDON
Surrey CR9 9EL

SEND NO MONEY NOW

resumed the crown. The throne is rightfully mine, and my uncle has stolen it.'

Mandala demurred. 'I can't dispute these facts, Your Grace, but the question is surely whether you can prove them? It seems to me that if there were incontrovertible evidence, your uncle would never have been able to accede in the first place.'

Monmouth smiled. 'I had been told you were as shrewd as you were beautiful,' he said. 'You're right. My paternity has never been in doubt, of course, only its legitimacy. You are fortunate that your inheritance was from your mother. That relationship can never be in doubt.'

'My mother took good care to name me in her will,' Mandala told him. 'I was doubly fortunate in that there were no other possible heirs to dispute it. In the eyes of the world, Your Grace, there is nothing between us: we are both bastards, and will be happiest if we accept that fact.'

'If the world brands us in the same way, we must support each other's interests, don't you think? I have taken the liberty of hiding my army in your densely wooded combes. Will you ride from here and deliver me to the Militia?'

Mandala hesitated, and then smiled ruefully. 'I should do so, no doubt. Had I stayed at home like a gently bred female and contented myself with a stroll in the knot-garden, I shouldn't even be aware of your presence here. I should be similarly ignorant if my ride had but taken me in another direction. To be truthful, sir, it matters not one jot to me who sits on the throne, and I have no desire to hand anyone over to the executioner. If I ride from here, it will be to forget your very existence—a forgetfulness which will be made much easier if you leave my land by morning.'

The Duke swept her an ostentatious bow, which made her laugh. 'I should be happy to do so, mistress, had we not already hoped to spend the night here. If we do so, we are bound still to be here in the morning, though I don't intend to linger: I have a campaign to wage. I undertake to remove my men as soon as may be, and certainly before noon tomorrow.' He paused as if wondering whether to broach something else. 'There is another small matter,' he said.

'And what is that?' Mandala asked warily. She was beginning to recognise that she was dealing with a man who was accustomed to use his very considerable charm to get anything he wanted.

'You are, I believe, *extremely* rich. I, on the other hand, am endeavouring, with very little funds, to assemble an army, an army which will inevitably, sooner or later, expect to be paid.'

Mandala laughed. 'And you would like me to contribute to this expense?'

He smiled. 'How quick you are to take a point!'

'It's not so easy, you know. I have the money, that's true enough, and it's mine to do with exactly as I choose. I still have to account to my steward for any large amounts, if only to prevent anyone else falling under a suspicion of theft. How do I do that without telling him the truth?'

'I'm sure you will contrive. You strike me as a very resourceful woman.'

'I learnt one thing from my mother, Your Grace. Every good turn deserves another. What return do I get for taking the risk of your remaining here and for giving you some of my fortune?'

The Duke sighed. 'And to think I imagined you might do so out of pure altruism!'

'Is there any such thing?'

'You sound more like Deveril York than a beautiful woman living remote from the world.'

'Deveril York!' Mandala exclaimed. 'You know him?'

'My acquaintance is large,' Monmouth replied evasively. 'We have met. A cynic through and through. Tell me,' he went on, anxious to slide over his unintentional slip of the tongue, 'what would you consider a fair return? Your beauty deserves a wider audience than the country bumpkins it encounters in this benighted spot. I can offer you acceptance at Court at every level of society. Some will perhaps jib at receiving the Scarlet

Woman, but not for long. Your beauty and charm will win them over even if your fortune doesn't. Within the year you will have made a brilliant match. Perhaps a title in your own right?'

These were generous offers indeed, and though Mandala had little interest in either, she knew she might in later life regret rejecting them. She also knew she was taking a great gamble. If Monmouth's rebellion failed —and surely the King's armies must already be marching to meet him?—she might be able to convince the King's men that she had been ignorant of the Duke's presence on her land. Such a plea could not be made if it became known that quantities of plate were missing; if word of her acceptance of Monmouth's offer were known, her fate would be sealed. On the other hand, if he succeeded, it could do her no harm at all to have the highest in the land under an obligation.

'You've convinced me, sir,' she said at last. 'I shall not be able to return until tomorrow morning, however. Will you be able to keep your men concealed for that length of time?'

'Leave my men to me, Miss Sorn. I am the best judge of how to dispose my troops. I shall hope to see you here at mid-morning.'

'I shall be here—unless I am prevented from doing so by the King's armies. In that event, I shall deny all knowledge of you.'

'I can ask no more than that. Come, let me assist you back on your horse.'

He led her out and threw her deftly into the saddle. As she gathered her reins together, he reached for one hand and pressed it lightly to his lips. 'It has been a pleasure to meet you, Miss Sorn. I only wish the circumstances had been more conventional. I look forward to seeing you again. *Au revoir*.'

Mandala inclined her head. 'And I you, sir. *Au revoir*.' She turned Fatima and put the whip and spur to her side, hurrying the little mare homeward through the deepening dusk.

As his leader turned back to the barn, Lord Grey shook his head. 'I don't like it, sir,' he said. 'We should have kept her here. She could get word to Dorchester, and we'd be finished.'

'She could, but she won't,' Monmouth told him. 'I recall York saying that if we met her, she would deal straight with us—either yes or no, but no duplicity. I'm inclined to believe him.'

Mandala was too much concerned with guiding Fatima safely through the darkening woods to give any thought during her ride to the events at the barn, and such thoughts as she did ponder were concerned with the story she must give Jonah Swinbrook.

The groom who rushed forward to take Fatima was easier to deal with.

'Wherever have you been, mistress?' he said. 'Martha's been worried half to death. We've been seeing you lying dead and bleeding somewhere, and that's a fact.'

Resisting the temptation to point out that she could hardly be both, Mandala thanked him for his concern. 'I'm sorry to have caused the household any anxiety. I went further than I intended, and came across a badger set with a whole family playing like puppies. I was so entranced by them that I made no note of the passing time. I hope Martha will forgive me.'

'I doubt it, mistress,' the groom told her cheerfully. 'She was right angry the last time she came out to see if you was back yet.'

'As bad as that? I'd better wear my penitential face. Can you have Fatima ready for me early tomorrow? I want to be sure I can find that set again.'

The groom shook his head. 'She's had a long day. Best if she stays at home tomorrow. I could put your saddle on the cob, as his leg has mended,' he added helpfully.

Mandala wrinkled her nose. The cob was a general-purpose saddle-horse used by any member of the household who had need of a mount. He was a sound, stolid animal with plenty of strength and stamina but little speed. 'Very well, he will have to do, though I doubt I shall enjoy the ride as much.'

It seemed as if Martha would never be done with exercising the privilege of an old servant to berate the mistress she had known since childhood. Mandala, anxious to be rid of her, agreed with all her strictures and was complimenting herself on having avoided any explanation concerning badgers—an explanation that would convince the maid less easily than the groom —when Martha concluded, 'That's all I've got to say on the subject, miss, but I'll tell you this! I've not asked you where you've been because I don't want to know, and like as not you'll tell me it's none of my business—and nor it is—but I know someone who's been up to mischief when I see them, and such a one is sitting before me right now. Goodnight, mistress.'

'Goodnight, Martha.' Mandala smiled to herself. When Martha started calling her 'miss' instead of 'mistress', she knew she had sunk beyond reproach, if only for the time being. An abject apology for her behaviour was usually enough to put them back on their old footing, but Mandala needed to keep Martha at a distance. Above all, she wanted no questions about where she was going tomorrow morning, and when she returned, she wanted none concerning where she had been.

Once she was certain her household was asleep, Mandala crept out of bed and made her way with her keys and her chaperon—the loose hood that protected her hair in sudden inclement weather—to the room where the treasure-chests were kept. Her goal was to take her contribution to the rebellion without Jonah's knowledge, since she could think of no satisfactory explanation for why she should suddenly need so much money. If Monmouth succeeded, she could safely tell Jonah the truth anyway. If he didn't—well, that was more difficult. For the present, it was more important that he knew nothing at all until the rebellion was over, one way or another. Her original intention had been to give the Duke some of the plate that had survived the demands of his grandfather, Charles I, during the Civil Wars, but she now decided that such items were too bulky and their absence too easily detected. Coin would be better, provided she could get out of the house and on to the cob without its chinking arousing curiosity.

She closed the door of the treasure-room behind her and knelt before the chests ranged on the floor. Her candle cast a distorting light that made the keyhole difficult to find, but finally it was located and the lid thrown back. She held the candle aloft, and the contents of the chest gleamed dully in its flickering light. Gold, that was the thing. Sovereigns and guineas. Not only would Monmouth be able to use them immediately without melting them down, but they were not traceable back to Abbas Manor. Mandala set to work scooping coins with her hands into the hood. Guineas, the new coins struck for the first time the year before her birth, predominated, but there were some of the old sovereigns of a hundred years ago, interspersed among them, a quantity of silver pounds. When she judged she had enough to please even Monmouth, who, she suspected, shared Sir Nuneham's genius for getting through money, she re-locked the chest and let herself out of the chamber, locking it behind her before making her way swiftly to her own room.

Thus far all had gone smoothly, she thought gratefully as she sank on to her bed with a sigh. She longed to sleep, but dared not. First, she must be sure she could deliver the money without detection. A workbox stood on a table by the window, and from it she took needle, thread and ribbons. Working as swiftly as the candlelight permitted, Mandala whipped the edge of the chaperon over so that she had a channel right round the hood through which to thread the ribbon. Once this was pulled up, the chaperone had become a sizeable bag and was easily filled with coin. The only problem now was how to carry it without attracting notice and where it would make the minimum of noise.

The obvious place was round her waist, whether under or over her skirts, but that quickly proved unsuitable because of the chinking. She even toyed with the idea of transferring it to saddle-bags, but since the groom would expect to attach them, it could scarely be done without his realising what they contained. She finally discovered that, if she hung the bag round her neck so that the ribbon passed between her breasts and the bag itself sat beneath their concealing curves, and if she then put a cloak over all, it was hidden from casual view and its contents made almost no sound. It was heavy and uncomfortable, but it worked. With a sigh of relief, Mandala hid the bag under the foot of the mattress and climbed into bed, falling instantaneously asleep.

The scheme worked admirably and when Mandala trotted off into the woods next morning, the bag nestled, entirely unsuspected, beneath the bosom of her riding-coat. The addition of a cloak was easily explained by the convenient chill of the morning air. This time, as she rode, she was looking for figures hidden in the bracken among the trees. She saw none. When she reached the Tilnorth Barn, there was but one sentry, who rapped on the barn door to give notice of her approach. Only two figures emerged: the Duke himself and one of his friends.

'Earlier than I expected,' he commented, and reached a hand up to her. 'Will you dismount, Miss Sorn?'

'There's no need,' Mandala told him, fumbling with the clasp of her cloak as she spoke. 'Where are all the others?' she asked.

'Gone,' he replied. 'I moved them on at dawn under Grey's command.'

'You waited here yourself? You had great faith that I would return without a military escort!'

'I had heard you were an honourable woman, though I won't deny there were those among my aides who were less sanguine than I.'

'Lord Grey among them, I imagine,' Mandala said without rancour, and handed him the bag.

He loosened the drawstring and peered inside, whistling softly when he saw what it contained. 'Beyond my expectations, Miss Sorn! A generous gift, indeed. You have bought yourself a dukedom at the very least.'

'You're very kind, sir, but I'm sure you won't take it amiss if I tell you I'll not order my coronet until you've won your campaign.'

'A cautious decision—and quite possibly a wise one,'

he told her. 'I hope that the next time we meet it will be in the Palace of Westminster.'

'Just so long as it's not at Tyburn Tree,' she replied drily, and turned the cob to return home. 'God be with you, Your Grace.'

'I think he is. *Au revoir*, Miss Sorn.'

Mandala made no attempt to hurry. Her task completed, she now had all the time she needed to mull over the events of the last twenty-four hours. She wasted no time contemplating the glory of a dukedom. There would be a certain malicious satisfaction to be gained from watching those who had refused to associate with a Scarlet Woman wriggling on the hook in order to entice a Duchess into their society, but Mandala was realist enough to know that at this moment the odds on the Duke's winning his campaign must be very long indeed and that, even if he emerged victorious, the promises of princes were not always to be relied on.

More intriguing was the name the Duke had let slip. Deveril York. It had been quite clear from his earlier comments that Monmouth had heard a lot about her from someone. She had not thought this very strange at the time, since she supposed her presence here, her fortune and, above all, her history must be the subject of much gossip. The mention of Deveril York put quite another complexion on it. She knew Deveril had spent time in France, and everyone knew that Charles's acknowledged bastard had been brought up there. There could not be much difference in their ages, so it was hardly surprising that they should be acquainted. More disturbing was the inference that they had been in touch sufficiently recently to discuss her. She flushed with private annoyance. What right had Deveril to discuss her with anyone, even if he did apparently do so in a complimentary vein? More importantly, what light did this information throw on his recent visit?

He had supposedly come down, on the pretext of seeing Courtenay Place, to meet Isobel Courtenay in order to decide whether he wanted to marry her. He had apparently—unless Isobel had misunderstood what she overheard, and it was hard to see how she could have done—told Sir Nuneham that he intended to offer for her, yet he had not seemed the least put out when Isobel had told him she had no intention of accepting him. His heart had not been involved, of course, but one would have expected his pride to be hurt. His visit had enabled him to be conducted all over the Courtenay estates, and when he introduced himself to Mandala and ingratiated himself into her good opinion, their rides had shown him most of her land as well.

Monmouth must have been plotting this uprising for some time: it was hardly the sort of thing one undertook on the spur of the moment. What could be more necessary to such a scheme than to have someone sniff out the lie of the land? In short, a spy. Yes, that was it. Deveril York was Monmouth's spy. The more she thought about it, the more convinced Mandala became that there was no other explanation that fitted all the facts so neatly. Of course he had been a pleasant companion: it was in his interest to be so. As for that episode that Isobel had so fortuitously interrupted, she supposed she had brought it on herself. She had been most indelicate in presuming to tell a man that he would make a bad husband, and it would appear that Deveril York was a man easily roused, whether to anger or to more physical passions.

She admitted to herself now, for the first time, that she had not entirely welcomed Isobel's interruption. She had responded to his embrace as she had responded to his companionship. The knowledge that everything had been part of a massive deception was hard to accept. It meant she was nothing in Deveril's eyes but a means to an end, and the end was treason.

It would serve him right if she rode now, this instant, to Axminster and laid information against him, she thought savagely, though even as the thought occurred to her, she knew she would do nothing of the sort. It would serve him right if the rebellion failed and he was caught. She would attend the hanging with glee. Her enjoyment of the picture thus conjured up was spoiled by the suspicion that anyone as clever as Deveril York would be likely to evade capture. He seemed to have disappeared already; he certainly had not been among Monmouth's aides.

She realised with sickening clarity that she wanted Deveril to be in Devon with Monmouth, not because she wanted to see him hang but because if he were, they might meet again, and she wanted to feel his arms around her once more, somewhere where there was no fear of interruption. For the first time she realised that she had wanted Deveril York to offer for her, not for timid Isobel. He had not done so, even when the conversation had turned in that direction, albeit with some animosity.

Nor would he, she thought suddenly. It was all very well for the Duke of Monmouth to be a bastard. His father was the King, and that excused everything. Mandala Sorn, bastard daughter of a brothel-keeper and an unknown and very ambitious young man, was another matter. No man worth having would wish to ally himself with such a one as that, no matter how large her fortune. Mandala pulled herself together with an effort. This was folly. The fact was that Deveril's sole purpose had been to spy for Monmouth. His goal achieved, he had disappeared as spies were presumably wont to do. He lived a life of duplicity and deviousness, characteristics that were hardly likely to augur a good husband. It was just as well he would consider her totally unsuitable. She would be far happier in the long run.

The undoubted logic of her argument provided her with remarkably little consolation.

Mandala's interest in politics might, as a general rule, have been minimal, but she was more than a little interested in the progress of Monmouth's campaign, and not only because she had invested in it. Devon had always been a stronghold of Protestantism, even, in the opinion of many, a hotbed of that particular heresy, and the population as a whole was not happy with an avowedly Catholic king. Unfortunately for the Duke's campaign, much of this support was tacit, the influential landowners preferring not to commit themselves at this stage. This situation meant, however, that news of the campaign spread swiftly and, in general, accurately through the countryside. Mandala reached for every scrap of gossip she could find, hoping to learn not only of Monmouth's success but of Deveril's presence in the action, if not necessarily at the Duke's side. She heard plenty of news about the Duke, but nothing at all about Deveril.

At Taunton on the 20th of June, Monmouth committed the ultimate treason by proclaiming himself king. He had not wanted to do this, since it might alienate those Puritans who hoped for a return of the Commonwealth, and it additionally set the final seal on his fate should he be caught. But he needed the support of the local landowners, the gentry and lesser aristocracy, whose example would be followed, and he was persuaded that they would throw in their lot with him if they knew there would be a Protestant king on the throne.

Mandala's encounter with him had left her in no doubt that his ultimate goal was the crown, but when news of the proclamation filtered down to Abbas St Antony, she wondered if it had been altogether wise to state it so baldly. As the local gentry still failed to come forward, her view was increasingly shared by Monmouth.

On the night of the 5th and 6th of July, the Duke decided to stage the challenge that could turn the campaign finally and conclusively in his direction. The royal army, totalling something under three thousand souls, was camped at Westonzoyland on the edge of the broad, flat, marshy expanse of Sedgemoor, while the rebels, numbering just over three and a half thousand, were at Bridgwater, on the opposite side of the moor. Numbers favoured the rebels, but the royalists had six times as many cannon. Mists rose at night from drainage rhines that criss-crossed the moor, providing excellent cover. It was Monmouth's plan to use this cover to march across the moor and attack the King's men before dawn without warning.

It was a daring plan, and no easy task to march so many men so far without betraying their presence— marching feet and the hooves of six hundred horses cannot be totally silent. Yet the element of surprise was crucial. The royal army was well deployed at Westonzoyland, its cannon advantageously positioned, and any attack that was less than a complete surprise was doomed to failure.

At first all went well. An army patrol passed them by and incredibly failed to detect the rebels in the thickly swirling mists. Some villagers saw them and hastened to Chedzoy to give word of what they had seen, but, miraculously, no one passed the word on to the royal camp. But at about one o'clock things began to go wrong.

The mists prevented their being seen, but also made it impossible for the rebels to see exactly where they were. No landmarks, no moon or stars, could identify their position. When they came up to the Langmoor Rhine, an eight-feet-wide water-filled ditch, they knew they had missed the crossing-point. But was the plungeon, as the narrow, flat, wooden bridges across the rhines were called, to the right or left? It was inevitable that in casting about for the crossing-place, and the attendant confusion, the level of sound should increase until traces of it penetrated the blanket of mist. They were heard, and a warning shot was fired by a patrol. An officer, hearing the shot and knowing that its sound might not reach the main body of the army through the mists, sent a messenger to rouse the King's men.

The rebels had no choice but to press on, even though the element of surprise was lost, and, by seven in the morning, so was the battle. The defeat was absolute. As the dead men were counted, it became clear that the rebels had suffered such losses as to put an end to Monmouth's dreams for ever. A thousand rebels died, and another five hundred, many of them wounded, were taken prisoner. Only eighty of the King's soldiers were killed, and something over two hundred wounded. In addition, the rebels lost all but one of their guns.

Those rebels that could, fled. Those regiments that could, pursued them. The Duke of Monmouth was among those who escaped, but his freedom was short lived. He was captured two days later, and by the 15th of July had been executed for treason.

News of the defeat spread swiftly through the land as fleeing rebels sought refuge with their families, hoping, by returning quietly to their jobs, to be overlooked by the King's retribution. No one was to be left for long in any doubt that such retribution would be meted out. Throughout the month of August, his soldiers descended on castle and cottage to arrest and imprison not just those who had taken part in the rebellion or who had supported the rebel cause, but also those believed, often on insubstantial evidence, to have sympathised with that cause.

Mandala maintained a calm face to the world, but she knew the danger she stood in if anyone knew how very substantial had been her own support. She had known it was a gamble, but had not bargained for the ferocity with which losers were to be treated.

It was at the beginning of August that Jonah Swinbrook came to her in some agitation and insisted upon seeing her alone. Even when the door of her sitting-room was safely closed, he seemed ill at ease, glancing over her shoulder as though in expectation of discovering an eavesdropper.

'I've just come back from over towards the Tilnorth Barn,' he began, having satisfied himself that they really were alone.

Mandala's fingers paused for an inconspicuous second in their embroidery. 'Where we store the wood after coppicing? That's Tilnorth, isn't it?'

'That's right, mistress. No one works there in high summer, so I was puzzled-like to see a plume of smoke coming from that direction. I rode over very quiet-like, not sure what to expect—I mean, poachers don't usually light a fire. They like to be gone with their pickings as fast as possible. Mistress, Tilnorth's being used by rebels—twenty or thirty of them, I estimate.'

'How do you know they're rebels?' Mandala asked. 'Did you speak to them?'

'And have my throat slit? No, mistress, I did not!'

'Then they might just as easily have been vagrants,' Mandala suggested.

He shook his head. 'No, mistress. These men looked

like respectable men fallen on hard times, not like
vagrants who've never known anything else. On their
way to Lyme or Poole or Weymouth, no doubt, hoping
to find a ship. What do we do, mistress?'

'Do they know you saw them?'

'No. I thought it best to slip back here and tell you.'

'Then I think we do nothing, Jonah. If you're right,
they'll soon be gone, and if you hadn't chanced upon
them, we'd be none the wiser until, perhaps, someone
stumbled on the remains of their fire. Let us remain none
the wiser until they've gone.'

'I wish them no harm, mistress, but they're traitors,
for all that,' Jonah said doubtfully.

'And if Sedgemoor had ended differently, they'd be
heroes.'

'With respect, mistress, if Sedgemoor had ended
differently, they'd not be there.'

'Nevertheless, we leave them—and pray God they're
soon away.'

Unfortunately, Jonah Swinbrook was not the only
person to spot that tell-tale plume of smoke. A trooper
in the Wiltshire militia saw it and drew his officer's
attention.

'Probably just a cottage.'

'Probably, sir, but a very remote one. Good place to
hide, I'd say.'

It was an opinion that the officer, upon consideration,
felt obliged to share.

In the interval between Jonah's sighting and the
trooper's, most of the rebels sheltering there had split up
and gone their separate ways, either down to the coast or
simply out of the western counties and consequently
—or so they hoped—away from suspicion. Only half a
dozen remained, and, since there was only one doorway
to the barn and the fugitives had not thought it necessary
to post a look-out, the soldiers had no difficulty in
creeping up and taking them unawares without a shot
being fired. Afraid that they might be local men and that
it might on that account be unwise to march them though
Abbas St Antony, the militia chose to use another route.
No hint of their capture therefore reached the Manor,

and when Jonah Swinbrook rode out towards the
Tilnorth Barn two days later, he assumed that they had
dispersed and heaved a sigh of relief, a sigh which was
echoed by Mandala when she heard his news.

'So that's that, Jonah. I admit I feel a lot easier to
know they've left us. Perhaps, now, life can return to
normal.'

Five of the men were summarily hanged in Bridport, a
lesson to the townsfolk in the fate of traitors, but the
sixth earned his freedom.

'You don't want the likes of me,' he told the com-
manding officer. 'What you want is the big people. The
people who planned this little upset. The people who
paid for it but kept out of the action. Not the fools, like
me, who got dragged in against our will.'

'Can you furnish us with the identity of these people?'
The officer could hardly believe his luck.

'Not all of them, naturally, but there's one very
important one I can point the finger to.'

'Go on.'

'Tilnorth Barn, we was taken at. Near Abbas St
Antony. Now why do you think we chose to stop there?
Because we knew if they stumbled across us, they'd not
hand us over, that's why. And how come we was so sure?
Because we'd stopped there before the proclamation at
Taunton. Monmouth himself slept in that barn, he did,
and while he was there, who should come a-visiting but
the Lady of the Manor—Miss Sorn, I think her name
was. Mighty pleased Monmouth was to see her, too.
Said he knew her mother. Helped her down off her horse
all gentlemanly-like, and they went into the barn for a
little chat. When she left, she said she looked forward to
seeing him again, and when she'd ridden off, the Duke
remarked that she could be trusted. She came back next
morning and handed him a bag that looked real heavy.
He peered inside and whistled, and said she'd earned a
dukedom.'

The officer looked at him suspiciously. 'This is a
mighty detailed story,' he said. 'How came you to know
so much of what was said?'

The man smiled the unpleasant, ingratiating smile of

one who knows his life is at stake. 'Wasn't it me as held the lady's horse? Wasn't it me as was sentry outside the barn next day when all his men had gone and the Duke was waiting for her?'

'He was waiting for her?'

'Oh, yes, sir. Everyone but him and one officer had gone—and me, of course. Once the lady'd ridden off, we left to rejoin the army. She was expected, all right.'

'Miss Sorn, you said?'

'That's right, sir. Of Abbas Manor. The barn stands on Manor lands.'

Mandala was not unduly concerned when a troop of soldiers rode up to the Manor House. Jonah had reported the night before that the barn was now empty, so she knew she had nothing to fear from a search. It was unsettling having troops going all over the countryside, rousing villagers, searching their cottages, asking about strangers in the locality, but it was to be expected. She was simply grateful that they had taken so long to get to Abbas St Antony. So far as she knew, there were now no fugitives on her land, and if the troopers discovered any, her surprise would be genuine.

Joan opened the door to them and soon came running to fetch Mandala. ''Tis you they want to see, mistress —and they mean it. I've said as how you're busy, but they insist. The officer said he'd come and find you himself if you didn't come quick.'

'I suppose they feel they should have the permission of the mistress of the house before they search it,' Mandala told her. 'There can be no other reason.' But even as she spoke, a faint, sickening whisper of doubt flickered somewhere in the region of her stomach.

She followed Joan to the door. 'Gentlemen?' she said, keeping her voice deliberately cheerful.

'Miss Sorn? Miss Mandala Sorn?' the young officer enquired.

'I gather you must see me and cannot be content with a maid or the housekeeper. I have no objection to your searching the house, the outbuildings, or any part of the estate,' Mandala told him.

'I'm sure you haven't,' the officer replied. 'We caught the last fugitives hiding on your land. They were there with your permission. We have come for you.'

'For me? I gave no fugitives permission to be here. If they said I did, they lied.' Mandala felt that this statement was no less than the truth and had the merit of not indicating that she had known of their presence.

The man smiled grimly. 'Funny, isn't it? No one ever admits their guilt, yet we know the rebels had support here or else why come this way? They certainly had support from you, Miss Sorn, didn't they?' He paused, waiting for a denial, and when his question was greeted by silence, he laughed. 'As good as an admission! Not that it makes any difference. I have a warrant for you. You're to be taken to Dorchester to await trial. The Assize has already started in Winchester—Dame Alice Lisle will be executed tomorrow. The Judge is at Salisbury by now, and at the rate he's dealing with rebels, he'll soon get to you. You've a long walk ahead of you, Miss Sorn. I suggest your maid fetches you more suitable footwear.'

'May I not ride?'

'A prisoner—ride? No, Miss Sorn, you may not.' He eyed her appreciatively. 'I don't doubt my men will enjoy the sight of you getting hot and breathless. You'd better hope they're too tired at the end of the day's march to want to do anything but sleep.'

Mandala wasted no time arguing with him but told Joan to fetch her warmest cloak and the leather boots she rode in: she judged these to be easier for walking a long way than pattens. It was not Joan, but Martha, who brought these articles after a delay which caused the officer some annoyance. He was tempted to cut short the wait, but there was a certain air of authority and an unexpected calmness about Mandala which made him think perhaps he would be wise to allow this delay to continue. The evidence against her seemed strong enough—there was a witness, after all—but Miss Sorn might be able to refute his testimony or, more probably, she was very likely to have friends in powerful places.

As Martha fastened the cloak round her shoulders,

Mandala realised that it was heavier than usual and that the additional weight was very one-sided. She looked questioningly at the old serving-woman and received in return an unusually bland and innocent smile. 'I chose this cloak, mistress. It's the one that will keep you warmest. It's the lining that does it,' Martha told her.

Mandala smiled. 'That explains it,' she said, and perched on the low stone wall beside the steps to have her satin slippers removed and the short, high-heeled boots put on in their place.

'Where are you taking her?' Martha asked. 'Her lawyers will want to know where she is.'

'Dorchester gaol,' the officer replied. 'We may get there tomorrow night, more likely the next day— depends on how fast we can push the prisoners. We've more to pick up in Bridport. Until then, it's up to this one what speed we make. Let's hope she's a good walker: I've no desire to spend two nights on the road!'

'Then don't be a fool,' Martha told him. 'If she's all you've got till then, put her up behind one of your troopers. You'll be in Bridport well before sunset if you do. That means comfortable beds tonight and in Dorchester by tomorrow night, with any luck.'

The officer looked at her. It was irregular, but the old woman was right. Of all the prisoners they were taking to Dorchester, Mandala was the least likely to be able to cover thirty miles without holding them back. She would almost certainly slow them down on the next leg of the journey anyway. Maybe it would be better to make what speed they could by this simple expedient. She would hardly be able to escape. He turned to the men behind him.

'Trooper Bruntish, take this prisoner behind you, pillion-style.'

Since the trooper's horse carried no pillion-saddle, Mandala found herself perched on the animal's back behind the cantle. It was not a particularly comfortable place to sit but walking would be far worse, so she made no complaint and smiled gratefully at Martha.

'Get word to Mr Leafield as fast as you can,' she said. 'Tell him what has happened and where I am.'

'I'll send Jonah to London right away,' Martha assured her. 'Doubtless he'll overtake you on the road.'

'If this is a London lawyer,' the officer intervened, 'you're wasting your time. By the time you get your message to him and he reaches Dorchester, it will all be over. The Judge will be there in two or three days, and he wastes no time. He's dealing with prisoners in batches, not singly.'

'But he can't do that, surely?' Mandala exclaimed.

The man shrugged. 'Why not? He's Lord Chief Justice. He can do what he likes, and I don't suppose he fancies spending years on the task—which is what it would mean, for there's hundreds accused. They say the King wants quick results, and that's what he's getting.'

This was hardly reassuring news, and the only consolation Mandala had on the ride to Bridport was the sight of Jonah Swinbrook overtaking them only two miles along the road, mounted not on the sturdy cob, but on Fatima. Presumably he intended to change horses several times on the way, but he could not have found a swifter one for the first stage of his journey.

The small gaol at Bridport was crammed with prisoners. Some bore still festering wounds from the battle, and Mandala was amazed that they had lived so long—and doubted whether all of them would survive the morrow's march. Most had been on the run for a long time, and looked it. They were ragged, dirty, and half-starved. Few of them were women. No food was given them, and although Mandala knew that Martha had quickly sewn a bag of money into the lining of her cloak for just such an eventuality, she dared not investigate to find out if there was enough to buy bread for them all. She had no wish to be overpowered and robbed. Such money as she had was not only to buy food but also to bribe gaolers and quite possibly men of much higher rank. A night of hunger would do her little harm. Better by far to give no hint of her hidden wealth. She slept little in the malodorous gaol, and as they filed out in the morning to be manacled together in a long double column, each prisoner was given a hunk of stale bread

and had the opportunity to drink some foul-looking
water from a pail with a common wooden dipper.

The march to Dorchester demonstrated to Mandala
just how lucky she had been the previous day. Her boots
were designed for riding, not walking. Within five miles,
she could feel the blisters on her feet. Within ten, she
knew they must be raw and bleeding. When they
stopped to rest the soldiers' horses, she asked permission to remove the manacle from her ankle so that
she might bind her feet, but the soldier she spoke to
shook his head.

'Shouldn't advise it,' he said, not unsympathetically.
'For one thing, you'll not get your boots back, with or
without bandaging your feet, and believe me, you'll not
be able to walk without them—we're less than half-way
there, yet.'

'But I certainly won't get there like this!' Mandala
exclaimed.

'You'd be surprised what you can do if you have to,'
the soldier told her. 'What do you think happens if you
really give up?'

'I don't know. I haven't thought about it. I suppose
they leave a soldier with me to get me there a bit later.'

He laughed. 'That'd be luxury, that would—and
every prisoner in the West Country would be trying it.
No, lady. The officer'd have no choice. You'd be hanged
from the nearest tree. Or shot. But hanging's more
likely: it costs less.'

Mandala found it was possible to keep walking even in
the most excruciating agony.

Dorchester gaol was an improvement upon Bridport's
only in being larger. Even so, it was not intended to
house over three hundred souls at one time, and was
consequently as crowded and filthy at this time as any
gaol in the land. It offered Mandala one reward, however: the opportunity to remove her boots. This was so
painful an exercise that she implored the help of one of
her fellow prisoners.

'I think the only thing to do is to pull them off so
fast that the pain is at least short lived,' Mandala told
him.

The man looked doubtful, but he obliged with agonising efficiency and Mandala looked at the raw red skin in disbelief. Another woman, one accused of seditious utterances, stood before Mandala, arms akimbo, and looked at her feet.

'Good job you didn't have to walk to London, I'd say,' she said dispassionately.

'I can't disagree with that,' Mandala replied. 'They need salves rubbed in, but I'll be wasting my time asking for them. One of the soldiers told me that if I took my boots off, I'd never get them on again. I think he's right. I'll be walking into court barefoot.'

'If you do, they'll fester. Let me tear up the bottom of your shift. We can bandage them with that. It will at least make it easier to walk—and cleaner.'

Mandala concurred with this excellent scheme, and once it had been executed, her feet felt a great deal easier.

'Let's hope you're not sentenced to transportation,' the other woman said. 'It's a long walk to Bristol. You'd be better off burned.'

Mandala could hardly agree with these sentiments, and said so. 'Besides,' she added, 'I see no reason why I should even be convicted.'

The woman snorted. 'You've been captured, haven't you? Conviction is a formality. The only choice will be death or transportation to the West Indies—and the choice will be the Judge's, not yours.'

When Mandala's time to appear in court arrived, she found that it was perfectly true that the Judge was dealing with people in batches, mostly composed of prisoners on similar charges. Mandala was to be charged not only with offering shelter to rebels both before and after the campaign but with having given money to Monmouth himself to try to ensure its success. Because these were singularly serious accusations and because she was a woman of considerable fortune, despite her social shortcomings, she was to stand trial alone. She had done her best to clean herself up, dipping another piece of torn shift into her drinking water to wipe her face clean and doing what she could, with only her fingers for a comb, to tidy her hair. She was not sure whether to be glad or sorry that she had no looking-glass.

As she paused outside the courtroom door until bidden to enter, she saw a man peering through a small opening. After a few seconds, he drew back and slid a small panel across the aperture. Mandala turned to her military escort.

'Who's that?' she whispered.

'Him? Oh, he's the hangman. Estimating the weight for the drop.'

Mandala wished she had not asked.

The trepidation with which she entered the courtroom was only slightly offset by the interest any enquiring mind could be expected to have in its surroundings on such an occasion. There was no courthouse in Dorchester, and assizes were held in a large upstairs room at the Antelope, a fashionable hostelry that stood across a busy, if narrow, thoroughfare. Although large as such rooms go, this one was smaller than Mandala would have expected for its present use, though she supposed that normally it would be dealing with no more than half a dozen cases—for which this space might well be ample. All four walls were heavily panelled from floor to ceiling, the panelling broken only by the stone fireplaces at either end, each surmounted by a heavily pilastered mantel.

The room was packed, and as Mandala made her way to the makeshift dock, she was far too preoccupied to try to identify any familiar faces, though she knew she should search for that of Mr Leafield. She tried to do so, and was brought to a temporary halt by the unmistakable fashionably dressed figure of Sir Nuneham Courtenay sitting under one of the windows opposite. For some reason she could not have explained, she had not expected there to be anyone present—except, perhaps, Mr Leafield—who knew her, and Sir Nuneham's presence was therefore doubly startling.

Once she was within the confines of the dock, raised on a small dais a few inches above the floor, she had more time to look about her until the Judge returned. There was no sign of the lawyer and no other face she recognised, but just as she turned back to await her ordeal, the door opened again. Mandala's eyes, expecting to see the Judge upon whom her fate depended, were drawn irresistibly by the sound. The newcomer was no judge, but Deveril York. As always, he wore dark colours—a blue as dark as the midnight sky, on this occasion—among a sea of jewel-hued velvets and satins with here and there the more practical broadcloths and homespun of the countryman. The effect of his choice of colour, coupled with his harsh features and black hair, was uncomfortably sinister, and Mandala caught herself shivering a little. He must feel very sure of himself, she thought, to walk into the enemy's camp like this, and she wondered what had brought him. She would not have taken him for the sort of person who found entertainment in trials or executions. He appeared not to see her, or, if he did, gave no sign, but took a seat at the back of the room near the smaller of the two fireplaces. Mandala would have her back to him throughout the trial.

She had no more time to think about Deveril York, for the Judge re-entered the room, not, as she had imagined, by the same door as she had, which she had taken to be the only one, but by a smaller one, disguised because it looked as if it were part of the panelling, to the right of the larger fireplace, in front of which was the judge's bench. This was a heavily carved throne-like chair, and a banner depicting the coat of arms of the Crown hung above the mantel, a fitting backdrop to the resplendent figure that now entered and would sit enthroned beneath it.

It was impossible not to be interested in the man who held her life in his hands, and, as the court rose in respect at his entrance, Mandala took her first look at the Lord Chief Justice of England.

Judge Jeffreys, Baron Jeffreys of Wem, was forty years old and quite the most extraordinarily handsome man Mandala had ever seen. His dark eyes were wide-spaced and looked out frankly on the world above a long but well-shaped nose. His mouth was sensitive without any hint of femininity, but there was at each corner the tell-tale muscle that betrayed the determined will of one accustomed to over-riding objecting views. His full brown wig fell over the scarlet robes of his office; a deep frill of fine lace edged the plain linen of a rudimentary Puritan collar, only partially hidden by the white fur band across his chest that held in place the hood hanging down his back over a fur-edged cape. The same fur trimmed the sleeves of the gown beneath the cape and continued down its front, while the ends of a broad black sash hung almost to the hem. Beneath all this, so far as she could see, he wore black, relieved only at the wrist by a narrow lace cuff turned back over the plain narrow sleeve. The gold chain of his high office lay round his shoulders.

He was a cultivated man of taste, discrimination and wit, one of the most able, as well as one of the most ambitious, lawyers of his time, and his keen legal mind seemed unimpaired by his formidable reputation for drinking, though Mandala could see nothing in the face before her to suggest that this well-known propensity was having any outward effect. It was perhaps unfortunate that the gallstones from which he was said to suffer undoubtedly affected his temper, and, according to some, the sentences he meted out. So far as Mandala could tell, he appeared to be in a benign enough mood today. He was, above all else, the King's man, the 'lion under the throne'. No one regarded this as a fault: the King appointed his judges and the King had the right to expect them to deliver the verdicts he wanted. In the majority of cases, the King had no views on the matter, but where treason was concerned, things were very different. King James demanded that the current crop of rebels be dealt with so severely that no one else would contemplate treason during his reign. George Jeffreys was the man charged with ensuring that he was not disappointed. A more capable instrument would have been hard to find.

All of this went through Mandala's mind as his surprisingly slight figure stepped the few paces to his chair. Much of it she had gleaned from the other prisoners. Something about him bothered her, and it was not a fear of his judgment. There was something in his face that was familiar. There was no reason why it should be: she had never seen the Lord Chief Justice before, she was sure. She cast her mind back, but was certain she had never encountered him in France or London. Indeed, she was increasingly sure she had never seen him before. It was not that sort of familiarity. It was more a matter of having seen someone who looked in some way similar. Such a puzzle was unlikely to be solved, and she put it firmly away to concentrate on the more important matter—her life.

The Judge took his seat, and the onlookers followed suit. He looked across at the woman in the dock and frowned slightly. The clerk rose and prepared to read the indictment, which was a simple one—treason.

Mandala had had no opportunity to seek legal advice, but she knew that, from the King's point of view, she was undoubtedly guilty even if she had no idea by what evidence they intended to prove it. She also knew that, if she pleaded guilty, she would be condemned to death out of her own mouth, and while her foolishness might have got her here in the first place, she was determined at least to make them prove it. She had drawn herself up, prepared to answer the indictment, when Judge Jeffreys beckoned the clerk over to the bench. They whispered together, each casting an occasional glance at Mandala. When the clerk had returned to his place, the Judge leaned forward.

'Before we proceed, there are matters which need clarification beyond doubt. Prisoner at the bar, identify yourself.'

Since her name had already been quite clearly read out, Mandala was more than a little surprised at this question.

'Mandala Sorn, my lord.'

'Mandala Sorn. S-O-R-N?'

'Yes, my lord.'

'Where do you live?'

'Abbas Manor—at Abbas St Antony in the county of Devon, my lord.'

'In what capacity do you live there?'

'I own it.'

'How did you come to do that?'

'I inherited it from my mother.'

'Who was she?'

'Purity Sorn.'

'And your father?'

Mandala flushed, and tilted her chin defiantly. 'I don't know, my lord.'

'Where did you live before you came into this rather splendid inheritance?'

'I was at a Huguenot school, my lord, but I suppose my home—although after my mother died, I was there but once—was in Paris, in the rue des Flandres.' She hesitated. 'Maman was known as Madame de Rouen.'

'But there was no Monsieur de Rouen?'

'Not that I ever heard of, my lord.'

He stared at her hard in a curious way, with his eyes very wide under glowering brows. It was not an expression that increased the comfort of the onlooker, and Mandala had the uncanny feeling that he was willing her to retract all that she had said. Finally he spoke.

'You do not look like a woman of great estate.'

'With respect, my lord, neither would you if you'd walked over twenty miles in riding-boots and then spent several nights in an extremely crowded and noisome gaol.'

The onlookers gasped. This was no way to speak to a judge, much less so notoriously short-tempered a judge as this one! A frown flickered briefly across his face and was replaced by the hint of a wry smile.

'I take your point, mistress.' He beckoned the clerk towards him again, and once more they conferred briefly though without glancing at Mandala this time. When they had finished, the clerk went to the door and whispered to someone outside. The Judge addressed the court. 'I am not entirely satisfied with certain aspects of this case. There are questions to be decided in chambers. The case is adjourned. It will not recommence until this afternoon.'

He rose, and the court followed his example. Without

a glance in Mandala's direction, he went towards the small door through which he had entered, and disappeared. Mandala, perplexed at this turn of events, just had time to observe that the door led, not into another room, but down a flight of steps, before she, too, was led away.

To her surprise she was taken neither to an anteroom to await the Judge's return nor back to gaol, but instead to a small bed-chamber in another part of the Antelope where she found a pitcher of hot water, a bowl, soap, towels, a small hand-mirror and a brush and comb laid out for her. The gaoler who had brought her went over to the one small window and looked out.

'Sheer drop,' he commented. 'That's all right, then. I'll be outside the door. You're to tidy yourself up properly.'

'Why?' Mandala was both mystified and suspicious.

He shrugged. 'How should I know? I'm just a gaoler.'

'Do you think someone could bring me clean linen for my feet—and some salve?' Mandala asked doubtfully.

'Don't see why not. I'll ask.'

He went out, and Mandala heard the key turn in the lock before his feet clattered down the stairs. She, too, crossed over and looked out of the window. As the gaoler had said, it was a sheer drop down to the ground. She was still very much a prisoner.

With a feeling of almost sybaritic relief, Mandala stripped down to what was left of her shift, and then she sat on the edge of the bed to unwind the now filthy bandages from her feet. Where they had stuck to the raw skin, it was painful in the extreme to remove them, and she decided she would probably have to soak them off in the warm water. First, then, she must make the most of this unexpected opportunity to wash herself.

The gaoler returned before she had finished, and when she heard the key turning in the lock, she clutched her discarded gown to her, expecting him to stand upon no ceremony. To her surprise, however, he tapped on the door before opening it and handed her a small bowl of salve, some neat linen strips and a pair of well-worn but serviceable mules.

'The landlady's compliments,' the gaoler said. 'These here overshoes had been left behind and she didn't like to throw them out, so you may as well have them. She said it don't seem right for a lady to appear in court without shoes.' His tone suggested that the landlady was guilty of the most misguided sentimentality.

'How very kind of you to bring them!' Mandala exclaimed.

'Yes, well, as to that, I'm told you're to hurry up,' the man said.

It was almost as painful to smooth the ointment on to her feet as it had been to get the bandages off, but the relief once it was done was worth the agony. She rebound them again with the fresh linen and found that the mules, which would otherwise have been too big, were now as comfortable a fit as she could hope for. She could do nothing about the dirt and creases in her gown, but at least she could once more brush her luxuriant curls and comb them into place so that, when she finally looked at herself in the mirror, she was reasonably pleased with the result.

When the gaoler unlocked the door at her knock and looked at her, he seemed surprised at her appearance.

'Who'd have thought you'd clean up so well?' he said. 'Maybe the Judge is a better judge than I gave him credit for.' He cackled at this witticism, which, not unnaturally, left Mandala feeling distinctly uneasy about what might be in store.

He led her back to the now empty courtroom and over to the little door, which he opened. As Mandala had noticed earlier, a flight of steps went down, but much further than she had suspected. She turned questioningly to her escort.

'Down there,' he said. 'I'm to stay up here on guard. Just keep going. Someone'll meet you at the other end.'

'"Just keep going"?' Mandala echoed. 'How far is it, for goodness' sake? Where does it lead?'

'Never been down there, myself, so I couldn't say, though I know what the local gossip says. Still, you'll find out for yourself, won't you? There's not many gets this sort of chance to earn their freedom, I can tell you.

Count yourself lucky. Keep a civil tongue in your head and do as you're told, and if the Judge's gallstones aren't playing him up, you'll likely walk out a free woman.'

Comments such as these were hardly calculated to dispel her unease, which deepened as she made her way down the twisting stair and found herself in the Antelope's cellars. These were both cold and dank, but small pitch-soaked torches guttered in wall-sconces at either side of an aisle between barrels, and when she reached the opposite end, she found a door. Since she could think of nothing else to do and was reasonably sure she would not have been allowed down here unescorted if there had been any means of escape, she opened this and found a short passage, followed by another flight of stairs upwards.

At the top of these she was met by a neatly-dressed manservant who looked the very soul of discretion. He glanced at her in the casual way of his kind. That is to say, he appeared to notice nothing, yet could have given an inventory and price-list to cover everything she was wearing. He took her up a broad oak staircase, its sides panelled from floor to ceiling, and came to a halt before a heavy door, upon which he knocked. Mandala heard no response from within, but the manservant must have done because he opened the door and stood aside to let her enter. He did not follow, but closed the door behind her.

She stood in a large panelled room. Ahead of her, overlooking a street, was a long, shallow, oriel window whose casements flooded the room with light. A fire burned in the stone hearth, and beside it, his robes of office cast aside in favour of a velvet robe of the more casual sort, sat the Lord Chief Justice of England. One black-stockinged foot was stretched out towards the warmth, and he held a glass of wine.

'Sit down, Miss Sorn,' he said, indicating a chair opposite. 'Madeira?'

CHAPTER EIGHT

MANDALA DID AS SHE was bid and accepted the offered wine, sipping it gratefully, partly for its welcome warmth and partly because it relieved her of the necessity of speaking.

For a few moments the judge scrutinised her very closely in silence, 'I suggest you remove your cloak, Miss Sorn,' he said eventually. 'If you don't, you will certainly feel the cold when you leave here.'

Mandala had no wish to remove it, for to do so would seem to accept that she might be here for some time, but Lord Jeffreys was obviously right: the combination of the fire and the wine was already making her warm enough to justify taking off the cloak. She undid the clasp and let it fall back over the chair. The weight with which one side of it hung down brought a faint smile to her observer's lips.

'A money pocket, Miss Sorn?'

She flushed. 'My maid sewed a small bag into the lining before they took me away. It has bought a few small comforts in gaol, such as almost-fresh bread.'

'And you have avoided having it stolen in the night? You are lucky, indeed.'

'Why am I here, my lord?' she asked bluntly.

'Have you no idea?'

Mandala had, but she did not intend to voice her suspicions just yet so instead she shook her head.

A cynical smile twisted the well-shaped lips. 'I think you have, but it is mistaken,' Lord Jeffreys said. 'Tell me this: can you prove your identity?'

She looked at him in some bewilderment. 'Prove it, my lord? I know who my mother was and there was no difficulty attached to my inheriting her estate—which surely there would have been, had there been any question that I was her daughter?'

'Do you have any proof that your mother was who you

say she was—this Purity Sorn, I think you said? After all, she was known in France by a very different name.'

'Madame de Rouen,' Mandala confirmed. 'She told me her name. That's all the proof I have, but she, too, certainly inherited Abbas Manor. Could she have done so if there had been any doubt?'

'I imagine the lawyers must have been satisfied,' he agreed. 'Do you know who they were?'

'Why, yes: my own dealings have been with them. I believe they have handled Sorn affairs for generations. Leafield and Leafield of Lincoln's Inn. I am personally acquainted with Thomas Leafield.'

'A respected firm. Yet they are not representing you in court? You might be allowed representation, you know.'

'I assumed I was, and my steward was sent to London to enlist their help. I know he went because he overtook us on the road, but there's no sign of Mr Leafield in court. I fear that either Jonah failed to get to London or Mr Leafield for some reason didn't wish to become involved with a treason trial.'

'I think you may assume that your steward reached Lincoln's Inn.'

Mandala's spirits sank. 'Then I am very much on my own if Mr Leafield won't help me.'

'Mr Leafield has been of far greater assistance to you than you can imagine,' Lord Jeffreys said. 'He rightly judged his presence here to be quite unnecessary. Will you permit me to order a luncheon for us both? I can at least promise something better than almost-fresh bread.'

Mandala laughed ruefully. 'I don't think I could possibly decline such an invitation! I don't suppose you have the least idea what prison food is like.'

'I'm happy to say it's an experience I have so far managed to avoid, and have every intention of continuing to do so.' He rang a small hand-bell on the table beside him, and the manservant who had brought Mandala in arrived so promptly that he could only have been waiting outside to be summoned. 'You may serve lunch now, Edward.' As the man left the room, Lord

Jeffreys turned to Mandala. 'The meal will be a light one, as I have to be careful what I eat, and Edward will have ordered what he judges will best suit me.'

The meal that was set upon a side-table might have been light by the standards of fashionable London, but it was sumptuous enough for Mandala after the last few days' diet of bread, water and, sometimes, cheese. There were no rich pies, though there was a venison stew. It included also a poached salmon, scallops in a wine sauce, a spit-roasted chicken, quails' eggs in aspic, a baked custard, an apple pie and a syllabub. Mandala could not feel that much of this was suitable for a man whose digestion caused him pain, but she noticed that he confined himself to the salmon, the quails' eggs and the baked custard, so perhaps the rest was simply there for show, or perhaps there were days when he chose to eat more lavishly.

While the servant was in the room, conversation between Mandala and the Lord Chief Justice was necessarily restricted and, on her part, constrained, though her host seemed unaffected. She still had no real idea of why she was here or the purpose of Lord Jeffrey's questions. She glanced at him surreptitiously across the table, still puzzled by that element in his features that seemed familiar but which she couldn't quite pin down.

He finally waved the manservant away and led her back to her chair. 'I hope you feel better now,' he remarked.

'Much,' she agreed. 'It's amazing how nothing seems quite so bad if one has a good meal inside one.' She hesitated. 'Lord Jeffreys, are you going to tell me why I'm here?'

'Since it doesn't look as if I'm going to seduce you?' he suggested, and laughed. 'I'm not a fool, Miss Sorn. I know what must have been in your mind and will certainly be in the minds of those who know you were brought here. The mystery will have to remain for a little longer, however; there are a few more questions first. Tell me, what do you know of the circumstances of your birth?'

'Very little. I gather my father was of respectable birth

and that both his parents and my mother's were anxious for a marriage to take place. Maman said that he refused; that he was very ambitious and had no wish to be held back by a provincial—and Puritan—wife. She did tell me he had realised his ambitions and had achieved a position of power and influence . . . ' Her voice trailed away as the implication of her words dawned on her.

There was a long silence while he allowed them to sink in. 'Precisely,' he said at last, ironically. 'It's the mouth, you know.'

'The mouth? I'm sorry, my lord—I don't quite follow.'

'You were wondering why there was something familiar about me. It's the mouth. You've seen it every time you look in the glass. Your mother's was softer, weaker, but apart from that, you bear a striking resemblance to her.'

'There was nothing weak about Maman!' Mandala protested.

'Not once she had to fend for herself, I agree, but I found her . . . malleable.'

'That's a horrid word to use!'

'Possibly. It doesn't make it untrue, however. There must have been unexpected iron in her soul for her to take the path she did and turn it to so much advantage. Perhaps you share that characteristic. I am certainly not weak willed and you do not strike me as being so, so why are you charged with treason? Did you really shelter Monmouth and give him money? It says little for your judgment if you did.'

Mandala was instantly wary. Was this a subtle way of trapping her? It would certainly lead to the removal of a possible embarrassment to him.

'I said I was no fool, Mandala,' he warned. 'I know what you're thinking, and you're wrong in this, as well. I want to know for my own curiosity.'

She was tempted to deny it all, but she had a strong suspicion not only that the Judge would know she was lying but that, in a few well-chosen questions, he would elicit the truth. Instead of answering, she put a question of her own.

'Did you recognise me through a resemblance to Maman? Or was it the name that made you look twice?'

'Neither. I never saw your mother covered in gaol-dirt! I told you that Mr Leafield had been of greater assistance than you realised. He had handled the Sorn side of the negotiations between the two families when your mother was with child. He therefore knew the identity of your father. When your steward reached him, he realised the embarrassment to the Lord Chief Justice of finding his daughter before him on a charge of treason. Such accusations have a nasty habit of rubbing off on others by association. He guessed that both our interests would be served by warning me that you were here in gaol. Unfortunately, the messenger's horse went lame and he didn't get here till breakfast-time today. Had he arrived earlier, you would have been released and the charges dropped, without a whole courtroom being any the wiser.'

'And now?'

'Now it becomes more difficult. You have appeared and been indicted. That is why I need to know just how deep your involvement with Monmouth's cause was. If there is some tiny loophole I can use to dismiss the charges, I shall do so. No one will believe it, of course. They will assume you earned your freedom in the time-honoured way, and I'm afraid I am not prepared to disabuse them of that idea—and neither must you.'

'Because the fact that such a charge was brought against your daughter would bring your own loyalty to the Crown under suspicion?'

'In part. If I dismiss charges against my own daughter instead of handing her over to another judge, that is nepotism. If I dismiss charges against a singularly beautiful young woman who is as obliging as she is beautiful, that is certainly reprehensible, but it's also human nature. I have no wish to ruin your reputation so surely, but, in the circumstances, I can see no other way.'

'I don't think you need worry too much about my reputation,' Mandala said bitterly. 'I don't have one. The people of Abbas St Antony know the circumstances of my birth, and I have—perhaps inadvisedly—made no

secret of how Maman earned our bread. Nor have I felt
obliged to be apologetic about it, or ashamed. Consequently, I am branded the same way. Your daughter, my
lord, is generally held to be a Jezebel—a Scarlet
Woman.'

'I'm sorry,' he said simply. 'But if that's the case, they
will be all the more ready to accept the least flattering
interpretation for your freedom. Now, what about
Monmouth?'

Mandala stared at him with something close to disgust. He had said he was sorry—and meant it—but what
he was sorry for was the reputation she had, not his part
in bringing it about. Everything else was a matter of
expedience.

'Did you love my mother?' she asked suddenly, and
had the satisfaction of seeing him, for the first time,
surprised.

'Love her? It was a long time ago. So long, I scarcely
remember it. Does that shock you? She was beautiful
and desirable and I enjoyed the snatched moments we
shared. I doubt if that constitutes love.'

Mandala doubted it, too, and thought it better to return
to her own problem rather than to press him further.

'You asked about Monmouth,' she said. 'He sheltered
on my land after he landed and before he reached
Taunton. He was there without my prior permission. I
stumbled upon him and his men when I was riding, and
he persuaded me to let them stay until morning. The
second time they were there—some of the rebels, that
is, for I never heard of Monmouth's presence—I knew
nothing about it until an estate worker brought word. I
decided to do nothing except hope they would soon be
gone.'

'And the money? It is said you gave him a substantial
sum.'

'A mistake.'

'Of some magnitude! But why?'

Mandala hesitated. It was difficult to analyse her
reasons, but she must try. 'I'm not sure. It certainly
wasn't because I was convinced of the justness of his
cause. It was partly to ensure that he left, and partly his

charm. He is—was—a very charming man, you know. I knew all along it was a gamble. I didn't think it was nearly so cut and dried as he believed it to be.'

'You said it was a gamble. That implies you had something to gain if he won.'

'Two things: he promised to have me received at Court—which may not seem a very great thing to you, my lord, but when even my neighbours won't receive me, it becomes a sizeable lure—and a dukedom in my own right.'

He looked at her curiously. 'Was that such a vast temptation? My acquaintance with you is slight, but I shouldn't have thought so.'

'It wasn't, and I have a strong suspicion he'd have forgotten all about it—but I should have held him to his first promise.'

'I can offer you nothing but your life and a brief notoriety and then obscurity, Mandala. I have no desire to see you at Court. To be honest, I should prefer never to hear of you again.'

'I'd rather have my life than a dukedom,' she pointed out.

He laughed and stood up, extending his hand as he did so to help her to her feet. 'It's time we got back to business,' he said. 'I think I see how it may be done.' He raised her hand to his lips, and kissed it. 'Do you know, I'm almost sorry you're my daughter. Had it been otherwise, you might well have gained your freedom by other means.'

Mandala chuckled. 'I think not, my lord. You'd not have noticed my attractions under all that gaol-dirt!'

He opened the door for her and handed her into Edward's care once more, and within minutes she found herself back in the re-assembled courtroom. Her changed appearance was remarked upon in whispers and nudges, and she had great difficulty in appearing oblivious of the comments of those nearest the dock. As she had entered the room, she had caught sight of Deveril York again, and Sir Nuneham had also returned for the afternoon session.

The Judge entered, attired once more in scarlet, white

and black, and the court hushed expectantly. He was in no hurry to satisfy their curiosity. He scowled at the spectators in the strangely ferocious way for which he was noted, his brows lowered but his eyes wide.

'There are factors in this case which I mislike,' he began. 'The charge against this woman has been brought on nothing more tangible than the word of a man who is a known traitor, caught in the act, and who laid information against the defendant solely to save his own skin. His fellow traitors, taken with him, were not prepared to sink to his depths, and have been hanged. Evidence such as his is suspect at best, and a warrant for his arrest has been issued.'

On the floor of the courtroom, glances were exchanged. There was nothing untoward in a man's escaping the noose by laying information elsewhere. It was to be expected, and there were few judges who objected. Certainly the Lord Chief Justice was not among them —or had not been until now. They transferred their gaze to the woman in the dock. She had used her time with the Judge to good effect, it seemed. More than one spectator nudged his neighbour.

'Consequently,' the Judge continued, fully conscious of the conclusions being drawn by his audience, 'I do not consider that any court can place dependence upon the accuracy of evidence such as this—evidence which any half-witted advocate could demolish in seconds. The charges should never have been brought, and the case is therefore dismissed.'

Mandala heaved a sigh of relief. Somehow she had not expected it to fall out quite so neatly, and she found herself shaking so much that she had to be assisted from the dock and the courtroom. She made her way to one of the Antelope's public rooms and sat down on a settle, requesting the potman to bring her some mulled wine.

It was while she was sipping this, the warm glass cupped between her still-shaking hands, that Deveril York strode into the room. She raised her eyes expectantly and half rose from her seat, but one glance at his face dashed whatever hope she had had.

'Congratulations,' he said in a voice so heavy with

sarcasm that the word was robbed of its meaning. 'What a clever, scheming hussy you turned out to be!'

She stared at him, shock at the venom in his words removing the tremor from her hands as the wine had not done. 'A compliment, I gather. Why, thank you, sir,' she retorted.

Outside the door, on his way to his horse, Sir Nuneham Courtenay paused, attracted by the sound of familiar voices raised in anger.

'I imagine you would regard it as such. You've learned the lessons of your upbringing well.'

Determined not to let him see how much his harsh jibes hurt her, Mandala forced herself to smile sweetly. 'My upbringing, Mr York, was largely in a seminary run by nuns, and later in a Huguenot school. I don't think either would consider that they had taught me those attributes.'

'Then they were bred in your bones—or learned from your esteemed mother. However, be that as it may, you can't deny that the Lord Chief Justice has played fair with you. Very fair.'

She flushed. 'Lord Jeffreys ascertained the truth, sir. It was not I who had Monmouth shelter on my land. Had it not been for you, he would have gone elsewhere. Fortunately for you, Lord Jeffreys did not enquire into that aspect of the matter.'

'I doubt if he had time. He had first to ascertain whether you were worth the trouble of setting free. I take it you were. What happens now? Do you follow discreetly to Exeter and Taunton until he tires of you?'

White with anger, Mandala stood up and dashed the remains of her wine in his face. 'How dare you!' she hissed. 'You know nothing of the matter at all. You just leap to the nastiest possible conclusion. I had thought that at least we met as friends, that you didn't pre-judge me by my mother, as everyone else did. But I was wrong, wasn't I? You have exactly the same opinion of me as they do. You chose to pretend otherwise so that you had the opportunity to spy out my land for Monmouth. 'Tis I must congratulate you, sir, for you had me completely fooled.'

It was Deveril's turn to blench at the implication of her words to anyone listening, and he inwardly thanked God that the room was empty for the present. 'You talk nonsense,' he said firmly. 'Dangerous nonsense! Such wild guesses in return for a few home truths will get you nowhere.'

'They're not wild guesses, and you know it,' Mandala retorted. 'Are you forgetting? I met Monmouth and talked with him. As a consequence, I nearly burned at the stake. Do you think I don't remember every word he said?'

He smiled unpleasantly. 'Oh, yes. I dare say he offered you a dukedom. James Scott is very free with promises of dukedoms.' Her face told him that his guess was accurate. 'And what recompense did he expect for that? He would have needed more than a few guineas.'

'It was not a promise I set any store by, and so I told Judge Jeffreys. At least he believed me,' she added.

He stared at her in silent disgust for a few minutes. 'I'm not sure how you did it, but you played your cards very cleverly indeed. When you came into court so dirty I wouldn't have believed it possible that you would take his eye. He is said to be fastidious.'

Mandala shook her head. 'That had nothing to do with it.'

'Obviously,' he sneered.

'Are you not prepared even to try to believe me?' she said despairingly. 'Have I always been such a complete liar in the past?'

'What do you expect me, or anyone else, to believe? A beautiful woman, with the faggots as good as cut, comes before a judge of some susceptibility. The case is adjourned to the judge's chambers, and when the court resumes some hours later, the lady is washed and combed and the judge quite uncharacteristically benign. Add to that the known facts of your birth and your mother's profession, and who do you think will believe you went to his chambers to read to him?'

Mandala flushed at the reference to her birth, and knew that the one thing she dared not reveal was the truth. 'I wish you were prepared to take what I say on

trust,' she whispered. 'It simply is not as you have
concluded.'

'I can think of no other likely explanation. Can you?'

Only the truth, she thought miserably. Aloud,
she said, 'Why is it so important to you to have that
explanation?'

'Don't delude yourself, Miss Sorn. I am merely
curious to see to what extent you are prepared to distort
probability in order to prove that you are not exactly
what everyone believes you to be and what you have
today demonstrated you are.'

'For someone who is "merely curious", you are
expending a great deal of energy and venom,' she
suggested. 'Why not just walk away?'

'Perhaps my dislike of deception equals your own. Be
that as it may, I strongly recommend you to return to
France as soon as your judicial obligations are fulfilled. I
think you will find yourself totally ostracised once
today's events are generally known. Good day, Miss
Sorn.'

Mandala made no reply but turned away from him and
stared into the fire, tears pricking her eyes. She heard his
boots on the flags outside, and then, after an interval, a
horse's hooves clattering out of the yard.

As soon as Sir Nuneham was satisfied that he was
unlikely to hear any more of interest, he hastened away
from the door before he should be discovered, claimed
his horse from the stable and set off on his homeward
journey. He was in no hurry: he should be able to reach
Bridport comfortably before evening, and he had been
given plenty to think about. There was no doubt in his
mind as to what lay behind the angry exchange of words
to which he had unashamedly listened.

He knew, because Deveril had told him so, that his
former guest had intended to offer for the heiress, even
though he had no need of her riches. He had warned
Mandala against the other man, and, even though she
had spurned his own advances in no uncertain terms, he
had thought she might heed the warning. His later
encounter with Deveril, however, had given him a fair

idea of the arrogance of the man. He had certainly not given up his plan to offer for her then, and had behaved in the proprietary manner of one who considered the battle won. Today's court appearance now put Mandala's reputation on so very public a level that no gentleman, not even Sir Nuneham, could consider allying himself with her, however great her fortune. Deveril's anger was no doubt due to that consideration. Mandala's, he suspected, was because, despite the warning she had received, she had been persuaded into imagining herself to have a fondness for him, and she must have also realised that any respectable marriage was now out of the question.

More intriguing by far was the titbit his eavesdropping had picked up. Mandala had claimed that she knew from Monmouth's own lips that Deveril had been spying out the land for him. If that was so, then Deveril York was the biggest traitor of them all. He had only to inform against him, and all those scores would be settled.

For several miles Sir Nuneham's journey was made more pleasurable by the contemplation of his revenge. Then a faint feeling of unease intervened. It was all very well to lay information against Deveril, but who had made it possible for him to spy out the lie of the land? It was Sir Nuneham himself who had invited him to Devon. He must somehow extricate himself from any suspicion of involvement. He cast his mind back. He had volunteered the invitation because he had hoped to interest Deveril in Isobel, but the initial advance had been Deveril's. He had expressed an interest in Courtenay Place. Clever! He must have guessed an invitation was inevitable. Once there, what had Deveril done? Got up at an obscenely unseasonable hour—sometimes as early as nine o'clock—and ridden about all over the place. He had known the Haddenhams, too. Now that *was* an interesting fact in the light of what he had just overheard. In the vigorous effort to purge the south-west of those sympathetic to Monmouth's cause, known Puritans were placed high on the list, since they objected most vociferously to the King's catholicism and therefore were the most likely to want to see a Protestant monarch on the throne. He did not know whether Deveril was a Puritan or just an opportunist, but the Haddenhams most certainly were. So, for that matter, had the Sorns been, though you would not think so to look at Mandala. When Deveril had left Courtenay Place, Sir Nuneham had assumed he had also left the county. His unexpected arrival at Abbas Manor had given the lie to that, so where had he been staying? Some hostelry was a possibility. So was Haddenham Hall.

It was not very difficult for Sir Nuneham to convince himself that the Haddenhams were thoroughly implicated and that Mandala's involvement was quite possibly much deeper than had emerged in court. However, even he knew that he dared not implicate the Lord Chief Justice's new mistress: the man had a nasty way of turning one's own words against one. He could get his own back on Deveril, and if the Haddenhams were convicted of treason, even Isobel would see the impossibility of allying herself with them. Not that much of an alliance would be possible once they had been hanged or, more probably, transported to Barbados. He would ride to the magistrate at Axminster with his information.

To Sir Nuneham's surprise, the magistrate seemed disinclined to snatch delightedly at his news.

'I know nothing of this Deveril York,' he said, 'but I am puzzled as to why, if you heard this conversation at Dorchester while the Assize was still in session, you didn't think to pass it on to the proper authorities there?'

'To be honest, the full implication didn't dawn on me until I was on my way home.' Sir Nuneham told him. 'I was anxious, too, not to implicate Miss Sorn further. You have heard what happened?' Sir Paul Bridlington had not, and was most interested. 'So, you see, what I overheard rather endorses her case, but I'm sure Lord Jeffreys won't want to see her produced as a witness.' Sir Paul had never met Lord Jeffreys but knew his reputation, and felt bound to agree with this rather unpleasant spendthrift fop.

'It's the Haddenhams' involvement I'm reluctant to accept,' he said. 'They are Puritans, of course, and as such are highly suspect at the present time. The fact remains that they take no part in politics. The boy, I know, is totally uninterested. Nathaniel is a good man and a peaceable one, and I just can't imagine his condoning a rebellion against the Crown, much less offering the rebels any assistance.'

'Which only goes to prove how very clever he is!' Sir Nuneham exclaimed triumphantly.

Since it was perfectly obvious that Sir Nuneham was not to be deflected from his goal, Sir Paul reluctantly agreed to take down the details his visitor offered and to pass them on to the militia. He showed Sir Nuneham to the door without his pleasure at his departure becoming too apparent, and delayed acting upon his information as long as he dared. He finally decided, on such evidence as he had, that there was nothing to implicate Mark Haddenham except the fact that he was his father's son, and so he issued only two warrants. He had no feelings about the one that bore Deveril York's name, but it cost him some anguish to inscribe the name of Nathaniel Haddenham.

CHAPTER NINE

MANDALA MADE SLOW progress home. She had enough
money left to be able to stay at an inn, but there were no
spare rooms because of the crowds in Dorchester for the
Assize. When she returned, dispirited, to the Antelope,
the landlady took pity on her and said she could sleep
over the stables with the kitchen-maids. Next day she
hired a straight-shouldered cob whose spirits matched
her own and set out for Abbas St Antony.

Only two good things had come out of this episode:
she was alive, and she had solved the mystery of her
parentage. That the latter must remain for ever a secret
was a source of regret, but at least she knew her father's
identity. Having met him, she could well understand
how her mother had been persuaded to part with her
virtue. 'Malleable' was the word Lord Jeffreys had used
to describe her mother. It did not fit the mother she
remembered, but doubtless sheer necessity had brought
the iron to the fore. It was ironic that the world should
now believe she had herself been seduced by him, but
since the truth could not be told, the world would
continue to believe that—and the world included
Deveril York.

He had made it perfectly clear what he believed and
what he thought of her as a result, and it mattered
terribly to her that it should be so, yet who could blame
him? She often thought she disliked him, and she knew
he had used her for his own traitorous ends. Yet the days
spent riding with him had showed that they could spend
hours in each other's company in complete amity, that
they often shared a common viewpoint, a similar sense
of the ridiculous. Nor was that all. On the occasion when
he had taken her into his arms, she had known there was
more. Perhaps it would be more true to say she had
sensed it, but, when Isobel came upon them, she had
known a deep, hungry yearning that his body told her he

shared. Now she had unwittingly forfeited any chance there might have been for something more to come of it. Now she was indelibly branded with her mother's mark. Her father had saved her life, but at a price. Mandala cared not a jot for the opinion of Devon's gentry: she had managed quite well without their approbation, and doubted if that was likely to change now. But she did care for Deveril's opinion. He had told her once that she did not deserve the reputation bestowed upon her. He was certainly no longer of that opinion and there was absolutely nothing she could do about it. He had never been hers, and now he never could be. He had advised her to return to France. Perhaps, in the circumstances, that would be the best thing to do.

Any journey on a poor horse accompanied by such thoughts was bound to seem interminable, and when, some ten miles from Abbas St Antony, she saw a familiar cob coming towards her and recognised the stalwart figure of Jonah Swinbrook, Mandala's spirits could only lift.

The steward cast over her mount the shocked eye of one accustomed only to seeing the best. 'Is that all Dorchester could offer?' he asked.

'It's all they would let me have,' she told him. 'I have never ridden a more uncomfortable brute in my life.'

'You should have taken him at a gallop,' Jonah said knowledgeably. 'The worse the horse, the faster you ride him.'

'I don't think he knows what a gallop is. Besides, how long do you think he could keep it up? Bad as he is, he's better than walking—and that is an opinion based on experience. I have to thank you for getting to London, Jonah. You served me well.'

He nodded. 'That Mr Leafield, he seemed to reckon he knew just what to do. Said to go home and leave it to him, but I couldn't rest easy back at the Manor, and Kate and Martha both agreed I should come to Dorchester and see what's happening. I've the pillion-saddle, mistress. What say you come up behind me and we'll tie the nag on behind?'

Mandala agreed with alacrity to this admirable

suggestion, thus completing the journey in relative comfort, and when they drew rein outside the Manor House, she slid gratefully down into Martha's waiting arms.

'Sweet Jesus!' the maid said in horrified tones. 'Whatever do you look like? It's a bath and bed for you, my girl, and no argument!'

'Oh, I'll not argue with that,' Mandala said tremulously, as though the last vestiges of strength had left her as her sore feet touched the gravel drive.

Within the hour she was tucked up between clean, sweet-smelling sheets, a clean night-shift against her skin and new bandages on her feet to which aromatic unguents from Kate Swinbrook's cupboard had been tenderly applied. Satisfied with Mandala's protestations that she was exhausted but not hungry, Martha brought her a glass of warm cinnamon milk and made her drink it down.

'I know it's not your favourite, but it will help you to sleep. Even if you think you won't need help, I've a strong suspicion you'll feel that prime bit of knacker's meat for hours yet. You'll not be disturbed until you wake up, and then I'll see to it there's a bite to eat, and it's my belief you'll drop right off again. After that, you'll be right as a trivet, I'll be bound.'

As she turned to go, Mandala touched her sleeve. 'Martha,' she whispered. 'I met my father.'

The maid's face expressed neither surprise nor curiosity. 'Did you now? I heard he was in Dorchester.'

'You knew how important he was?'

'Of course I did! Wasn't I your mother's nursemaid? I've followed his career as well as I could. You'd do well to forget him, though: I doubt he wants to be reminded, and he's not a man to cross, by all accounts. Sleep well, mistress.'

'You won't tell anyone?' Mandala said, suddenly anxious.

'I've not told anyone these past one-and-twenty years. Why should I start tittle-tattling now? Just you go to sleep. Things will look much more simple when you wake up.'

While Mandala slept, she had a visitor. Mark

Haddenham rode over in some haste and implored Mrs Swinbrook to let him speak to Miss Sorn. Instead, he had to make do with Martha Rissington, and found her adamant.

'Miss Sorn's asleep, and asleep she stays, young man. There's no business so pressing that I'm prepared to wake her up.'

'You don't understand,' he protested. 'My father has been taken, falsely accused of being involved in the recent uprising. I need Miss Sorn's help urgently.'

'She has herself only just returned from facing similar charges. You have my sympathy, Mr Haddenham, and I'm sure your father would have Miss Sorn's, but what on earth do you think she can do to help him?'

Mark hesitated. Was it possible that the gossip from Dorchester that had already reached some households had not yet reached here? If that were the case, he had no desire to be the one to pass it on. 'It was just . . .' he began. 'It occurred to me . . .' He gave up. 'When will she wake up?'

'I've not the slightest idea, but it will be two or three days before she's in any condition to tackle her own problems, let alone yours.'

'Will you tell her that I called?'

'Naturally.'

'And why?'

Martha considered. 'Probably not, since I don't see how she can be expected to help. Good day, Mr Haddenham.'

The gossip had reached Abbas Manor, and there was much speculation as to its accuracy. It did not sound like the Mandala Sorn everyone knew, but there was no denying that desperate situations called for desperate measures, and it was only to be expected that, given her upbringing, she was likely to be less reluctant than most to employ that particular measure. Martha's unwavering refusal to believe one word of it was the only thing to encourage the rest of the household to doubt the story. Even though she refused to give reasons for her firmly-held belief, she managed to convey the impression that she was party to some hitherto undisclosed information, and because she was known to be truthful, she more than half convinced her audience.

Mark returned the next day, and the next. Each time he was sent away, but on his third visit Martha relented a little.

'Come back tomorrow, Mr Haddenham, and maybe she'll be recovered enough to see you. I make no promises, mind you, but I'll undertake to let her know you've been calling, which I haven't done so far. Just remember that she needs rest, not someone else's problems.'

He had no choice but to be content with that, which at least had the merit of being the most hopeful reception yet.

When he returned the next day, he learned that Mandala was, in Martha's opinion, sufficiently recovered to receive visitors and that she had been advised of his intention to call. So great was his agitation at the delay in seeing her that he quite forgot the customary social niceties and instead of bowing or taking her hand, burst straight into the purpose of his visit.

'You've no idea how glad I am to see you sufficiently recovered to talk to me,' he said. 'Miss Sorn, I need your help on my father's behalf.'

Mandala looked surprised. 'Your father? What help can I possibly be to him?'

'Your maid hasn't told you?' Mandala shook her head. 'They have taken him in connection with recent unhappy events, and he lies in Taunton gaol, charged with treason.'

Mandala blenched. 'I've never formally met your father, but anyone in that unfortunate position has my sympathy.' She paused briefly. 'You said you needed my help on his behalf. Forgive me, but I can't imagine how I can help him.'

For the first time it crossed Mark's mind that there might be some awkwardness if he revealed that he had not only heard some very insalubrious gossip about her but also believed it, to the extent that it formed the basis for his belief that she could assist him. 'He will appear at Taunton Assize,' he began awkwardly. 'He and Deveril

York were taken at much the same time, and . . .'

'Deveril!' Mandala exclaimed, her interest sharpening beyond mere sympathy.

'Yes, Deveril York. They are both on a similar charge, though I fancy from something my father once said, that in his case the charges may not be without foundation.'

'And what is my part in all this, Mr Haddenham?'

He shifted his feet uneasily. 'I would there were a—a discreet way of wording this, Miss Sorn, but I can't think of one. The word is that you escaped conviction because you took Judge Jeffreys' eye. That you went to his chambers and returned a free woman. The inference is . . .' He faltered.

'Let me make it easy for you, Mr Haddenham. The inference is that my virtue was the price of my freedom.'

'Yes.'

'Rumour moves fast through the narrow Devon lanes!' she commented sarcastically. 'Now, pray, enlighten me further. What relevance does this gossip have to your father's unfortunate situation?'

'Don't you see?' he said eagerly. 'If you could but intervene with the Judge, plead my father's case, surely you could sway him?'

'Do you really think pleading would be enough?' Mandala asked drily. 'I think you mean that what's gone already won't be missed, and why should I not seduce the Lord Chief Justice again, only this time for your father?'

Mark coloured. She had put it rather too baldly. It made it sound rather nasty, rather sordid. 'Well, yes,' he admitted sheepishly. 'That is what I meant.'

Mandala turned from him and stared out of the window and she saw before her neither the knot-garden or Nathaniel Haddenham, but Deveril York. Lord Jeffreys had been quite unequivocal: he never wanted to hear of her again. Mandala had no quarrel with this desire. It was enough that she knew who her father was, and that she had her freedom. She was perfectly willing that they should continue along the separate paths they had been pursuing for over twenty years without those paths ever

crossing again. Much as she sympathised with Mark
Haddenham and pitied his father, she would not even
have paused to consider Mark's suggestion had Deveril
York not been involved.

She loved him. She had no reason to believe that he
had ever returned that feeling, and every reason to
believe that he now held her in disgust. To use her
connection with the Lord Chief Justice to free him would
only deepen the contempt in which he held her. If she
did not, he would die. She knew, as Mark did not, that
he was guilty, and she had no doubt that, somehow,
information to that effect had been laid. It was just
possible that she could, by pleading for Nathaniel Haddenham, include Deveril in her arguments. If guilt by
association was possible, then why not innocence by
association? She turned back to Mark.

'Very well,' she said. 'I'll try. No, don't become too
hopeful. I can't just say, "Free this man because I ask
it." I must have some evidence, some grounds, for
believing him innocent. What grounds can you give
me?'

Mark looked despairing. 'He's my father. I know him
well. It's just not in his character, Miss Sorn.'

'You'll have to find a better argument than that,' she
pointed out. 'You can't deny that he's a Puritan, and as
such is highly suspect.'

'We have always been Puritans. My grandfather
fought for Parliament, but he opposed the regicide and
took no part in politics after that event. This path has
been followed by my father, and I intend to pursue it
myself. He cannot approve of the present King, and
would be happy to learn that the succession was settled
on his Protestant daughters rather than face the possibility of a Catholic son being born to his second wife. He
would do nothing to remove the rightful king from his
throne. To do so would run counter to his principles.'

'He didn't believe Monmouth's claims?'

Mark shook his head. 'He maintained that there was
so much doubt as to his legitimacy, that if he sat on the
throne we should have civil war. He believed that the
supporters of Princess Mary and Princess Anne would

seek to overturn King Monmouth and we'd be back where we were forty-five years ago.'

Mandala sighed. 'I believe you—and with those views, I'm sure your father could have had no part in the rebellion. But you must see that it is a purely theoretical argument. We have to assume they have some information, however inaccurate, from somewhere, in order to have arrested him in the first place. I shall try to find out when the Assize is due to sit in Taunton. In the meantime, rack your brains. You must find something more conclusive than long-held opinions.'

Mark rode away in low spirits, clutching to his heart the only straw of hope he had—that Mandala was willing to speak for his father. He had gone to her as the only person he knew who could conceivably exert the sort of influence that was needed, knowing that there was absolutely no reason why she should. By some miracle, she was willing to, but he had to find further, better, evidence, and that was going to be difficult, if not impossible.

He did not make his way directly back to Haddenham Hall but rode in a wide arc that brought him to the fringes of the Courtenay estate. Here he followed a convoluted track, more used by deer than men, that led far into Sir Nuneham's land and eventually to a small clearing where there stood the remains of a charcoal-burner's hut. He paused among the trees on the edge of the little glade. He could never be quite sure, in the week that elapsed between visits, that he would not be met by his neighbour or his neighbour's keepers. He stayed where he was for a long time, but there was no sign of life beyond the occasional rabbit, and he was beginning to think his détour had been wasted time when a faint rustle across the glade caught his ear. It was very soon followed by its cause, as Isobel stepped gingerly into the glade, looking about her with nervous apprehension.

One might have thought that the sudden appearance in such circumstances of a man on horseback would lead so obviously fearful a girl to scream and run, but instead, Isobel's face flooded with relief and she ran forward to meet him.

'You remembered!' she exclaimed. 'I had heard about your father, and feared you would forget—or never wish to see me again. I am so sorry at the news. Is there anything you can do?'

Mark sprang from his horse and swept her into his arms. 'As if I could forget our assignation! It is so like you to rate yourself low in my estimation.'

It was a few moments before Isobel was able to answer, for her mouth was otherwise occupied. When she was able to do so, she whispered, 'But your father must always come first. Oh, Mark, I am so sorry! Nuneham is mad, quite mad—and so I told him.'

Mark was understandably bemused by her apparently disconnected train of thought. 'Why should you tell Sir Nuneham any such thing? Has he found out about our clandestine meetings? Has he threatened to part us?' He sighed. 'He disapproved of me before this. With my father due to stand trial for treason, his view is unlikely to change.'

'Then you don't know?'

'What should I know?'

'It was Nuneham who informed against your father and Mr York.'

Mark stared at her in disbelief. 'Sir Nuneham? But why should he do such a thing? What evidence did he have?'

Isobel shook her head. 'As to the evidence, I've no idea, though from something he said, it was something he overheard. The reason is clear enough: he made no secret of it. Mr York was his first target and the more important of the two. Nuneham really hates him, Mark. Partly because he didn't offer for me and thereby give Nuneham access to his fortune, and partly because he thinks Mandala Sorn prefers Mr York. Nuneham had offered for her—he was prepared to overlook her background in order to get control of her fortune—but she turned him down in no uncertain terms, and he thinks it was for Mr York. The thing is, Deveril York won't offer for her now that her reputation is irretrievably lost, but, of course, Nuneham can't either, for the same reason. He blames Mr York for all this; which is nonsense, and so I told him. Anyway, he overheard something that implicates Mr York quite deeply, and has informed on him to get his own back.'

'I suppose I can see his reasoning,' Mark said doubtfully. 'At least, I can if I remember that Sir Nuneham isn't very bright. I'm sorry, Isobel: I should not disparage your brother, but it's true, you know. I still don't see where my father fits into this.'

'It gets worse,' she told him. 'It seems he had what he describes as a brilliant idea. (You're quite right: I've often thought that, while he can be really very cunning, he isn't always very clever. It seems disrespectful to think that about one's own brother, but I have done —often). Anyway, he thought that if he could somehow drag your father into it, the Haddenhams would be so discredited—to say nothing of losing all their lands —that I would have to give up any idea of marrying into the family.'

'He's mad!' Mark exclaimed. 'What evidence has he produced to implicate my father?'

'I don't think he has any, beyond the fact that he is a well-known Puritan and acquainted with Mr York.'

'That's all?' Mark was incredulous.

'As far as I know, yes.' She hesitated. 'I thought you should know all this. That was why I was afraid you wouldn't want to see me again.'

He hugged her fondly. 'Foolish girl! As if I would visit your brother's sins on your shoulders!'

There was a long silence, during which he convinced her of the folly of her imagination. 'If I had judged you by your brother, I should never have fallen in love with you,' he said at last, and then, reluctantly, released her. 'I must return to Abbas Manor with this news,' he said. 'Miss Sorn may be able to make use of it.'

'Mandala! What do you mean? Have you already been there?' She sounded a little shocked.

'I could think of no one else in a position to plead for my father, so I asked her. It was a faint hope on my part, but, somewhat to my surprise, she has agreed to intercede with Lord Jeffreys on his behalf. She said she needed more evidence than his son's opinion that he was innocent. What better evidence could there be than that the information was given out of spite?'

Isobel looked doubtful. 'Mandala was kind to me, and I liked her very much,' she said. 'How she could bear to—to give herself to a perfectly dreadful man like Judge Jeffreys, I just can't imagine. Though, of course, it's very good of her to speak for your father, whom she hardly knows,' she added.

'Perhaps Judge Jeffreys was preferable to the stake,' Mark suggested gently.

Isobel shuddered. 'I should prefer to die,' she said dramatically.

Mark kissed her again. Honour should not be diluted by practical considerations, and he was glad Isobel felt that, too. 'You understand that I must leave you now, my love. I shall have difficulty as it is to get to Abbas Manor and back home before nightfall.'

'Of course. You must be on your way. Oh, Mark, I do so hope you are able to resolve it all.'

'Our hope must lie with Mandala Sorn,' he reminded her.

'Yes, of course, only that does not somehow seem to be quite proper.'

Perhaps wisely, Mark refrained from asking for an explanation of this somewhat cryptic remark, and, after a rather less prolonged leave-taking than usual, remounted his horse and set off back the way he had come.

Mandala judged that the Lord Chief Justice would probably prefer not to be intercepted on the road to Taunton, as she had at first planned, and that it might be wiser to reach there before him and seek an audience in a manner which might be more conducive to discretion. It was a matter of personal pride that, on this occasion, at least, he should not see her as he had done before. She was a woman of wealth and fashion, and it was as such that she would appear before him. She was also determined that her arrival in Taunton should occasion no comment, even if her departure after seeing the Judge did. To that end she was accompanied by a groom who carried Martha on the pillion-saddle, and a baggage-horse to ensure that she need never sit down twice in the same gown.

Taunton was packed for the Assize, but the landlord of the Red Lion was very happy to find a room for such an obviously fashionable a lady as Miss Sorn. He was obliged to express the hope that she would not object to her maid's sleeping on a small truckle-bed in her room. Mandala graciously accepted this arrangement, and, as soon as Martha had shaken out her gowns and laid them out in a way best calculated to diminish the creases, she sent the maid abroad to ascertain where Judge Jeffreys would be lodging and when he was expected.

When Martha returned with the information, she also brought the news that Mark Haddenham, too, was in Taunton. Mandala supposed it was only to be expected that he should be here at so critical a time, but she was rather sorry that she was now unlikely to attend to the business that brought her here without being seen by someone from her own locality. She knew this was an irrational feeling, since Mark thought he knew perfectly well the means she was going to employ to free his father. All the same, she would have preferred him not to have been there.

Her father—it seemed strange to think of him in those terms—was expected in the late afternoon, and would be in court the following morning. Mandala toyed with the idea of being at his lodging to meet him, but rejected it: his temper was known to be difficult, and the long ride from Exeter was unlikely to put anyone in the best of humours. Better to wait until he had rested and eaten. His temper could not be guaranteed, but at least there was a chance it might not be at its worst.

Mandala dressed with very great care in the dark green that she knew became her colouring so well. The lines of the gown itself were simple: a plain boned bodice with a low scooped neckline to the shoulder and the very briefest of sleeves, but both the neck and sleeves were edged with ermine, as were the centre edges and the hem of the overskirt, which parted to show the matching heavy brocade petticoat. This overskirt was neither looped back nor trained, but it was of an immense fullness which gave it a sumptuousness belied by its apparent simplicity. No smock was visible except on the arms where, below the narrow, ermine-edged sleeves, it fell in two huge puffs of starched lawn, ending in broad lace cuffs that hung halfway to the wrist.

She wore her hair in the current mode with a centre parting and long, horizontal curls at either side. Caught in at the nape, the rest was artfully arranged in two long ringlets that lay over her left shoulder, accentuating the unflawed whiteness of her neck and shoulders. She wore a single strand of pearls, and at the centre of the fur-trimmed neckline she pinned an antique brooch depicting St George and the dragon, the body of the saint's horse being a huge baroque pearl and its head a smaller one, while the rest of the scene was enamelled in bright colours on a gold ground. Three pendent pearls hung from the bottom of this, and two more from her ears.

She viewed herself in the mirror, and saw no reason for dissatisfaction.

Martha looked at her, and sniffed. 'It's as well his lordship knows who you are,' she said. 'Dressed like that, you're a target for every fortune-hunter ever born —and those who weren't interested in the fortune would be after something else. At least, where you're going, both will be safe!'

A cloak and pattens hid these riches from passers-by, and the presence of a maid and an armed groom ensured her safe arrival at the Judge's lodgings. Mandala removed her pattens and bade the landlord show her to Judge Jeffreys' rooms. Startled at first, and then bestowing upon her a knowing wink, he said he would enquire if she was expected.

'I'm not,' she told him. 'But I think if you fetch his manservant, Edward, you will find I am to be received.'

Intrigued, the landlord wasted no time. Edward, too well trained to betray his surprise at seeing her at all or at seeing her attired in so very different a style, looked at her briefly in silence, before bowing and saying, 'Very well, mistress, follow me. I don't know whether his lordship will see you, but he will certainly wish to know you are here.'

When he emerged to say that the Judge would receive his visitor, Mandala unclasped her cloak and handed it to him before going past him through the door.

This room was smaller than the one in Dorchester and seemed much darker, but Mandala recognised that this was probably because the light was fast fading from the sky and the candles had been lit. Judge Jeffreys appeared to be wearing exactly what he had worn at their previous meeting, but this time he stood up as she came in. His eyes widened when they saw her, and she thought she heard him catch his breath. His opening words implied that she had been correct.

'I only wish I were ignorant of our relationship,' he said frankly, and extended a hand to lift her from the deep curtsy she had swept.

She smiled as he bowed over her hand. 'I think that is best interpreted as a compliment, my lord,' she said.

'It is, but it is best *not* interpreted as meaning that I am pleased to see you. I thought we agreed that I would never set eyes on you again?'

'We did, my lord, and I fully intended to keep to that, but then something happened.'

He led her to a chair opposite his. 'Sit down. Madeira? I find it most restorative.' He poured out a glass and handed it to her before resuming his seat. He eyed her appreciatively. 'Purity did very well for herself, it seems. Abbas Manor never provided the income needed for those pearls, let alone everything else.'

'Maman was very successful,' Mandala told him. 'The rue des Flandres was so convenient to Versailles, and her patrons were so very generous.'

'The assets she acquired are certainly not wasted on her daughter. Now, Mandala, what are you here for? I have a busy day tomorrow, and have no desire to be long out of my bed.' He glanced towards a pile of documents tied with pink tape and lying on the table.

She hesitated. He had been perfectly affable so far, but there was something, an edge to his voice, that made her cautious. 'May I first ask how you are, my lord?'

'If you refer to my temper, my dear, I should advise you to tread warily. A long journey has left it somewhat frayed, and it hasn't been improved by your unexpected arrival. Nor does it get better the longer it waits,' he added drily.

'Then I'll take the hint and come straight to the point. You knew how my release would be interpreted, and you were quite right. I am now generally held to be your mistress, and therefore able to exert influence over you.'

'Do you mind?' he asked suddenly.

'Being regarded as your mistress? I would it were otherwise, but it's better than being dead.'

'You share my appreciation of the value of expedience. Go on. You referred to your influence over me.'

Mandala looked at him thoughtfully. 'I don't think you are the sort of man who is very easily influenced,' she said. 'Not unless it's to your advantage.'

'Take care. You could be too shrewd for your own good.'

'I'm sorry. That was a view better kept to myself. I had a visitor: the son of a neighbour who has been taken for treason, along with . . . with someone else.' She hoped the Judge would not notice that tell-tale hesitation. 'A certain Nathaniel Haddenham. He is a most upright man, my lord. A Puritan, it's true, but one who eschews politics and supported neither Monmouth's claim to legitimacy nor his effort to gain the throne.'

The Lord Chief Justice reached across the table and took a bundle of papers, selecting one and putting the others back. He untied the tape and read the contents.

'You are familiar with Nathaniel Haddenham?' he asked at last.

'No, my lord. I scarcely know him, even though he is a neighbour. His son's view is endorsed by those who do, and I understand the information was laid by someone who had reason to discredit him.'

'Who was this person?'

Mandala hesitated. She had not expected to have to name Sir Nuneham, but she could hardly draw back now. 'Sir Nuneham Courtenay,' she said.

'And his reason?'

'Mr Haddenham's son would like to marry Sir Nuneham's sister—and she shares his feelings. However,

Sir Nuneham needs her to marry well to ease his own
financial difficulties, and the Haddenhams, who are
perfectly respectable country gentlefolk, are not rich
enough or well enough connected to suit him. If they are
disgraced, Isobel can be easily persuaded against an
alliance that will reflect badly uopon the Courtenay
name. Or so he believes.'

'You do not share that belief?'

'Isobel has a stubborn streak that I suspect Sir
Nuneham underestimates.'

'If his fortunes are at so low an ebb, why doesn't he
push his interest with you?'

'He has tried.'

Her father permitted himself the hint of a smile. 'I
take it you discouraged him?'

'I think that sums it up rather well,' she admitted. 'I
was obliged to smash a vase over his head, and, indeed, I
was half afraid I'd killed him. It turned out I hadn't,' she
concluded.

'It sounds almost a pity.'

'That's what . . . someone else said,' she agreed.

'There is no evidence of guilt here other than the
information originally laid, and the fact that the man is a
Puritan,' Judge Jeffreys said, returning to the document
in his hand. 'Furthermore, it was the opinion of the
magistrate that it was a trumped-up charge. An opinion
of greater weight than that of the man's own son—or a
neighbour who scarcely knows him. I should probably
have dismissed it in any case.' He looked at her. 'I do
dismiss some of them, you know.'

'That isn't what they're saying.'

'Doubtless! But, then, they're saying you're my mistress, aren't they?' Her face told him that the point was
well taken. 'And now, Mandala,' he went on, 'for whom
are you really here to plead?'

Startled, she stared at him. 'My lord?'

His voice was tetchy. 'Don't fence with me, my girl.
You didn't come here to plead for some barely-known
neighbour, and I'm not a fool. Who is this "someone
else" who was taken with Haddenham? The same
"someone else" who thought it a pity you'd not killed

Courtenay, I imagine. I presume he has a name?'

Mandala flushed. Her father was a great deal too astute. 'Deveril York,' she said.

There was a long silence. 'Deveril York,' he repeated at last. 'You've come here to plead for him?' She nodded. 'Using Haddenham as a lever?' She nodded again. 'I take it you are rather better acquainted with York than with Haddenham?' Again Mandala nodded. Judge Jeffreys' mouth was set in a hard, straight line. 'I think you'd better explain your involvement with him.'

Mandala shook her head. 'I can't . . . I mean, there really isn't any "involvement" to explain.'

'Then why plead for him?' He waited for a few moments, and then since Mandala seemed unable to answer his question, he said, 'Perhaps you'd better explain about him from the beginning.'

Quite suddenly Mandala realised that, of all the people in the world, the last one to whom she could give a truthful explanation was her father, because it would inevitably include Deveril's reason for visiting her, and that would condemn him utterly. She twisted her fingers together in her lap, frantically seeking the right words until finally they were wrenched from her by some force beyond herself.

'I love him, you see.'

He groaned. 'God's Death! Couldn't you find something simple—like a debt he owed you? Besides, how can you say you love a man and at the same time deny an involvement?'

'I don't think he loves me,' she whispered. 'At least, I did think at one time that he might, but I know it's impossible now.'

'What has suddenly rendered it impossible?'

'He was in court at Dorchester.'

'I see. He now believes what everyone else believes?'

Mandala nodded. 'I don't blame him for that, but I don't want him to hang.' She glanced towards the papers on the table. 'Can't you look through the indictment, or whatever those are, and see if it is as unsubstantiated as Mr Haddenham's? It was the same person who laid information, and for a similar reason. I rejected him, and he thought Deveril—Mr York—would offer for me.'

'The case is not at all similar,' the Judge told her. 'I have no need to refresh my mind as to the details. Deveril York is a name well known to me. He has been sought for a long time—or, at least, firm evidence against him has been sought.' He smiled grimly. 'Your choice in men is as ill judged as your mother's,' he said. 'I had no intention at that time of marrying a provincial. Deveril York will never marry. He has for a long time been destined to be hanged, drawn and quartered.'

'No,' Mandala protested. 'I don't believe that! Many people supported Monmouth who never had a treasonable thought in their heads before, and I'm not at all sure that Deveril did really believe in Monmouth's claim!'

'Oh, he didn't. I think we may safely assume that he is perfectly well aware that the traitor Monmouth had absolutely no legitimate claim to the throne.'

'Then why . . .?'

'Your Mr York is in the pay of Stadtholder William —Princess Mary's husband. He, like a lot of other people, wants to see an undisputed Protestant on the throne, with a Protestant wife and Protestant children. Preferably, one suspects, himself. There have been a number of plots designed to bring that about. All have so far failed. Always Deveril York has been somewhere in the background, and, behind him in the shadows, William of Orange. If Monmouth had succeeded, there would have been a Protestant king, and later, when it suited William, Monmouth's legitimacy would once more have been called into question and Mary's superior claim to the throne brought out. In the meantime, in case the rebellion failed—as it did—William has been pledging his support for his father-in-law, hoping to persuade him later to name Mary as his heir.'

Mandala digested this. 'I understand that—I think,' she said. 'It doesn't explain what Deveril—Mr York —was doing.'

'He was facilitating Monmouth's chances of success. William judged that his best route to the throne might be that one. It also enabled him to gauge the support there would be from the people for a Protestant king. If James has a son by his second wife, he will never be persuaded after that to will the throne to his eldest daughter.'

'But surely that's the flaw in this devious scheme?' Mandala said. 'It would be Mary who sat on the throne, not William. He would be nothing more than her consort.'

'I don't pretend to know how things will fall out,' the Judge said. 'But if James proves unable to hold the throne, I wouldn't be too sure that William won't find some way of sitting there in his place. At all events, I'm unlikely to live to see it.'

Mandala looked at him. It was true that his face was looking tired and drawn, but she had attributed that to a combination of the candle-light and the enormous pressures under which he must have been working since the Assize started some six weeks earlier.

'I'm sure you overstate the case, my lord,' she said. 'Once this Assize is finished, you will be able to rest, and I'm sure your view of your future will be more sanguine.' She rose to her feet. 'For my part, I will leave you free to seek that bed you mentioned.' She hesitated. 'I'm truly sorry to have broken our agreement, my lord, but you do understand, don't you? . . . And what about Deveril York?'

He sighed and got to his feet. 'I'm sorry, my dear. I do understand, but I can see little choice but to let York hang. The King will require it.'

'Is there no hope, then?' she asked, the despair in her voice echoed in her face.

He took her hands and kissed them. 'Be thankful that one of your pleas has succeeded,' he said. 'Will you be in court?'

'I don't know. I've given the matter little thought. I'm not sure I could bear it.'

'Where are you lodging?'

'At the Red Lion.'

He nodded as if, by doing so, he stored the information away for future reference. 'Mandala, you're a beautiful woman—a daughter of whom I would have been proud, a woman after my own heart—but please, I beg you, do not seek me out again, ever.'

'I won't,' she said. 'Ever.' On an impulse, she kissed him briefly on the cheek and was gone before he could speak. She collected her cloak from the ever-patient Edward, and ran down the stairs to Martha.

'Well?' the maid demanded.

'Nathaniel Haddenham is safe,' Mandala told her, and pulled her hood far down over her face to hide the tears now suddenly released.

The Great Hall of Taunton Castle was a far cry from the Antelope. Its cold stone walls soared up to smoke-stained rafters, and the only touches of colour, apart from the clothes of the onlookers, were those provided by the crimson cloth over the judge's throne and the banner carrying the royal coat of arms above it. The intimacy of that other courtroom, the closeness that permitted the smallest eyebrow-flicker to be seen, was lost. The dock was vast, possibly because the judge's list showed that he had five hundred and twenty-six cases to hear in three days, a schedule which necessitated his newly instituted practice of judging defendants in batches.

Mandala, with Martha at her side, pushed her way among the crowds and found a place to stand a few feet from the route by which prisoners would cross to the dock. She found she was standing not far from Mark Haddenham, and each acknowledged the other's presence with a tight-lipped nod.

The Judge entered with the customary pomp, and Mandala was forced to admit that it was a far more awe-inspiring spectacle in these imposing and imper-sonal surroundings than it had been in the panelled upper room of the Antelope. No one among the first batch of prisoners was known to her, and if she had not been consumed with apprehension about what was to follow, she would have found an interesting study in her father's method of dealing with each individual's attempt at defence. She knew from her own experience how he had a genius for appearing to miss a relevant point and then unexpectedly referring back to it in a way that threw one entirely off balance. It was a skill he demonstrated over and over, as he cross-examined defendants and the few witnesses who were so sure they could not be implicated that they were prepared to give evidence. When Nathaniel Haddenham's turn came, she saw the same strategy employed against Sir Nuneham Courtenay to some effect.

Sir Nuneham had plainly never expected to have to appear and, had he guessed it would be so, he would almost certainly have had second thoughts about including Nathaniel Haddenham in his information. It was one thing to inform on a neighbour in secret and for one's own purposes, but quite another to stand up in court and testify against him. When a messenger had arrived from Taunton in the early hours with a demand from no less a person than the Lord Chief Justice that he appear in court, Sir Nuneham toyed with the idea of refusing, but he had no time to find out whether he had any right to do so and very soon decided that, even if he had, Lord Jeffreys was perhaps not the man in front of whom to exercise that right. Accordingly, he lent the messenger a fresh horse and accompanied him through the night back to Taunton. When he took his place on the stand, he had had only a few hours' sleep before the messenger's arrival, and, since he reached Taunton, only time for a hastily consumed breakfast of pie, ham and devilled kidneys washed down with a tankard of ale—a far less substantial start to the day that he was accustomed to.

The Judge turned to him. 'Does it surprise you that the defendant has pleaded "Not guilty"?'

It seemed a rather unnecessary question. 'No, my lord. I mean, he would, wouldn't he?'

'You know him well?'

'For many years, my lord.'

'And his family?'

Sir Nuneham nodded. 'If you mean his son—yes. Mrs Haddenham died a long time ago.'

'His son would, I think, be younger than you but older than your sister?'

'Yes, my lord.' The questions seemed more than ever pointless.

'You rode over to Sir Paul Bridlington and laid information against the defendant concerning his activities in the recent uprising?'

'Yes, my lord.'

'What was the nature of the defendant's activities?'

Sir Nuneham shifted uncomfortably. 'He is a known Puritan, my lord.'

'That is not in itself illegal,' the Judge pointed out. 'What is the nature of his treason?'

'His views are well known, my lord. He is opposed to a Catholic king on the throne of England.'

'Then he is a fool to express them. That doesn't make him a traitor.' The Judge was clearly unperturbed that he had already condemned to transportation many whose crime was precisely that. 'Has the defendant ever made a secret of his Puritan views?'

'No, my lord.'

'They are well known in the county?'

'Yes, my lord.'

'His father was of a like mind?'

'So I have heard, my lord.'

'In other words, he is the very person to come under suspicion in the present circumstances?'

'Yes, my lord.'

'Yet his name had never been mentioned until you informed. What had he done to make you take such a step?'

Frantically, Sir Nuneham cast about in his mind, but could think of nothing, so he kept silent.

'Let me help you. How well acquainted with each other are the defendant's son and your sister?'

'Quite well, my lord,' Sir Nuneham replied cautiously.

'Would you describe the defendant as wealthy?'

Sir Nuneham considered. 'No, my lord. Comfortable, perhaps.'

'Are you in debt?'

Sir Nuneham flushed. 'What has that to do with it?'

The Judge's face darkened. 'You will answer my

questions, not ask your own, or be held in contempt. Are you in debt?'

'Yes, my lord.'

'So either you or your sister—and preferably both —needs to make a good match?'

'It would help, my lord. It wouldn't be the first time it had been done.'

'Indeed not, nor the last. A very prudent step. I believe your sister and young Haddenham wish to marry?'

'He hasn't offered for her, my lord,' Sir Nuneham said defensively, and then, after a glance at the Judge's face, added, 'but I believe it may be so.'

'A match which won't help you out of your difficulties. Of course, if the family is discredited, your sister would naturally ally herself elsewhere. Sir Nuneham, I put it to you that the defendant has done nothing. His only "treason" is in having a son who aspires to your sister.'

'It is a quite unsuitable match, my lord!' Sir Nuneham protested.

'Quite possibly, but happily that is not for me to pass judgment on. Do you deny that you said you were not surprised he pleaded "Not guilty"?'

'No . . . but . . .'

'The absence of surprise was because you knew perfectly well that he was not guilty—that you had made the whole accusation up. It is quite clear that there is no evidence to support the charge of treason in this case. Sheer malice was behind the indictment. The case is dismissed.'

A gasp of incredulity went up from the court, and doomed hopes were raised in many breasts that they, too, might escape on similar grounds. Unalloyed delight swept over Mark Haddenham's face. He made his way through the press of onlookers, and as he passed Mandala, he paused.

'I don't know how to thank you, Miss Sorn,' he whispered. 'My father will, I know, wish to add his gratitude to mine. Perhaps we may call on you?'

She smiled perfunctorily. The fate of Nathaniel

Haddenham had been of limited interest to her; it was the fate of Deveril York that was her concern. 'I shall not leave the court yet awhile,' she told him. 'I'm staying at the Red Lion. By all means bring your father, but not today.'

Mark bowed, puzzled by such seeming indifference from the person who had made it all possible, and made his way from the Great Hall to meet his father.

Deveril's case was due to be heard in the afternoon, and Mandala nursed a hope that perhaps, if Sir Nuneham's evidence had been so soundly discredited in the morning, her father might treat it similarly in the afternoon. When the court adjourned at mid-day, she stayed where she was, unwilling to risk not being able to get back into the courtroom or to find so advantageous a position if once she left it.

In fact, she found herself rather closer to the path of the prisoners as their shackles clattered across the floor. Her heart cried out as she saw Deveril thus chained. She did not doubt the truth of anything her father had told her, but the truth could not alter the fact that she loved this man, traitor or not. He stood a good head taller than his fellows, and somehow managed not to look as if he had spent several days in gaol. Only the harsh lines of his face seemed deeper-etched now, and she saw his eyes ranging over the assembled onlookers as though he sought an individual.

She could not keep her eyes from his face, and it was inevitable that such a concentration on her part should draw its object to her. His eyes found hers, and held them in a cold, hard grasp that she found impossible to break. His fetters enabled him to pause only briefly as he came level with her.

'So you have followed him to Taunton,' he said. 'I hope you are both well pleased with the bargain you made.'

Mandala flinched as if she had been slapped and turned her head, the cold injustice of his words permitting her to break away from his gaze. There was no retort she could offer. She could not tell him the truth, and, without it, he believed what everyone else would believe. She could only hope her journey here had not been in vain.

As the trial progressed, her heart sank deeper and deeper. There had been an initial burst of renewed hope when she realised that Sir Nuneham Courtenay was to be the only witness against him, but on this occasion Lord Jeffreys handled him very carefully, almost reverentially, and Mandala, to her horror, learnt for the first time that her conversation with Deveril had been overheard. The Judge led Sir Nuneham carefully through what he had heard, punctiliously avoiding anything that might serve to identify the recipient of Deveril's ill-judged remarks. The verdict was never in doubt. Neither was the sentence.

Mandala longed to rush from the court, but dared not. To do so while the Judge still spoke might risk a charge of contempt. She sank her head in her hands, and Martha put her arms round her mistress's shoulders.

'Bear up,' she whispered. 'Just a little longer. Let no one see how you feel.'

Mandala was unsure whether to be glad or sorry that Deveril looked to neither left nor right as he left the court.

The groom, who had waited for them outside the castle, joined with Martha in helping their mistress back to the Red Lion.

'We'll not be leaving today,' Martha told him. 'Have the horses ready for tomorrow.' She judged that the sooner Mandala was back at Abbas Manor, the sooner she would be able to resume the life she had uncomplainingly led before the events of this summer. She told Mandala they would return home next day, and, when Mandala raised no objections, set about packing some of her mistress's gowns.

Mandala talked little, and refused to eat. Not even Martha's coaxings could induce her to partake of anything at all, and the old maid eventually persuaded her to go to bed in readiness for the next day's long ride. She tucked her in and then set by the firelight, wrapped in thought. *I've trod this road before*, Martha thought. *First*

the mother, then the daughter, though at least the daugh-
ter isn't with child. Both Purity and Mandala had been
women whose passions, once roused, could over-ride
their judgment. Both had fallen in love with men who
put their own interest first. Most men did that, of course,
but these two to a quite remarkable degree, the one
refusing to make good his dishonourable behaviour, the
other leading the woman who loved him to the very foot
of the stake. Purity had never recovered from George
Jeffreys' treatment of her. She had never allowed herself
to love again and became hard and calculating, using
men's weakness for her own ends. Martha had no desire
to see Mandala tread the same road, but feared that she
might: she resembled her mother in many ways, despite
having the added assurance her age and wealth had
given her. Martha was very much of the opinion that
marriages contracted for purely practical considerations
were more likely to result in lasting happiness than any
based on this new-fangled idea of making love a pre-
requisite. So often there was the love without the marriage, and, in Mandala's case, Martha could not see her
easily loving someone else and even less easily marrying
for any other reason.

A tap at the door broke in on these reflections and she
eased herself to her feet. *Old age creeps on*, she thought
as she opened the door softly, her finger to her lips in
warning to whoever stood outside.

The caller was a neatly-dressed manservant of the sort
accustomed to gliding unobtrusively about his business.
He observed the warning finger, but would not have
dreamed of raising his voice even had there been no
warning.

'Is this Miss Sorn's room?' he asked softly. 'Miss
Mandala Sorn?'

'It is.' Martha's voice was suspicious. 'You'll not
speak with her, however, for I've just this past hour
persuaded her to sleep. I'm her maid.'

'Then give her these before morning,' the stranger
said, handing her two sealed papers, and then bowed
at precisely the angle calculated to indicate that they
stood on equal footing, before disappearing into the

darkness of the corridor.

Martha took both documents over to the firelight. The directions on each meant nothing to her because she could not read, but she could see they were not identical. The seals on each, however, were. Nor was the wax sealed with the insignia of a private individual. This was very much a Seal of State, and if Martha guessed accurately, the Seal of the Lord Chief Justice. She hesitated. 'Before morning', the messenger had said. She looked across at Mandala, sleeping peacefully at last. She was very loath to wake her, but this might be important. She lit a taper at the fire and set it to the candles beside the bed, and then shook her mistress gently until she stirred and woke.

'What is it?' Mandala murmured. 'Morning already?'

'No, not morning. These have come. The messenger said you were to read them before then.'

Mandala sat up, still sleepy but curious, and took the folded papers, holding each in turn to the candle-light. 'One is addressed to me, the other to the Governor of Taunton Gaol,' she said.

'Open it,' Martha directed, holding the iron candelabrum up so that the paper was more clearly lit.

Mandala needed little urging, and broke the seal of the letter bearing her name. It was undated and unsigned, and she had never seen the writing before. The contents left her in little doubt of their author.

> The prisoner York has this evening had his sentence commuted to transportation as an indentured labourer to the West Indies for a period of not less than ten years. The prisoners will leave for Bristol and transportation in two days' time. The accompanying letter will authorise you to meet the prisoner within the gaol's confines to bid him farewell, should you wish to do so.

That was all, but its effect on Mandala was immediate. 'He does not die!' she exclaimed. 'Martha—Deveril York does not die!'

'They've never released him! Not after the evidence!'

'Alas, no. He goes to the West Indies as an indentured

labourer. Martha, it means he will be able to return one day.'

'If he doesn't die first,' the maid pointed out. 'I've heard the hulks they use aren't seaworthy, and if they do get there without mishap, they die of the fever. So don't you expect to be wearing the willow until he gets back, for, as like as not, he won't be back.'

'It doesn't matter, Martha. What's to stop me going there, too?'

'Only common-sense, I suppose, and I don't reckon you'll pay much heed to that. Is that all? What was so urgent about that that it couldn't wait till tomorrow?'

'Nothing, but there's more. This letter to the Governor gives me permission to visit Deveril in gaol to say goodbye—if I wish to.'

'Hmm. What makes you think he'll want you to?'

Mandala's face clouded. 'I've no way of knowing, though, if his words are any indication, I may not be welcome. Martha, I can't sit here and *not* go, knowing I have the means to do so.'

Martha sighed. 'So we shan't return to Abbas St Antony tomorrow—or, rather, later today. Very well. I suppose it's inevitable. If you don't want him to see you quite hagged, you'll go back to bed and sleep the rest of the night, though I don't doubt you'll find it hard.'

Mandala dressed with as much care for her visit to Taunton Gaol as she had when she went to see her father—but very differently, preferring the simple, more modest lines of the dress she had put on after repulsing Sir Nuneham's advances.

She handed the Governor the sealed letter, and he read it two or three times with raised eyebrows, looking at her steadily but in silence between each reading.

'You appreciate that there must be a guard outside the door at all time?' he finally asked. Mandala nodded. 'Very well. We shall not be long. Please be seated. Your maid will have to wait outside.'

Mandala and Martha exchanged puzzled glances. They had both assumed that Mandala would be taken to the cell Deveril presumably shared with others similarly condemned. Martha was told to wait outside the Governor's room while that gentleman accompanied a turnkey into the farther parts of the prison, returning in a few minutes with Deveril York. Deveril frowned slightly as he passed Martha, but said nothing as his fetters were removed, the door opened and he was told to go inside. The door closed behind him, and as he stood there rubbing his wrists, he heard the heavy key turning in the lock. He glanced round the room without appearing to see Mandala, and went over to the single window high up in one wall.

'You're wasting your time. It doesn't open,' Mandala told him.

He turned towards her and swept her an exaggerated bow. 'What's the purpose of this visit, Mandala? I compliment you on your influence: only Jeffreys' signature could have obtained a private interview with a condemned man in the Governor's own office. But why?'

Mandala was quite unable to answer this entirely reasonable question. She had not asked for this visit, but when the opportunity was given to her she had accepted with alacrity: it was likely to be the last time she saw him. Even if she followed him to the West Indies, it would not be easy to discover his whereabouts in those scattered islands.

'I came because I wanted to see you before you went,' she said.

'You know the death sentence has been commuted?'

'I was told so.'

'How very close you must be to the Lord Chief Justice of England! I only knew myself half an hour ago. Or have you come straight from his bed?'

'No, I have not!' Mandala exclaimed. 'I have never . . .' She suddenly realised that to say she had never been in Lord Jeffreys' bed would either not be believed or would give rise to questions she dared not answer. "It is nothing like that,' she amended feebly.

'What have you never?' Deveril asked, and it seemed to Mandala that he was looking at her with a suddenly concentrated interest.

She stood, and turned towards the window so that he could not see any confusion in her face. 'Nothing,' she said. 'Lord Jeffreys has nothing to do with my visit.'

'Nonsense, girl! He authorised it, just as he commuted my sentence. I can think of no reason why he should have done either. Agents of the Crown have known about me for years, but failed to find any evidence they could use. Then I have an ill-advised conversation which is overheard by that malicious nincompoop, and I find —interestingly—that his lordship words his questions so carefully that the recipient of my guilty admission is never mentioned.' He took her roughly by the shoulders and turned her so that she had no choice but to look at him. 'You must please his lordship mightily to win not only your own freedom but the power to visit another man. What puzzles me is why you should want to. After all, what are you to me?'

Nothing, she thought despairingly, *but you are everything to me*. Aloud, she said, 'I don't envy anyone in gaol, though you seem to be coping with it better than I did. I—I wondered if there was anyone—any family, perhaps—who need to be told what has happened?'

'I have no family, and there's certainly no one else to be informed. Lord Jeffreys could probably have told you that.'

'Lord Jeffreys! Does everything have to get back to him?'

'I wish it didn't, but his name, his influence, seem to crop up all the time.' He looked at her speculatively, as though he were seeing her for the first time, and when he spoke, his voice was softer. 'I read you wrong, Mandala, and it hurts to find I was mistaken.'

Mandala was bewildered. 'What do you mean? I don't understand.'

'I thought you were different from your mother. I don't blame you for saving your life by any means you can, and yet, somehow, I wouldn't have expected you to choose that way. Not like your mother: it would have been the first thing she thought of.'

Mandala hesitated. She was on the brink of telling him the truth, but stopped herself in time. After all, she had no way of knowing how much of this conversation could be heard outside. The door seemed solid enough, but she remembered the Antelope: the panelling had seemed solid enough from the inside, but the hangman had his peephole none the less.

She tossed her head defiantly. 'Then we are closer than you thought.'

'And I'm disappointed. I had thought that with you . . . But it's all too late, in any case. Tomorrow we go to Bristol.'

'Do you know your destination?'

'The West Indies. Barbados is the most likely, or Jamaica, perhaps. Who knows?'

'Is there no way of evading the sentence?'

'Many people are buying their pardons. I've been told there's no hope of that for me. Although my indentures are only for four years, I'll not be allowed off the islands for ten. How rigidly that is applied will depend upon how long King James lives—and who succeeds him.'

'Of course! If it's Stadtholder William and his wife, they will very likely permit your earlier return.'

Deveril's eyes narrowed. 'What do you know of Stadtholder William? His name has never been mentioned in court.'

'But I heard . . . I mean, I thought . . .' Mandala's voice tailed off.

'You heard.' His voice was hard again, and had a biting edge. 'So My Lord Jeffreys talks in his bed, does he? How inadvisable when he's sharing it with one who has no discretion. He's one man I never took for a fool! You must have skills for making a man relax that go beyond the merely accomplished. I almost envy him. I would that I'd guessed at your talents before I found myself in this predicament, where they can be of little use or interest to me.'

Mandala flushed. 'You're insufferable!' she said. 'You take the slightest little thing and twist it out of all recognition. You read into it things that simply aren't there and use them to other people's disadvantage.'

'A characteristic I share with your lover,' he said savagely.

'The West Indies are welcome to you!' Mandala cried, furious that she dared not dispel his illusion. 'They say it is a most inhospitable climate, and you are certainly not accustomed to labouring. Very likely your sentence will be the death of you, one way or another—and a good thing, too. They say the hulks they send you on are little better than coffin-ships. With any luck, yours will go down before it clears the harbour.'

Infuriatingly, Deveril did not seem to be in the least disconcerted by this attack. He grinned. 'Sorry, Mandala—I can swim.'

'In fetters?' she flashed.

'To annoy you, in anything,' he replied. 'Be under no illusion, I shall survive. I'm a great deal tougher than you give me credit for. I'll survive—and I'll be back. It may well be several years and I dare say your noble lover will have cast you aside by then and you'll be back on your own considerable resources. I'll visit you, Mandala, and I've a shrewd idea what I'll find: Abbas Manor will far outdo the rue des Flandres. It's a long way from Town, of course, but that can be turned to advantage. Such seclusion! Your mother's establishment offered variety enough, one would have thought, but a woman who can in so short a time coax secrets from the Lord Chief Justice himself—not to mention unheard-of privileges . . . Such a woman will doubtless devise hitherto undreamt-of delights. And I, Mandala, shall be there to sample them, I promise you.'

Almost before the last word was out of his mouth, her hand dealt him a stinging blow to his face, and was on its way back with another one when he caught it.

'You're a deal too fond of using your hand,' he said grimly, forcing it down to her side and then up behind her back till she flinched and involuntarily moved closer to him to ease the pain. His grip was immediately shifted to her waist and she found herself drawn close against his body. His mouth found her upturned lips and a lingering, yearning hunger swept over her for what could never be. It seemed that Deveril felt it, too, and his caresses were those of a lover who knows the end is near yet dares not express what he feels except with his lips, his tongue and the tensed urgency of his body.

When they drew apart, the atmosphere between them was subtly changed. Deveril put out a hand and gently stroked her hair, and Mandala's head turned to nestle in the palm of his hand. He bent down and kissed her gently. 'My deepest regret is that it is too late,' he said.

Mandala nodded, uncertain whether he referred to his imminent transportation or her supposed liaison with Lord Jeffreys—and afraid to ask. 'I wish you hadn't been here this summer on—on . . . business,' she said instead.

'So do I, but if "business" hadn't brought me, nothing would, and we should not have met. Mandala, if I survive this exile and return here, I shall let you know. If you—or your husband—do not object, I shall perhaps seek permission to visit you.'

She smiled tremulously. 'If I am running a successful brothel, the wealthy Mr York will need no permission to visit, I promise.'

He smiled ruefully. 'Forgive me, Mandala. That was an unkind jibe—and unwarranted. Besides, Abbas Manor would not be a suitable location at all, as you must surely know.'

'From my vast experience?'

'From your common-sense. Come, we must part. Let us at least part friends.'

'There was a time, when we went riding together at Abbas, that I thought we were,' she said wistfully. 'Then I discovered the only reason was to enable you to find a place for King Monmouth to spend the night in safe seclusion on his way to Taunton.'

'No, Mandala. That was certainly my initial reason for seeking you out, but I had all the information I needed days before I left. I enjoyed those rides, too.'

Mandala sniffed. 'I'm glad of that. At least, I am if you're not just easing my wounded pride.' She hesitated before continuing. 'If you come to Abbas, you won't have to worry about my husband's permission. There won't be one.'

'That would be foolish, Mandala. Sooner or later you'll find someone who doesn't give a damn for your

mother and who, maybe, won't hear about Lord Jeffreys
—or won't care. You'd be a fool not to marry him.' He
raised her fingers to his lips and kissed the tips of them
lightly. 'You were made for love, Mandala. I envy
George Jeffreys, and that's the truth. I doubt if he can
deny you anything.'

Tears welled in Mandala's eyes. 'No, Deveril, it's
not . . . you still don't . . . Oh, *why* have I come to this
pass?'

He kissed her again. 'Don't think such bitter
thoughts,' he whispered. 'Your mother and I had a
characteristic in common: we're both survivors, and, if
I'm not mistaken, so are you. The last few weeks have
been enought to deprive anyone of the ability to make
wise decisions, balanced judgments. God go with you,
Mandala.'

She shook her head. 'His place is with you, Deveril;
your need is the greater.'

He longed to take her in his arms again, to kiss away
the agony he saw in her eyes, but that would only
prolong this already painful farewell. Besides, he
thought bitterly, someone else has given himself the
right to solace her now.

'Goodbye, Mandala.'

'Farewell,' she whispered, her voice barely audible.

A tap on the door brought the turnkey, who let
Mandala out before returning to escort Deveril back to
his cell. Martha made no attempt to console her mistress. One brief glance at Mandala's stricken face told
her all there was to know.

CHAPTER TEN

THE HADDENHAMS were awaiting Mandala's return to her lodgings, anxious to express their gratitude. As soon as she appeared, supported by her maid, they realised that they had not picked the happiest moment, a feeling reinforced by Martha's frown and shake of head in their direction. It had been their intention to return to Abbas St Antony as soon as possible, but since it was unthinkable that they should do so while Mandala was still in Taunton, they decided to stay a little longer. They had no idea where she had been or why she should be so distressed, but they felt they could easily spare another day or two for something so important.

Once back in her room, Mandala told Martha she wanted to be left alone, and the maid, deeming this the best thing, left her and resolved to return in an hour or so with some refreshment. Nathaniel Haddenham and his son were waiting in one of the public rooms, and she told them she thought it unlikely that Mandala would be able to see them until the afternoon at the very earliest, though she added that she could hold out no hope of certainty even then.

Left to herself, Mandala threw herself down on the bed, buried her face in the soft feather pillows and burst into tears. The deep, shattering sobs were not all for Deveril York, though she might not have been ready to acknowledge that fact. The turn events had taken in the last few weeks: her own arrest, the discovery of her father's identity, his action on her behalf and the fact that she must forever live with the knowledge that it would always misinterpreted, Deveril's arrest and, finally, the necessity of appealing once more to Judge Jeffreys—all these had steadily increased the tension to which she had been subject. Most of that had now suddenly been relaxed, and the tears were as much an expression of relief as of her deep sadness that, while

Deveril's life might have been saved, he was to be taken out of her reach.

To what extent he had ever been within it, she was uncertain. She knew that each of them had the power to rouse the other to physical desire, and, for her part, she knew the feeling went far deeper than that. There had been very little indication that Deveril might feel the same. During those long rides over her land they had conversed like friends of long standing, with no references to her background intruding upon their easy intercourse, yet even then, things had not been as they had seemed. Deveril had been using their rides to become acquainted with the wooded combes of Manor land for his own ends. He had even initiated their acquaintance with that in mind. That had been devious of him, and duplicity was, if her father was to be believed, the very essence of his whole life. Mandala longed to be able to discount Judge Jeffreys' assessment of Deveril York, but she could not: the Judge had no reason to lie to her, and her own brief acquaintance with Deveril, the way he had used her himself, bore out the Lord Chief Justice's opinion. As a matter of common-sense, of cold reason, she would be better off if he were in the West Indies. This seemed particularly true when she recalled with a shudder the scorn and derision he had made no attempt to hide when he thought he knew how she had gained her freedom and, later, access to him in gaol. It was true that he had said on the latter occasion that he did not blame her for what he believed her to have done, but she knew that his first reaction had been the true expression of his feelings, and no man who felt like that about a woman would easily overcome his repugnance. Only by telling him the truth could that be done, and that was now impossible.

Mandala supposed that perhaps, within the privacy and confidentiality of the marriage bed, a husband could be told, though, even then, it might rather depend upon who the husband was. She knew that Deveril was a man who, once told, would never reveal the information, nor, despite his deviousness, did she think he would use it for his own ends if he were aware of the distress his

doing so would cause the innocent subject concerned.
This knowledge was small consolation. Even if he were
not to be transported in the very near future, even
though his parting words had been devoid of rancour,
there was no thought in his mind of anything beyond
friendship. He had even exhorted her to marry. As if,
having known him, she could ever consider doing so! It
was inconceivable that any man could possibly fill the
gap in her heart that Deveril York had so unwittingly
filled. No, even if by some miracle, he evaded transportation, he would look elsewhere for a wife—or
remain unwed.

Suddenly Mandala sat up on her bed, her tears
checked. Why should he not evade the fate decreed by
law? He had already evaded the noose. Why should the
miracle not occur? And why should she not be the
instrument that made the miracle happen?

Tomorrow the prisoners set out for Bristol. The distance was so great that there was always the possibility
they would be transported in wagons, but their numbers
were such that she thought it unlikely. Men linked by
shackles could not move fast. Allowing for a late start on
the morrow, such as would be occasioned by the necessity of signing various documents and the unwillingness of
the accompanying troops to leave the relative comfort of
their quarters, it seemed highly likely that the first of
several nights on the road would be spent at Bridgwater.

Wherever the prisoners were put for the night—and
Mandala doubted whether the small gaols of little towns
could possibly be made to hold the numbers involved
—there would be a minimum guard, and as a consequence, a maximum opportunity then for one of them to
be removed from the group. It required initiative, which
she felt she had, and help, which at the moment she
lacked. There was a considerable risk in engaging the
help of others, and if she were betrayed in this, not even
the Lord Chief Justice would be prepared to help her.
But what if she could enlist the help of people who had
every reason to be willing to repay a debt? The
Haddenhams, for example. Were they still in Taunton,
or had they already returned to Abbas St Antony?

Mandala wasted no more time. She poured cold water into the bowl on the little toilet table, took a deep breath, closed her eyes and immersed her face in the water for as long as her breath held. She repeated this twice more before groping for a towel and patting her face dry. Then she looked at herself in the mirror. Most of the puffiness caused by her tears had gone, and her face no longer had the blotched look that disfigures all but a few fortunate women when they cry. She tidied her hair and went in search of her maid.

'Martha,' she said when she found her. 'The Haddenhams. Did I see them when we returned this morning?'

'You did. They wanted to talk to you, but I sent them away. You needed to be alone. They said they'd be back this afternoon.'

Mandala heaved a sigh of relief. 'Thank goodness for that! I was afraid they'd have gone back to Haddenham Hall. When they return, send them both up to my room straight away.'

'That I shall not!' Martha declared. 'What are you thinking of, mistress? It would be most improper. I doubt if anything they have to say needs to be that private, in any case. One of the public rooms will do perfectly well—or even a private room downstairs, if you insist.'

'A public room will *not* do perfectly well, Martha! As for a private room, yes, it might be wiser. After all, I don't want to frighten Nathaniel Haddenham entirely away, and after the means he thinks I used to gain his freedom, that might well be the effect.'

Martha looked at her suspiciously. 'What little plot are you hatching, my girl?' she said, forgetting for the moment that this was no way to speak to her mistress.

Mandala laughed. 'Why should I be hatching a plot? You've a suspicious mind, Martha! Never mind. Reserve me a room, and ask them to lay a luncheon there: I find my appetite is quite returned.'

Martha sniffed. 'For someone who a short time ago was prostrate with grief, you've made a mighty swift recovery, and that's a fact.'

'I've cried myself out, that's all. You know how it is.'

'I do, indeed. You've cried yourself out, all right. And you've hit upon some scheme or other, and it's ten to one I'd not approve or you'd tell me about it.'

Mandala flushed and tossed her head. 'It's not for you to approve or disapprove, Martha. Any more than I am under any obligation to tell you anything at all.'

If this set-down was intended to put Martha in her place, it failed. She nodded knowingly. 'That settles it. Once you start telling me my place, I *know* you're up to something. Very well, miss. Since it's none of my business, I'll ask no more—but sooner or later it'll get back to me, you mark my words.'

Accordingly, when the Haddenhams returned, they were delighted to find that their benefactress was well enough to receive them and more than a little surprised to see that she seemed to have made a most dramatic recovery since her return earlier that day.

'I am delighted to see that your spirits have taken so sharp a turn for the better,' Nathaniel began, conscious of a little awkwardness in meeting the neighbour who had for so long been ostracised and who had but recently proved herself to be precisely as others had deemed her to be. 'I understand from my son that I owe my freedom to your intercession on my behalf. Miss Sorn, I can only be grateful, though it is well-nigh intolerable to contemplate the high price you paid. I am for ever in your debt. If ever there is the chance to repay you, you have only to say the word.'

Mandala coloured with the consciousness that, had Deveril not been involved, she would have done nothing, and that, in any case, Judge Jeffreys had, without her intervention, already decided that there was no case to answer. Nor could she tell him that the price he believed her to have paid was far, far less than he—and everyone else—imagined. She was going to use his gratitude as shamelessly as Deveril had used her company, and he had just given her the opening he sought. Before she could devise a tactful way of sayng, 'Well, as a matter of fact, since you mention it . . .', Mark was speaking.

'I have a two-fold reason for thanking you, Miss Sorn. Not only is my father free because of your efforts on his behalf, but he has agreed to my marrying Isobel, provided Sir Nuneham's objections can be overcome.'

Mandala's delight was unfeigned. 'I'm so glad! I imagine you've not yet been able to tell Isobel?'

'Not yet. I can hardly wait to do so. The sooner we are back at Abbas St Antony, the better!' said Mark.

'There can't be much doubt about Isobel's reaction,' Mandala commented, uncomfortably aware that the scheme she hoped to persuade them to follow would delay their return by several days, or, if it failed, for ever. She turned to his father. 'Mr Haddenham, Isobel is not the least like her brother, and I believe her to be very much attached to your son. She will make him an excellent wife: running a country house is exactly the sort of thing she will do with quiet efficiency.'

'So my son tells me. You were kind enough to give the girl shelter when she needed it, so you must know her better than I. If both of you concur, I feel sure you must be right. Persuading Sir Nuneham could prove difficult, though, and I have made it clear to Mark that I'll have no hole-and-corner affair. I insist upon there being a marriage that has the full blessing of the bride's family for everyone to see.'

Mandala smiled. 'I don't think you need worry about that, sir,' she said. 'When Isobel knows that you have been brought round, I have no doubt at all of her ability to work on her brother until he can hold out no longer. Since some of his other schemes have failed, I fancy he will be quite willing to see her comfortably settled and thus save himself the expense of launching her on London society.'

Nathaniel smiled. 'I hope you may prove to be right,' he said, and rose from his seat. 'Miss Sorn, we have expressed our gratitude. I'm sure you will understand if I say that we—or more particularly, Mark—would like to be on our way home. A home I never expected to see again,' he added.

'No, Mr Haddenham. Don't go just yet,' Mandala

said, trying to ignore his look of hastily disguised surprise at her extraordinary manners in thus preventing their immediate departure. 'You mentioned your gratitude and—and your wish to repay the debt you feel you owe. I am going to trade quite unashamedly upon that wish.'

Nathaniel thought he understood. He smiled, if a little stiffly. 'Miss Sorn, you have been badly received in Abbas St Antony. You may rest assured that, no matter what your past or your mother's may have been, no matter what you had to do to secure my release, you will always be received at Haddenham Hall, and I hope will permit my son and me to visit you at Abbas Manor.'

Mandala laughed, though there was some nervousness in the sound. 'If you will but help me in what I ask, Mr Haddenham, I shan't mind if you never speak to me again.'

He was clearly startled. 'I'm almost afraid to ask you to enlarge upon your meaning,' he said.

'You will recall that Deveril York was taken at the same time as you, and on information laid by the same informant.' He nodded. 'Like you, he escaped the death penalty, but in his case it was only commuted to transportation to the West Indies. I had just returned from seeing him when you saw me this morning.' She hesitated. 'You must know how slender is the chance of his ever returning here safely.' Again he nodded. 'Tomorrow they move the prisoners on the first leg of their journey to Bristol. They are going to have to spend two or, more probably, three nights on the road. Mr Haddenham, I want to free Deveril York during one of those nights. There would be a minimum guard on them at night in order to let the rest of the escort sleep. It should be entirely possible to free one man. What do you think?'

Nathaniel Haddenham's heart had begun to sink long before Mandala had finished. He was a law-abiding man, and had never been anything else, yet here was Mandala, to whom he owed a great debt, asking him to repay it by breaking the law in a way which was not only fraught with difficulties but which, if it failed (as in his opinion was all too probable), would guarantee the walk to the scaffold which he had just escaped. And she asked him what he thought!

'I think it might be possible,' he said cautiously. 'I doubt very much if it is wise. Miss Sorn, stop and think, I beg you. We have both narrowly escaped death. If this scheme failed, nothing could prevent our execution.'

'Oh, I've thought, Mr Haddenham. I've thought very hard. What you say is quite true, but I believe that the knowledge of our fate if we fail is sufficient to force us to take very good care that we succeed. I can't think of a better incentive for success than fear of the noose or the stake, can you?'

Nathaniel could not, but he had a strong suspicion that that made a very good case for not trying at all. Yet how could he, in all honour, avoid repaying the debt he owed, even if the cost of repayment was so very high?

'And what if we succeed?' he asked. 'The hunt will be on. Do you expect to be able to hide him in one of your barns?'

'Goodness me, no! I should think Abbas St Antony would be the first place they'd start to look once they'd recalled my visit this morning. No, Mr York must make his way as fast as may be to Lyme or Weymouth—or even Poole. To any place where he may find passage to France or the Low Countries. He is well known across the Channel, and I suspect he keeps some of his fortune over there. He certainly has spent much time there in the past, so it will be no hardship to him. I shall be obliged to live abroad myself, but, since I was brought up in France, that is not a prospect which worries me unduly.'

'Do Mark and I also go abroad?' Nathaniel asked, unable to keep an ironic edge out of his voice at what was beginning to sound like a wholesale disposal of every-one's future to suit Mandala's present plans.

'Certainly not! Why should you? If my plan works, no one will see you or even guess that you're involved. You and Mark will return to Haddenham Hall as if you were just returned from the Assize—as, indeed, you will be,' she concluded triumphantly.

Nathaniel was uncertain whether or not to be glad that

she had given the matter so much thought. Mark's early apprehensions were beginning to dissolve. If Mandala had really made plans in such detail, it might be very exciting, and excitement was a commodity generally lacking in Abbas St Antony.

'I think we should listen to Miss Sorn's plan,' he said. 'That, at least, can do no harm and, who knows, it may be perfectly feasible.'

His father had a sinking feeling that it might sound more feasible than it would be in practice, but his debt to Mandala was such that he could hardly refuse to listen. He sighed, but pulled his chair closer to Mandala's. 'Very well,' he said. 'You'd better tell us your full plan of campaign, Miss Sorn, but I warn you, if I can pick holes in it, I shall do so.'

'Good. That's the only way we can make it entirely foolproof,' she replied.

She talked swiftly for a long time and neither man interrupted her. When she had finished, they both sat back exchanging glances.

'You really have worked it all out, haven't you?' said Mark.

'Where are the flaws?' she demanded, looking first at Nathaniel.

'Apart from the initial premise, which is quite insane, there is none that I can see,' he admitted grudgingly. 'There is one detail I don't altogether like, though: I don't think it's a good idea for you to dress as a man. Most improper.'

'Propriety!' Mandala exclaimed scornfully. 'I've got beyond the stage where that matters, don't you think? If I wear a man's clothes, my appearance from a distance will arouse no comment, whereas a woman would certainly be noticed and, later, recognised. If I'm dressed as a man, their attention, when I reveal myself in that guise, will be all the more intent, don't you think?'

'Quite possibly. They will also start asking themselves why? As a woman, you will attract attention, but no more than any woman travelling with an escort. A woman travelling as a man invites a lot of questions that are better left unasked.'

Mandala considered his argument and finally conceded the point. 'A pity,' she sighed. 'I was quite looking forward to it.'

Nathaniel frowned. 'This enterprise is not something to be taken lightly. If it is to be entered upon at all, the only criterion by which to judge any of it is its likelihood of success. Now, there is one suggestion I can make to help Mr York's escape from England. Yours, too, my dear, if you choose to avail yourself of it.'

'That's the only aspect of the affair that I've had to be unsatisfactorily vague about,' she said. 'Any suggestion that makes our flight easier is very welcome.'

He nodded. 'I mislike the idea of either of you traipsing from port to port seeking a vessel, and it would be equally dangerous to stay in one place trying to find a captain who will take you. There's a ship in Lyme now—the *Harbinger*—bound for the Low Countries. I own a share of her, and she will take whatever passengers I tell Captain Scratby to carry. There is a snag: she is due to leave on tomorrow night's tide. If we can get a message to Lyme, I can delay that sailing for twenty-four hours, but not for longer. The problem is how to get a message to him in time.'

'Let me go, Father? I have a fast horse, and Captain Scratby knows me,' Mark suggested.

His father shook his head. 'No, we need you for the greater plan. A message can be safely carried by someone who knows nothing about the other scheme.' He turned to Mandala. 'You have a groom with you in Taunton?'

'Yes. Jem. He can certainly carry a message.' She hesitated. 'Can we give him time to take Martha up behind him to Abbas? Otherwise she will be stranded in Taunton and that might give rise to comment—not least from her.'

Nathaniel thought about that before nodding slowly. 'As long as Jem is aware of the need for urgency, and goes on to Lyme on a fresh horse straight away. If they leave this afternoon and break the journey at Chard for the night, he should reach Lyme by noon or soon afterwards. That will give him plenty of time. However,

you realise that this means we must free Mr York
tomorrow night without fail?' Mandala nodded. 'Let us
hope your guess that Bridgwater will be the place is
correct. Leave it to us to procure a good, fast horse for
Mr York. Be ready to leave in the morning. Either Mark
or I will come for you. But first, a note for your groom to
deliver to Captain Scratby.'

When the two visitors had gone, Martha entered the
room and stood with her arms folded. There was a
suppressed excitement about her mistress that was at
complete variance with her earlier mood. 'And just what
are you up to, I should like to know? You've been
closeted with those two for over an hour, and I see them
leave with faces full of portent. Something's brewing,
and you're behind it, unless I'm very much mistaken
—and I'd like to know what it is.'

Mandala crossed over to her and kissed her on the
cheek. 'You've a suspicious mind, Martha Rissington,
and that's a fact! I've decided that maybe I'll return to
France, and I've heard of a ship going there that will
perhaps delay her sailing. You and Jem are to return to
Abbas Manor this very day, and he will take a fresh
horse from there to Lyme and deliver this note to the
captain of the *Harbinger*. If you spend tonight at Chard,
you'll not need a fresh horse tomorrow. Pack up everything except my riding-habit and put it on the baggage-
horse. I can't see that he will slow you down much, since
Jem will already have you on the pillion-saddle.'

'I see,' said Martha warily. 'We return to Devon, but
you stay here. On your own. No maid, no groom, no
chaperon. When do you return to Abbas? Are you
foolish enough to ride that distance unescorted? Why
don't you come with us? Or why don't we wait for you?'

'No, Martha. I'll send for you as soon as I'm settled.
Besides, I may not reach the *Harbinger* in time, and in
that event you'll be necessary for my comfort at Abbas
Manor.

'Where there's a houseful of servants to look after
your comfort, which there won't be on any ship—or in
France, for that matter. Still, if that's the arrangement
you want, who am I to quarrel with it? I'll send Jem to

you. I dare say he'll see nothing amiss with your scheme.' With a final derisive sniff, she left the room.

As Martha had predicted, Jem saw nothing unusual in his mistress's instructions. These he painstakingly repeated. 'I'm to make as much speed as I can to Chard, where we're to rest the horses for the night. When I've delivered Martha to the Manor, I'm to take a fresh horse and get to Lyme as fast as possible, seek out the captain of the *Harbinger* and give him this letter.' He patted his jerkin to show that the letter was safely stowed away.

'That's it exactly, Jem. Can you be sure to reach Lyme by tomorrow afternoon?'

He thought about that. 'With a fresh horse from the Manor, I can get there by noon—but I'll have to take my time returning. Might not be back till evening.'

'That's all right, Jem. Take as long as you like to get back *after* you've delivered the letter, but waste no time before that. If you can get there by mid-day, that will be even better.' She handed him a pouch of money, enough to cover all eventualities with plenty left over, and sent him on his way.

Within the hour he and Martha had set out, the baggage-horse trotting behind, and Mandala returned to her own room to pass the time until nightfall, when the need for sleep would give her something to do.

Sleep did not come easily. Her mind was whirring over her plans for the day, and more particularly, the night, ahead. So much could go wrong. About the only thing she felt she could rely on was the firm, if rather unwilling, support of the Haddenhams. There were so many imponderables. What if the prisoners left unexpectedly early and got a long way beyond Bridgwater by night? What if, for whatever reason, the officer in charge deployed a number of sentries and not just one or two? What if one of the other prisoners, annoyed that only one of their number was being freed, gave warning? These and many other uncomfortable questions chased each other round her head, and sleep out of the window, for many hours. Eventually she fell into an uneasy doze which must have been deeper than she thought, for when she awoke, the sun was well up. With Martha absent, she had not thought to ask a serving-woman to wake her. She leapt out of bed and resisted an impulse not to take her usual care with her appearance. When she finally went downstairs, she was as well turned out as ever. She ordered a substantial breakfast, and asked the serving-girl to send a message to the stables that Fatima was to be saddled ready for her owner to go riding when she had eaten.

Mandala was drinking her second cup of coffee when Mark came in, the mud on his boots suggesting that he had already been riding that morning.

'Good morning, Man—Miss Sorn,' he amended hastily.

She smiled at him. '"Mandala" will do very well. After all, Isobel calls me that, and you are shortly to be married to her, so you may as well follow her example.'

He sighed. 'You make it sound like a certainty. I wish I could be so confident!'

'Only let Isobel know what your father has decided, and I guarantee she will bring Sir Nuneham round. Are we ready to go?'

'No, not yet. As you suspected, the quarry is in no hurry to leave its earth. My father is in a small coffee-house opposite, and will let us know when we should set out.'

'You've already been riding this morning, I see,' Mandala commented.

'We had some difficulty locating a horse of sufficient size and calibre that was also for sale,' he told her. 'We finally heard of one at North Newton, so I've been out there to see it. The ride had the added advantage of giving me the opportunity to see the lie of the land over towards Bridgwater.'

'Did you get the horse?'

'Yes. A handsome beast, though not quite so good as the gentleman concerned is accustomed to riding. Still, it has the size, it's very sound, and the previous owner says it has plenty of bottom, and that's what we need. It's a bit too cold-blooded for my taste, but it'll go for ever, and that's more important for our purpose than breeding.'

Mandala agreed that he was probably right and they

passed an agreeable half-hour exchanging their views on horseflesh and debating whether a Turk, a Barb or an Arabian produced the greatest turn of speed, though for his part, Mark said he could not see much difference between them. 'It's my belief they're all the same breed, and the name given to each is simply dependent upon which part of Morocco or Asia Minor the animal comes from,' he said. 'Look at their heads, look at their tails: the same.'

'Their speed, too,' Mandala offered. 'If you mix any of them with our racing English Galloways, you should get an animal with substance as well as speed.'

Mark was about to tell her that many interested landowners were doing exactly that, and the results were, he was told, to be seen at Newmarket and Salisbury, Chester and Burford Down, when their engrossing conversation was brought to an end by the arrival of Nathaniel Haddenham.

He sat down beside his son and leant across the table, lowering his voice to a level which, while it was no whisper, would have been difficult to overhear. 'They've left,' he said. 'They've taken the road we expected. It looks as if they've set a slow but steady pace. I think Miss Sorn is right. I can't see them getting much beyond Bridgwater before dark.'

'And Deveril?' Mandala asked anxiously. 'Is he with them?'

'My dear, if he weren't, I should be only interested in suggesting we return home,' Nathaniel said with unwonted astringency.

There was still no immediate need for them to hurry. Three riders would have no difficulty overtaking a column of shambling, shackled men, and they had no desire to be seen by the accompanying soldiery except from a distance. Above all, there must be no hint that they might be shadowing the penal column.

It was a full hour before Mandala had Fatima brought round, and Mark threw her up into the saddle before mounting his own useful animal; together they rode round to the stable where Nathaniel's horse and the newly-acquired mount for Deveril York stood waiting.

Nathaniel handed his son the reins of this latter animal and mounted his own. Then the four horses made their unhurried way through the town and out on to the road that led northward towards Bridgwater.

There was no need to take the horses out of a walk. Even at that gait, they must be going at least twice as fast as the prisoners, but when, after an hour's ride, there was no sign of the column and they were already half way to their destination, they drew rein and looked at each other apprehensively.

'Where are they?' Mandala asked, looking ahead across the expanse of level ground that lay between them and the distant curves of the Polden Hills.

Nathaniel looked worried. 'We should surely have caught up with them by now,' he agreed. 'There can be only one explanation: they're not on this road.'

'But they must be!' Mark exclaimed. 'How can they reach Bristol by any other route?'

'Could the orders have been changed?' Mandala asked. 'Could they be making for some other port instead?'

Nathaniel shook his head. 'They set out upon the Bridgwater road. There's only one alternative, and it means we must retrace our steps. They might have taken the road to Othery.'

'Why should they do that?' Mark asked. 'It leads ultimately to Bristol, but the route is longer and it means a climb over the Mendips. No, Father, it doesn't make sense.'

'Whatever the reason, we shall be well advised to try it. If I'm right, then at least we can cut across country to the Othery road from here. Come on.'

It proved to be an inspired guess. When they stopped to buy bread, cheese and ale from a cottager's wife, she was full of the rebel column that had only just passed through.

'As miserable a bunch as you'd ever wish to see,' she said, 'and serves them right, says I. Still, I don't see as how they're going to get all the way to Bristol, not looking at them on their first day out. I reckon there'll be more than one roadside grave, and that's a fact.'

'This seems a strange route to follow if Bristol's where they're going,' Nathaniel commented.

'It is that. It's my belief they mistook the road. 'Tis easy done, and the soldiers are none of them Somerset men, I don't reckon.'

The pursuers went on their way, their minds easier in that at least they knew they were on the right road. But when they had crossed the Parrett, Mark drew rein again. 'Look,' he said, pointing to the ground.

The road was little better than a cart-track, its surface churned by the autumn rains that had begun. The additional churning caused by the passage of over a hundred shuffling men and several horses was something they had taken for granted, and thus had not even noticed its absence when the road had forked, so sure had they been that the column would be on the Bridgwater road. That confidence eroded by one mistake, Mark had been keeping a rather closer eye on the road surface, and now that they were over the river he observed that the column must have turned sharply to the north-west up a narrow lane, because the road ahead showed no sign of the recent passage of so many feet.

'Why?' Mark asked.

'I don't know these lanes,' his father said doubtfully. 'If it continues in this direction, it will return to Bridgwater, I think. Maybe the old woman was right, and they did take the wrong turn and have taken this opportunity to get back on the original route.'

'Then she was wrong about none of them being Somerset men,' Mark pointed out. 'You'd have to be local to know where this leads. You know country lanes as well as I do, Father: how often they lead only to an isolated farm or turn back on themselves.'

They turned into the lane and followed it along the river. Already there was the faint chill in the air that presaged evening, and with that chill, the first faint hint of mist was forming over the network of rhines that drained the levels and created pasture out of marshland. Mandala shivered, not because of the chill but because of the eeriness of a scene that she knew would only get even more eerie as the twilight drew on.

Then they saw the column. The lane had apparently turned sharply to the right, and they could see the men moving slowly at right-angles to them some little distance ahead. They stopped and watched. Now they had them in their sights, there was even less need to hurry. Indeed, as the mists thickened, it would be possible to approach more closely, confident that the sounds of the soldiers' horses would disguise the sound of their own.

In fact, there was nothing accidental about the column's route. The citizens of Bridgwater, having heard the outcome of the Taunton session of the Assize, made it perfectly clear to those concerned that their own gaol was itself packed solid with rebels and they could not possibly accommodate over a hundred more, with others to follow on subsequent days. Other arrangements would have to be made. Lieutenant Nisbet was to have charge of this particular consignment, and he was a Somerset man born and bred. His suggestion was that if they swung round towards Othery and then turned off, they could reach Westonzoyland and use the church as a temporary gaol. It had been used to that purpose after the last decisive battle, so why not again?

His colonel was less happy about it. 'Not a good idea, Lieutenant. Some of these prisoners will have fought at Sedgemoor. The place will have too much significance to them. It's a bit like rubbing salt in, don't you think?'

Lieutenant Nisbet conceded the point. 'Yet what can they do about it except resent it?' he said. 'In any case, we'll get no further by tonight, and in the morning we'll be able to swing round and avoid Bridgwater altogether.'

'I still don't like it. Didn't one of the prisoners taken at the battle escape from the church?'

'Yes, sir. Through a little door—and they'll all know about it, of course. I'll make sure that way out is sealed, and I'll have a guard on it as well as on the front.'

'Very well, since you're convinced it's the best plan. If you fail, Nisbet, it's your head that will roll!'

'Yes, sir. I fully understand.'

Thus it was that the watching riders saw the column enter the little village of Westonzoyland and halt outside the church. They heard the massive door open and the clank of chains as the men trooped inside. They heard the heavy key turn in the lock.

'How many guards do you think they'll set?' Mandala asked anxiously.

'No more than two, I fancy,' Nathaniel answered. 'They take a risk, though. If I mistake not, this is Westonzoyland, and prisoners were held here before. One escaped through a side door.'

'Then that will be guarded as well as the front,' Mark commented. 'It will be hours before we can move: they'll have to feed the prisoners, and that will take time.'

'I wouldn't be too sure,' his father said grimly. 'Feeding rebels is not likely to come high on their list, I imagine.'

In this he did Lieutenant Nisbet a disservice. The lieutenant had no time for rebels, but marching them to Bristol was going to be a tedious business that he had no desire to prolong because of the need to stop and bury anyone who died on the way. All it would take to keep them going was bread and water, so bread and water they would have, and he supervised its distribution himself. Satisfied that every man had eaten, he then personally checked the little door by which someone else had escaped.

'Afraid we'll all vanish in the night?' quipped one prisoner whose wit was not yet entirely doused.

'Making sure you can't,' the lieutenant replied affably. 'I'm setting a guard or two on the other side of that door, just in case, and more on the main one. No, you'll not get out of here.'

When he was satisfied that everything inside the church was as secure as he could make it, he left and turned the key before removing it from the lock. 'Pity it doesn't bolt on the outside,' he commented. He handed the key to a burly soldier. 'Here, Bolton, thread it on to your belt. You'll be on guard outside this door. You'll be relieved at midnight. Make sure your successor does the same. And let neither of you be hoodwinked into entering that church. So long as you're safely outside, they can't escape. Cuxton, you stand guard by that little door.'

'With respect, sir,' intervened a sergeant old enough to be his father and a tough veteran of Kirke's campaign in Tangier. 'Is two sentries enough? They're expecting you to post more.'

'If they're expecting more, they won't know there are fewer, will they? No, that will be sufficient. We shall be at the inn, and no disturbance can occur without our hearing it, Sergeant.'

The sergeant was by no means as certain as his commander that several hours in an inn would keep the men alert, but if that was how Lieutenant Nisbet wanted it . . . well, the prisoners were a sorry lot, and marching them about was no job for a professional soldier, so he hawked and spat and followed the lieutenant to the inn.

Although the thud of the church door closing and the turn of the iron key were sounds that carried clearly through the mist to the watchers, the rise and fall of voices was muffled so that only rarely did individual words come to them. When silence had descended once more, they retraced their steps to a barn they had previously noticed and led their horses inside. At this time of day the barn's owner was unlikely to put in an appearance. They held a hurried conference.

'Do you stay here, Miss Sorn,' Nathaniel told her. 'It's best if there's no risk of your being seen until it becomes desirable. Mark and I will cut across the fields and hope to come upon the road that leads past the church. We'll ride slowly, not intending to stop when we reach the church. We must hope the mists are not too thick for us to be able to ascertain how many guards they've posted. We'll try to find out where the rest of the escort is, and then we'll be back.'

Mandala nodded. 'Have you any idea how long you'll be?' she asked.

'None at all, though it's likely to be less than an hour. We'll leave the spare horse: no point in there being anything untoward to attract notice. If you brought a cloak, I suggest you put it on. The mists bring with them a chill that eats into the marrow.'

Mandala had already discovered that during their inactivity while the prisoners were locked inside the church, and since her cloak was strapped behind her saddle, she wasted no time in putting it on. Nathaniel and his son put theirs on, too, and slipped unobtrusively out of the barn, leaving her with nothing to do but strain her ears to catch a hint of their progress and try to convince herself that she was no longer cold. She failed in both endeavours.

She had no way of telling how much time had elapsed before the Haddenhams returned, but it had seemed an interminable wait. She was beginning to fear that they had been caught and that at any moment she, too, would be taken by a search-party sent out as a result of their discovery. When Mark told her they had been away less than three-quarters of an hour, she simply did not believe him.

'So far as we can tell, there are only two sentries: one round the far side of the church and the other at the front door,' Nathaniel said. 'We asked the one at the front door the way to the inn, and I noticed he had a heavy key threaded on his belt. I'm guessing that's the key to the church, and, if so, that will make things much easier: one of my greatest fears was that the sound of forcing the door would be heard at the inn—it isn't all that far away.'

'Was it wise to let him see you?' Mandala asked doubtfully.

'There was little choice. He saw us approach and hailed us—through boredom as much as anything, I think. It made sense to ask a civil question, and he volunteered the additional information that the inn would be crowded out this night with his luckier colleagues. So our enforced stop proved very useful. Now, Miss Sorn, this is what we're going to do.'

He explained his plan, and the others listened in silence until he had done. They both nodded their understanding and their acceptance.

'There's just one thing,' Mandala said. 'Deveril won't know of my part in this unless you tell him. I don't want you to do so.'

Nathaniel looked mystified. 'How else do I explain our involvement?' he asked.

'I don't know. Just think of something—but don't tell him the truth, I beg you.'

A long, cold hour later, Mandala was thrown up into the saddle and guided Fatima carefully out of the barn and along the lane until she came to the little inn. Lamps had been lit inside and she could see through the small casements that it was crowded. The sounds that she could hear indicated that, however cold and cheerless the night outside, inside was warmth and conviviality. She surveyed the scene with a sinking heart. Then she took a deep breath to strengthen her resolve and slid from the saddle, tethering Fatima beside the cavalry horses and as close to the mounting-block as she could. She lifted the latch and went in. The smell of tobacco, sawdust and ale mingled with the smell of men who had been riding all day hit her, and she had to force herself to go on in. As she closed the door behind her, one or two heads turned to see this new arrival, and when they did not turn back, others turned round as well. Gradually all talk subsided, and everyone was staring.

Mandala appeared not to have noticed the attention suddenly focused on her. Unhurriedly she unfastened her cloak, slipped it from her shoulders and shook it gently before laying it carefully across a table without seeming to be aware that soldiers were sitting at the table, their tankards before them. Then she removed her feather-trimmed hat and laid it, brim uppermost, on top of the cloak. Next, she took off her kid gloves carefully, finger by finger, and placed each in its turn inside the crown of her hat. Finally, she shook out her coppery curls and negligently drew two ringlets over her shoulder before stepping over to the bar.

She had no need to summon the landlord. So elegantly fashionable a female had never before crossed his threshold, and he was staring at her open-mouthed.

'A glass of mulled wine,' Mandala said with a confidence she was far from feeling. 'Also, something to eat, and perhaps you have a room for the night?'

The landlord shook his head. 'There's food and drink a-plenty, but the rooms is all taken. That's to say, both of 'em.' He nodded in the direction of his customers, almost all of whom were soldiers. 'You've picked the one night in the year when I could have done with twenty rooms,' he added. He took the mug of wine over to the fire and thrust the red-hot poker, hissing, into it. 'There's a game pie and a pasty and maybe a bit of cold roast duck. Then we've a ham in the kitchen we've not yet cut into, but it'll be good. If there's one thing my wife's good at, it's smoking hams.'

'Ay, and that's the truth,' someone called out.

Mandala flashed him her most brilliant smile. 'Then I must most certainly sample your ham. That and some game pie will do very well, I think.' She took the mug from him and cupped her hands gratefully round its warmth before sipping, and as she sipped, she looked over the top of the mug at her audience and her eyes smiled at them beneath fluttering lashes. 'That was very welcome,' she sighed as the warm liquid filtered down inside her. She turned back to the landlord. 'Is there really no room?' she asked, taking care to sound anxious.

Lieutenant Nisbet stepped forward and bowed. 'One of those rooms is mine, madam. It will give me great pleasure to vacate it on your behalf.'

Mandala looked him steadily up and down, her gaze indicating appreciation of both his offer and his person. She shook her head regretfully. 'No, sir, I cannot deprive you of your bed. I'm sure the need of a soldier is greater than mine, but the offer is most generous, Captain . . .?'

'Nisbet. Lieutenant Nisbet—James,' he told her, blushing slightly. 'The need of a beautiful woman must always be paramount, Miss . . .?'

Mandala hesitated. 'De Rouen,' she said. 'Marguerite de Rouen.'

'Marguerite! Such a pretty name—and so well deserved.'

It was Mandala's turn to blush, which she did delightfully. 'You're too kind, Lieutenant.'

There is no knowing how long this exchange of compliments might have lasted, had not the landlord's wife appeared at this juncture with a platter generously heaped with ham and pie and set it down on a table from which she unceremoniously ejected its previous occupants. Mandala gratefully accepted the seat thus made available and resisted the temptation to tuck into the food too heartily. She had to play for time, to keep the attention of her audience, and so, despite the healthy appetite brought about by a day in the saddle, she ate quite slowly. When she sensed that interest in her was waning, she would ask a question or address a remark to one or other of the bystanders.

When she had finished, she pushed her stool back with satisfaction, unlaced her Steinkirk cravat from its buttonhole and stood up to take off her mannish riding-coat. She shook out her lawn sleeves and untied her cravat altogether, revealing a low, wide-cut neck on the bodice beneath.

'It's very quiet in here,' she said. 'Does no one play the flute or the mandoline?'

One soldier admitted bashfully that he played the fife a little, and, with some urging from her, took his pipe from his pocket and began, somewhat diffidently, to play a tune which was unfamiliar, though the soldiers seemed to know it. His friends joined in with the words, and soon his diffidence vanished; when that song had reached its end, he went straight into 'Lilibulero'. Everyone, including Mandala, knew this, and before anyone was quite sure how it happened, she was in the centre of the room, leading them all. By the end of that song, everyone was feeling particularly warm and friendly and she asked the young soldier if he knew the old song, 'Greensleeves'. He did, and she sang the words in a clear, pure voice. The men listened, and she saw the tears glistening in some eyes, though they did not fall. *Good*, she thought. *The drink and the music is having its effect.*

When that was over, she turned to Lieutenant Nisbet. 'Come, Lieutenant. Do you know "Oh, no, John"?'

He blushed and confessed that he did, but said he was not one to make an exhibition of himself.

'Meaning that I am?' Mandala upbraided him. 'Nonsense, Lieutenant! This is just good fun. Don't spoil it.'

He was persuaded, but his self-consciousness made it difficult for him to throw himself into the song with quite the gusto that Mandala displayed. She coquetted her way through her responses with an archness that had the men first chuckling and then roaring with laughter.

The sounds of merriment from the inn drifted across the sleeping village and could be clearly heard by the two men guarding the church. The cold was creeping up through their boots and down through their fingers, and they stamped their feet and blew on their hands. Each at his lonely post wondered how much longer he had to wait until midnight, and how much dependence he could place on the new watch remembering to take over. Each strained his ears to catch the sounds from the inn as if fearful that the merriment would have stopped by the time he was free to enjoy it. Neither of them heard the soft *clump, clump* of unridden horses approaching: a *clump, clump* that stopped in the shelter of some trees a short distance from the churchyard. Neither saw two darkly cloaked figures glide from shadow to shadow among the tombstones.

The man guarding the little side door was the first to suffer from the effects of his lack of vigilance, and soon lay unconscious in the shadows cast by the church itself. The second man was the easier target, with his musket propped up against the tombstone. Beside it, the sentry also leant and enjoyed a pipe of tobacco, his attention given entirely to the sounds from the inn. These he could hear more distinctly than his colleague, because he did not have the bulk of the church in the way. He did glance round once, thinking he had heard a rustle. There was nothing. A rabbit, perhaps: he had heard one or two before.

He knew nothing of the blow to the back of his neck that caused his knees to buckle, nor did he feel himself being lowered carefully to the ground and pulled out of sight into the shadows behind the porch.

'The tools,' Nathaniel whispered, and while the cloaked form of Mark sped silently back to the horses, he unbuckled the soldier's belt and removed the key. Holding this precious object, he hid within the porch until Mark returned with a heavy iron crowbar and a sledge-hammer. The greatest danger now lay with the prisoners themselves. Any sound from them that carried to the inn or even to a neighbouring cottage was likely to attract someone's attention, and the key, as they knew, did not turn silently.

Once inside the church, they dared not immediately step forward: it would be fatally easy to stumble over one of the prisoners. Nathaniel took his tinder-box from his pocket and struck a flint. The brief flame enabled him to see something of the disposal of dozing prisoners, most of whom were now stirring. 'York,' he whispered as loudly as he dared. 'Deveril York'.

'Over here.' Thankfully, the man he sought was close at hand. Nathaniel took a candle-end from his pocket, lit it and secured it to a piece of projecting stone. One ill-lit glance told him that only one of Deveril's feet was fettered. An iron anklet clamped hard round his boot had a ring attached, and through this ran the chain that linked him to the men on either side. His hands were free.

When he saw the tools with which the Haddenhams intended to free him, he shuddered. 'For the love of God, take care, or 'tis my ankle you'll break, and not the shackle!'

'I'm not going to try to break the shackle,' Nathaniel told him. 'Only the ring. You'd do better to pray God no one hears the sound. This church will echo like the grave.'

'Put this under it,' Mark said, removing his cloak and folding it so that it formed a cushion between the ring and the floor.

'Well thought, lad,' Deveril told him, and tensed against the vibration of the blows that would be needed to sever the ring. It seemed an eternity of hammer on bar before the join, the weakest part of the ring, finally opened. Even though they had thought to muffle the hammer-head before they began, it seemed as though every blow must be heard the length and breadth of the village, and all three men heaved a sigh of relief when they had at last finished.

'Leave the tools,' hissed another of the prisoners.

Nathaniel hesitated. Which was worse? To have disappointed, disgruntled prisoners raising the alarm out of spite or to risk the noise of their attempts to free each other raising the alarm before they were all away? Deveril took the decision.

'We'll leave them at the door,' he said. 'Give us a slow hundred to get away before you move.'

'Agreed.'

Deveril and his rescuers doused the candle and made their way back to the door. Mark stood the tools just outside. They closed the door, and Nathaniel removed the key and put it back on the sentry's belt. 'The fewer clues as to how we got in, the better,' he said.

Deveril chuckled. 'I hardly think it matters,' he said. 'Where are the horses? We don't have long before those poor devils make so much noise reaching the door that someone comes to investigate.'

'Behind those trees,' Mark told him, pointing, and they ran as swiftly as they could to their waiting mounts.

'I don't know why you did it, Haddenham,' Deveril said when they were safely mounted, 'and this is no time for explanations, but I'm grateful.' He paused and looked towards the village. The church was still silent but every so often the faint muffled sounds of music came through the mists. 'Whatever's going on in the inn is fortuitously loud. With any luck, they'll not hear the prisoners for some time. Where do we go?'

'There's a ship waiting for you at Lyme,' Nathaniel told him. 'We'll nurse these horses along to Abbas St Antony and I'll remount you there. The *Harbinger* sails on tomorrow night's tide.'

The soldiers could not remember when they had enjoyed themselves so much. Certainly not when they were escorting prisoners. The songs got louder and bawdier, and this Frenchie—not that she sounded like one, but with a name like that, she must be—certainly knew how to get the fun going. The only person not enjoying the evening was Mandala. She had assumed it would be relatively easy to encourage the men to drink enough to see them under the table, and when that happened, she had intended to slip away. It looked as if soldiers had harder heads than she realised, and unless she was very careful, it would be morning before she could leave. Even on Fatima it would be no easy matter to reach Lyme by nightfall, particularly since, if she dared go to sleep, she would undoubtedly wake very late.

The landlady had changed her mind about this fashionable female. The deference, the willingness to please, had gone. Miss de Whatsit might dress very expensively but she behaved like any lightskirt, and Mrs Golspie had never had that in her hostelry before and was not at all sure she wanted it now, though there was no denying it made the men part with their money all the easier. She told herself it was only for one night and tomorrow the lot of them would be gone, but what she was not having was any carrying-on in her bedrooms, though how that was to be avoided, she couldn't quite see, because if the young officer did not take advantage of what was on offer, that sergeant certainly would.

Had she but known it, Mandala was pondering the same problem. The lieutenant had offered her his room, but if his present attentions were anything to go by, he no longer had any intention of vacating it himself. She managed to extricate herself from his wandering hands with the appearance of undiminished good humour, but she had a strong suspicion he would follow her upstairs; since she knew perfectly well that nothing in her behaviour had given him any serious hint that his attentions were unwelcome, she could not blame him if he did. She supposed, if the worst came to the worst, that she could lay him out with a well-directed bottle. How she then got out of the inn, she was uncertain. She would like to be gone before the guard changed and discovered the sentries. Once men were despatched all over the levels to find the culprits and the missing prisoner, it would be difficult to get away herself without someone at least noticing her direction. Perhaps if she asked to stable Fatima, she could take that opportunity to get away.

Mandala picked up her coat and her hat and went over to the bar. 'What an evening!' she said. 'I can't remember when I've enjoyed myself so much, but I've a long way to go tomorrow. So, with your permission, Mr Golspie, I'll settle my mare in your stable and take advantage of the lieutenant's kind offer to let me have his room.'

Lieutenant Nisbet was at her side, his hand resting negligently just below her waist. 'Let me settle the horse,' he suggested. 'That will give you time to settle yourself. This is not an acquaintance I intend to let drop.' His laugh was echoed by that of his men. They looked at the inviting swell of Mandala's hips and wished they, too, had a room to put at her disposal.

Mandala opened her mouth to say quite untruthfully that Fatima was accustomed to being managed only by her owner, when Mrs Golspie intervened.

'This is a respectable hostelry, I'll have you know, and you, miss, for all your fine clothes, are no better than you ought to be! I don't know where you're headed, and to tell the truth, I don't much care, but you can put that grand coat back on and the hat and the cloak and get back on that horse (which is surely rested by now) and be on your way.'

'But it's dark!' Mandala protested, disguising her delight at the landlady's intervention.

'It was dark when you came, as I recall, and since I reckon you does most of your work at night, I dare say you're quite used to it.'

'Oh, come, Mrs Golspie,' the lieutenant protested. 'You can't turn a lady out into the dark like this!'

'I wouldn't dream of turning a lady out,' the landlady retorted tartly. 'You just let her go, young man. At least that way you'll be sure you don't catch anything.' She sniffed. 'Not but what you won't somewhere else, I dare say. No, miss. Off you go, and I don't want to see you here again.'

Rejoicing inwardly at thus being given the best possible reason for going, Mandala managed to maintain an
expression of disappointment. She turned to Lieutenant
Nisbet, fluttered her eyelashes at him, and said, 'She
means it, you know.' She kissed him full on the lips to a
roar of approval, and then handed him her coat. 'Help
me on with it, Jimmy,' she said. 'Then you can put me up
into my saddle. I'm going to Bath. Will you be there?'

'No, Bristol,' he said sadly. 'Could you change your
destination?'

'I might. I'll think about it.'

He helped her into her coat and put her cloak round
her shoulders, his hands slipping carelessly over her
breasts as he did so, and she smiled up at him, playing
this game to the last. Once she was in the saddle, his
hand stayed on her thigh unnecessarily, and she resisted
the temptation to knock it away.

'Where will you go now?' he asked.

'On to Bridgwater. It's only a couple of miles. I'll find
somewhere there and be on my way in the morning.'

'Damn that landlady! We'd have had a good night.'

Mandala bent down and pecked him on the cheek. 'I
know we would,' she said. 'You'll just have to dream of
it—until Bristol, at all events. They do say anticipation
whets the appetite.'

She gathered up her reins and set off towards
Bridgwater, and then, when out of sight of that part of
the village, she turned back across the open land behind
the houses and headed towards Taunton, intending to
cut across country to Ilminster and thence to Abbas St
Antony and Lyme. Somewhere along this route she
should catch up with the other three.

A faint sound of muffled hammering drifted across
from the direction of the church, and as Fatima picked
her way over the soft ground, Mandala heard the clock
strike midnight.

CHAPTER ELEVEN

THE THREE MEN rode as fast as they dared through the swirling mists of an unfamiliar landscape. They knew that at any moment a false step could send them and their horses into one of the intersecting rhines that were invisible in these conditions. It would be safer to keep to the roads, but they needed to put a greater distance between themselves and Westonzoyland before they risked being seen on a highway. It was true there would be few people about to see them, but those few would be sure to remember anything so unusual as three night-riders.

None of these considerations was discussed, no words exchanged. They were facts so self-evident that there was no need to mention them, just as there was no need for consultation when the need to ease the pace for the horses' sakes became more important than increasing their distance from the inevitable search-party. Similarly, there was a tacit agreement when the time had come to return to the safer going on the roads. Had the night been milder, they would have rested their horses for half an hour after every hour of travelling, but the night chill was too great to risk that, so the only way to give the animals any respite was to reduce the pace to a walk for long stretches and sometimes to dismount and lead them. This last strategy was made more difficult for Deveril by the weight of his shackle and because he had already walked fairly steadily during most of the preceding day. Fortunately the horse Mark had bought for him proved to be all the younger man had hoped for.

'I'll buy this animal from you, Haddenham,' were the first words Deveril spoke.

'As you wish, though you'll hardly be able to get him aboard the *Harbinger*,' the Puritan replied.

No further converse was exchanged, and as the dark of the eastern sky began to lift, they drew rein by a field in which there were two tempting sights: a small stream and a large stone barn. They looked about, but could see no sign of the farmhouse to which the barn must belong.

'We'll need a look-out,' Deveril said.

'I'll do that,' Mark volunteered. 'Someone can spell me after a couple of hours.'

'After an hour,' Deveril corrected him. 'That way, we each get two hours' sleep and the horses three hours' rest.' He turned to Nathaniel. 'Can we spare that much time?'

'I estimate we're well over half-way to Abbas,' the older man told him. 'We can still be there soon after mid-day. We'll be able to make better time in daylight: I doubt if we've averaged more than five miles to the hour.'

'Good. I've business to attend to before I board that boat.'

They let the horses drink their fill and then led them to the barn. A wagon stood there, and they tethered the horses to it and loosened their girths before wrapping themselves in their cloaks and lying down in the straw stacked at one end. Mark kept watch at the door.

Mandala did not enjoy her ride that night, and she knew that if she succeeded in hitting the right road, it would be more by luck than judgment. It had not been pleasant riding through the mists with an escort. Without one, it was positively frightening. It was not so much that the mists obscured both the path and the stars, making navigation a chancy business, but they swirled in patches of varying density and uneven degrees of movement so that it was easy for the imagination to conjure up wraiths and spirits, boggarts and demons. Her common-sense told her such fancies were nonsense. Her imagination was not convinced. She found it difficult to resist the urge to put Fatima into a gallop, the sooner to reach the higher ground above the rhine-mists.

She forced herself to resist. She knew that, if she succumbed, there was a good chance that Fatima would stumble and she herself break her neck or be thrown head first into an invisibly waiting rhine. It took time to

walk the length of a ditch—which daylight would probably prove to have been jumpable—searching for the
wooden plungeon that crossed it, but she knew it to be
time essentially spent. That knowledge did not prevent
her frequently looking over her shoulder, and it was not
a fear of being followed by soldiers that made her so
apprehensive. With no means of telling the time, the
Somerset levels seemed to last for ever, and when at last
she crossed a plungeon to find, not another pasture but
the harder, stone-scattered surface of a road, Mandala
heaved a sigh of relief and patted Fatima's neck.

'Well done, old girl! It should be easier now.'

She turned the mare into what she hoped would be the
right direction, but the only thing easier about it was that
the pathway was at least clearly defined by the banks of
rising ground at either side. The biggest hazard was that
of Fatima's stumbling on a larger than usual rock that
had worked its way to the top of the track, so it was still
not possible for her to increase her speed. Mandala
acknowledged that this was probably no bad thing.
Fatima was a game little animal, but quite unused to
what amounted to the forced march she was being
expected to undertake. She longed to stop and give them
both a rest, but even if she had found an inn not
shuttered and blind to the night, she knew that no
respectable place would be willing to accommodate a
mud-bespattered female who rode alone at night. Nor
dared she seek shelter in some barn or hay-rick: once she
laid her head down with no one to waken her, she knew
she would sleep the clock round. From time to time she
wondered what were the chances of meeting the
Haddenhams and Deveril York, and reluctantly decided
they were minimal. She had no guarantee she was on the
same route—or, indeed, on the right one—and they had
certainly set off a long time before she had.

Soon after the sun had risen, she drew rein briefly to
look with longing at an isolated barn standing back in a
field not far from a stream. It was a perfect place to rest,
but she knew she could not. When the stream crossed
the road, Mandala allowed Fatima to slake her thirst.
The little horse had travelled well but was now obviously

close to total exhaustion, and Mandala knew she must limit what she allowed her to drink. Very soon she would need a complete rest, which would mean that Mandala had to find a replacement.

She stopped by a cottager hoeing in his garden. 'Can you tell me where I can get a fresh horse?' she asked. 'This one's about all-in.'

The man looked at Fatima. 'Ay, she is, that. You'd better make for Ilminster. It's only two miles or so. Think she'll manage it?'

'She'll have to,' Mandala told him, but she let Fatima pick her own pace until the little market town was reached.

Mandala was well provided with money, and although the horse she found was larger and heavier than she liked, he was not badly put together. The owner was happy to agree, for a very generous remuneration, to look after Fatima as if she were his own, and to return her to Abbas Manor, where he would collect his own horse.

A fresh mount and a knowledge of exactly where she was had a most invigorating effect on Mandala, and she set off again feeling almost as refreshed as if she had had a few hours' sleep. No doubt this feeling was enhanced by the hurried breakfast she had snatched, and, in particular, a liberal supply of coffee. It was less than twenty miles to Lyme—four hours' riding if she kept to a sensible, horse-sparing pace—but her mount was fresh, and she had not gone far before she realised that his owner had not lied when he said the animal had not been out for a couple of days. She could afford to push him, at least for the first part of the journey, and put him to a steady, mile-consuming canter. He was not as comfortable a ride as Fatima, but he had no difficulty in sustaining that gait for two miles at a stretch, alternating with a mile of walking. They rode through Chard, and at Axminster she felt she could spare time for a quick luncheon while the horse had half an hour's complete rest. She considered whether to stop at Abbas St Antony to tell them where Fatima was, but decided against it. Lyme was so near that she would be there in less than an hour, and what she wanted more than anything else now was to see Deveril at last. She would press on to Lyme.

As the horse clattered down the cobbled road that led to the little main street of the small fishing-port, the sea air and a sense of achievement combined to give her a feeling of exultation that temporarily overcame her nearly total exhaustion. Over the roofs of the cottages stretched the sea in its gently curving bay, the waves folding white scallops of gentle foam upon the sand. To her left, the cliffs dropped sheer to the sea, to the right was the smooth, undisturbed surface of the lagoon created within the sheltering arms of the Cobb. The tall masts of a ship that was no fishing vessel soared above the Cobb's stone walls. The *Harbinger*, she thought, and her heart soared. Deveril would be down there awaiting the night tide.

But Deveril must wait. First she must leave the horse at the little inn, with enough money to pay for his stabling that night and for a boy to take him to Abbas Manor on the morrow. The landlord confirmed her impression. The large vessel was indeed the *Harbinger*.

'Due to leave yesterday, she was, but there was lots of comings and goings, and lo and behold, she's still here. They say she sails tonight, regardless. Didn't say regardless what of, though,' the landlord added hopefully.

Mandala saw no need to enlighten him. She thanked him for his help and ran along the cobbled street and down towards the Cobb. The top of the wall was wide, but it sloped disconcertingly seawards, and since fatigue and long hours in the saddle made her stumble once or twice, she gave up the attempt to run and picked her way with some care.

Because the tide was still out, the deck was about level with the wall, and a narrow gangplank stretched across between the two. There were seamen on deck in the attitudes of those whose immediate work is finished and who only await the command to be busy once more. One man was splicing rope with the aid of a vicious-looking iron marlinspike. He was the only one to look up when Mandala hailed them.

'Is Captain Scratby on board?' she called.

'Maybe he is and maybe he isn't. Who's asking?' was the unpromising reply.

'He's expecting me.' Mandala was not prepared to identify herself. Word of Deveril's escape must be all over the south-west by this time, and at least one influential man would associate her name with that fact. He would certainly connect her with Marguerite de Rouen. Any of these seamen still had time to go ashore. Anonymity was safer.

'Amos, go below and fetch the Cap'n,' the splicer called out. 'Looks like we've got a passenger.'

Captain Scratby was small and weatherbeaten, with a bluff manner and shrewd eyes. 'And who sent you, young lady?' he asked.

'Nathaniel Haddenham. You should have had a letter.'

'I did, but I wouldn't want to risk setting sail with the wrong passenger, would I? Step aboard.'

The gangplank was no narrower than some of the plungeons she had ridden over in the dark, yet she hesitated. Perhaps it was easier when one could not see the water at the bottom of the chasm. The captain and the man he later identified as his first mate extended a hand towards her, and she clutched them with gratitude as she stepped across the last few feet.

'Come below, I've a cabin for you,' he said, and looked her up and down in some amusement. 'You'll be wanting a wash and some sleep, no doubt. A meal, too, I expect.'

'No, I'm not hungry,' Mandala told him. 'Sleep, however, will be most welcome. As for a wash, well, it's probably just as well I haven't seen a mirror for some time. If my habit's anything to go by . . .' She indicated her mud-encrusted skirt and coat, and had no need to complete the sentence.

The cabin was small and comfortable, and the bed with its deep feather mattress the most inviting thing Mandala could remember ever having seen. There was just one thing before she succumbed to its lures.

'Where is Mr York?' she asked. 'I'd like to see him

first—unless he's asleep already,' she added, remembering that his last few days had been even more tiring than hers.

'The other passenger we're expecting isn't here yet,' Captain Scratby said.

'Not here? But he left before me!'

The Captain shrugged. 'Be that as it may, my dear, he's not here yet. Don't worry: there's still plenty of time—three or four hours before high tide.'

'But what happens if he doesn't get here?'

'With him or without him, we sail on the tide. Now you make yourself comfortable and go to sleep. If the crossing proves rough, you'll get little enough later on.'

CHAPTER TWELVE

IT WAS NOT until the three men reached Haddenham Hall that any converse took place between them apart from that necessitated by making decisions connected with their flight.

'Stop and eat and take some time for a rest,' Nathaniel urged Deveril. 'I'll have a fresh horse saddled. A groom can ride over to Lyme tomorrow to pick it up. You've plenty of time.'

'I'll take refreshment and gladly, but not a rest. Time for that on board. I've business to attend to first.'

'You mentioned that before. Is it presumptuous to ask what business is so pressing that you must risk missing the tide for it?'

'It's not presumptuous—not from one who has made it possible for me to be free—but I think perhaps you'd rather not be told. If I'm successful, you'll find out soon enough.'

Mark looked at him speculatively. 'Does it concern Mandala Sorn?'

Deveril's brow clouded. 'Mandala? No, why should it?'

Mark reddened and shook his head. 'Nothing. I just wondered.'

The meal to which the three men sat down was a cold one, but there was plenty of it and they all tucked in ravenously, not having realised until it was set before them just how hungry they had been.

'There's just one thing that puzzles me, Haddenham,' Deveril said, addressing the elder of his two hosts. 'Why did you go to so much trouble to free me? You, of all people, can have been under few illusions as to what I was doing here.'

Nathaniel shrugged. 'I'm a Puritan. I've no more liking for a Catholic king than the next man. I don't condone the rebellion because I don't believe

Monmouth's claim was a just one, but I like still less the draconian retribution being exacted from those who may—and in many cases, may not—have had some small part in it.'

Deveril smiled tightly. 'Agreed—but you know there was no doubt in my case, and it was no small part.'

'Nor, I suspect, were you working entirely for King Monmouth.' A quick glance at his guest told Nathaniel that his random shot, fired in a desperate bid not to have to hint at Mandala's part in Deveril's escape, had hit very close to the bull.

Deveril gazed at him steadily. 'Do you believe James will keep the throne for long?' he asked.

'Do you?'

So traitorous a conversation had gone on long enough, and both men by tacit agreement returned to their victuals, Nathaniel very satisfied at having deflected his guest from the truth without having lied except, perhaps, by omission. The meal over, Deveril again refused the repeated invitation to rest, and mounted the fresh horse that had been prepared for him. As he swung himself into the saddle, Mark suddenly realised that he still wore his shackle.

'Delay a little longer, Mr York,' he said. 'We can get that off.'

Deveril hesitated. 'No, I think not. There will be time enough once we're at sea. I dare not use up any more time ashore in doing something that I need not do just yet.' He hesitated. 'There is just one thing. Although it is but a short journey, I feel naked without a weapon. Could I beg a sword of you? I will leave it with the horse in Lyme.'

Nathaniel did not altogether believe his visitor's reason though there was nothing unreasonable in the request, and he sent Mark to fetch a sword and swordbelt.

Deveril fastened it on and leaned out of the saddle, extending his hand to each in turn. 'For what you've done, I thank you. I trust none of this business ricochets back to you.'

'We trust so, too, I assure you,' Nathaniel told

him with a dry smile. 'Good luck, York—and God speed!'

Deveril swung the horse round and headed him out of the yard and down the drive to the lane. He headed swiftly in an easterly direction, slowing down only when he came abreast of the lane that led to Abbas Manor. Here he checked his horse briefly as if considering whether to turn off. An observer would have seen his scowl deepen and the lines of his mouth appear deeper etched before he spurred on and past the turning as if he had made a great decision.

There was no hesitation in his approach to Courtenay Place. He pulled up at the foot of the steps leading to the front door and tethered the horse to a rose-bush before running up them two at a time, his cloak flying out behind him. His knock was swiftly answered: Sir Nuneham put great store on such things. Deveril pushed past the manservant who opened it and handed him his cloak.

'Your master?' he asked curtly.

'The library, sir.'

'Always the library, yet I swear he's never opened a book in his life!' Deveril commented, and strode through the adjoining rooms. He wasted no time in knocking on the library door but burst straight in. Sir Nuneham looked up from the letter he was writing. His initial expression of surprise at so unceremonious an entry soon gave way to a mixture of fear and indignation.

'You!' he exclaimed. 'You're meant to be on your way to Barbados.' His eye caught sight of the shackle, and an unpleasant smirk crossed his face. 'Oh, I see! You escaped. Well, that's soon remedied.' He reached towards a little bell sitting at the far end of his desk, but before his fingers could close on its handle, the flat of Deveril's sword-blade smashed down on his hand.

'Not yet, Courtenay, not yet. I'm here to settle my account with you.'

Sir Nuneham essayed a feeble grin and an even more feeble joke. 'Don't tell me you've changed your mind about Isobel,' he said.

'Don't be a fool! If she's any sense, she'll wed young

Haddenham. You did your damnedest to get me hanged, Courtenay, but thanks to friends—of one sort or another—I've cheated the hangman and now I'm free. If you had found me committing treason or had reason to believe I was plotting it, then to inform on me would, I suppose, have been the act of a patriot. But you did neither, did you? You listened at keyholes like any sneak-thief. You heard a private conversation with a woman who had repulsed you. You thought I'd be adding her fortune to my own, didn't you? So you passed on what you had heard. You didn't dare to name the woman, though. That might have brought the Lord Chief Justice's fury down on you. You would have done better to consider whether I'm the sort of man to want another man's leavings. I'm more fastidious than you, Courtenay! I'm sure you could have overcome your squeamishness when you reminded yourself of her fortune and the fact that I was no longer in the running.'

There was a bitterness in his voice which Sir Nuneham heard with satisfaction. The older man was right. He would try his chances with the heiress once more, but first he must get rid of Deveril York, and at the moment he was not at all sure how that was to be achieved. He cleared his throat nervously. 'I only did what I saw to be my duty,' he said self-righteously. 'You can't hold that against me.'

'I can—and I do.' Deveril jerked his head to one side without taking his eyes from Sir Nuneham's face. 'Your sword's over there. Pick it up, and we'll settle this.'

'A dress-sword only!' Sir Nuneham exclaimed. 'Not intended for use at all!'

'I could have sworn it looked like Toledo workman-ship,' Deveril remarked.

Sir Nuneham smiled with satisfaction. 'It is. The very best—and a pretty penny it cost me, too, I can tell you!'

'If it's a Toledo blade, it's fit for more than show. Pick it up. You *can* fence, I take it?' he added scornfully.

Sir Nuneham flushed. 'Only the best masters taught me,' he said, not realising that boasts such as these would only serve to put his opponent on his mettle.

'Then you have the edge on me,' Deveril told him. 'I
honed my skills in battle.'

This remark did nothing to put Sir Nuneham at his
ease, nor was it intended to. If he could have thought of a
way of deflecting his visitor from his purpose, he would
have done so, but Deveril York looked uncomfortably
determined. Reluctantly, Sir Nuneham reached for his
sword and withdrew the beautifully wrought blade from
its scabbard. Although both weapons were rapiers, Sir
Nuneham's was lighter and more flexible than the one
Deveril had borrowed, a fact from which Sir Nuneham
derived considerable comfort. It might not have quite
the cutting-edge of the older weapon, but it would be
much better for the quick thrust that killed. For Sir
Nuneham had no illusions. He was reasonably sure
Deveril meant to kill him. He was quite certain that he
must kill Deveril first. The consequences did not bother
him at all—no one would condemn him for killing a
convicted traitor and an escaped prisoner. It was the
achievement of this satisfactory goal that might prove
difficult.

The two men faced each other, and Sir Nuneham
mentally notched up another advantage to himself: he
did not have the handicap of a leg-shackle.

As the two men parried and thrust, testing each
other's strengths and weaknesses, it soon became clear
that neither a shackle nor an old-fashioned weapon was
much of a hindrance to Deveril York, and that the
ruthless single-mindedness essential in battle was a dis-
tinct advantage. Soon after Sir Nuneham acknowledged
those facts, he was obliged to face another. Deveril York
was by far the fitter and stronger of the two.

It seemed to him that Deveril was making no serious
attempt to drive home his advantages, but he fought
with such speed and in a style which Sir Nuneham had
never been taught to counter that, in all too short a time,
the baronet was panting for breath. Not until that happened did Deveril begin to press the attack home. Sir
Nuneham avoided one lunge only just in time, and felt
his opponent's sword slice through the skin of his arm
instead of piercing the muscle, as it so nearly did. Drops

of blood fell on the marble floor and made it slippery. The fact of a wound, even a superficial one, was sufficient to erode Sir Nuneham's powers of judgment. His sword-strokes became wilder, more indiscriminate, as if he sought to engage his opponent by chance. Suddenly he saw his opening. He lunged forward, his Spanish blade pointed directly at Deveril's heart, and, as he lunged, his foot slipped in his own blood, he overbalanced and fell back on to the floor, his sword crashing from his hand as his wrist hit the marble.

Sir Nuneham's eyes dilated with fear when he saw Deveril York standing over him, the point of that old-fashioned sword at his throat. Sweat broke out on his brow and he gurgled incoherently. He had never expected to die so ignominiously!

Deveril looked down scornfully at the abject figure beneath his sword-tip. 'If I could rid the world of you, I'd have done a service to mankind,' he said. 'But I can't kill a cringing dog and that's what you are, Courtenay—a whimpering, snivelling cur! Your sister's worth a dozen of you.' He bent down and picked up Sir Nuneham's blade. 'I'll give this to your man on my way out. And, Courtenay——' he pressed the point slightly harder against his opponent's throat'—if you lay information of this visit with anyone, I'll make you a laughing-stock, and then, one way or another, I'll kill you.'

Not for a moment did Sir Nuneham doubt that he meant it, nor did he doubt that somehow or other, Deveril would carry out his promise.

When his visitor left, he sat up, shaking with a mixture of fear and relief, but made no attempt to leave the library. The further away his opponent was before Sir Nuneham had to face the not-quite-disguised smiles of his servants, the better. He was suddenly very glad indeed that so unpleasant a man as Deveril York was not destined to be his brother-in-law.

Mandala was woken out of a deep sleep by sounds of activity above her: men shouting, feet running and the creak of rope and timber. It took several minutes to recollect where she was, and when she remembered, she still had to make sense of what she heard. When she had done so, she sat suddenly bolt upright. They must be at sea! She leapt out of bed and ran over to the window that overhung the ship's stern, but it looked out at nothing but a moon-silvered sea. In the distance she could see one or two pinpricks of light that must be land. They could not be too far out. Then she remembered that this cabin faced away from the Cobb, so perhaps they had not yet set sail and were still in the process of casting off.

It was not until she had assimilated these conclusions that the most important question struck her. Had Deveril York come aboard? She swung her feet over the edge of the bed and reached for her riding-coat. She pulled this on over her shift and made her way up the gangway on to the deck. She rushed to the side. The *Harbinger* now rode high on the tide, and the wall of the Cobb was below the deck. She looked up at the quarter-deck where Captain Scratby and his first mate were standing. They would know. She ran bare-foot up the steps towards them, clutching her coat to her.

'Has Deveril York come aboard, Captain?' she asked breathlessly.

'No, our other passenger has not arrived, I'm afraid,' he said.

Panic swept over her. 'Then put me ashore! I must go back!' she cried.

He shook his head. 'I'm sorry, Miss Sorn. It just isn't possible. We have to take the tide, and you have only to look over the side to realise that you can't be landed safely. They're about to cast off the last cable, and then we shall be riding free. Then the gap between us and the Cobb will widen by the minute.'

He had barely finished speaking when a shout went up from the deck below and everyone's eyes followed the line of the seaman's pointing arm. A horse and rider had just turned on to the sloping top of the Cobb, and the clatter of galloping hooves could be clearly heard. The watchers saw a hat sail through the air, and then the irrgular shape of a coat followed it.

'Stop, Captain!' Mandala cried. 'That's Mr York, I

know it is. We must stop! It can only be for a very few minutes.'

'I can't. It isn't possible,' the captain told her. 'There is just the chance that he may be able to leap the gap.' He turned and shouted down to the man who was about to release the stern cable. 'Leave it!'

The horse was reined back hard on its haunches and the rider threw himself off. Deveril needed only one glance at the hull looming above him to know he had no real likelihood of making a successful leap for the rail. He saw the cable straining at its bollard. This was his only chance. He lowered himself on to it and hung, monkey-fashion, by the hands and feet, and with the skill taught of desperation, scrambled along until helping hands reached over and pulled him on to the deck.

'Stand back!' shouted the first mate, who had come down to the deck and now stood with his sword drawn. Realising his intention, the seamen scuttled away, dragging Deveril with them. It was too late to free the cable, and rope was too expensive to be completely discarded. It took two blows from the sword to cut through the cable, and when it was finally severed, the end whipped back on deck, only narrowly missing the officer who had ducked at precisely the right moment. He sheathed his sword. 'Get that spliced. We'll need it,' he said, and returned to his captain's side.

Deveril followed him. 'My thanks, Captain,' he said.

Captain Scratby smiled wryly. 'Don't thank me, Mr York. If I hadn't been afraid that this young lady would try to jump ashore, that cable would have been cast off before you dismounted. She's the one you must thank.'

Mystified, Deveril turned to the figure he had scarcely noticed before. He recognised Mandala, and frowned. 'You!' he said. 'What are you doing here?'

Mandala flushed. 'I go to the Low Countries, and then—who knows? France, perhaps.'

'You should feel at home there,' he told her, a touch of bitterness in his voice. 'Captain, forgive me for mentioning this at a time when your vessel must take your attention, but if you have on board someone who can rid me of this shackle, I'd be particularly grateful.'

Captain Scratby directed him to the orlop deck, where tools were kept which would free his ankle, and Mandala watched him go. There was no backward glance from him, no smile. She felt suddenly very small and very insignificant. He did not know her part in all this, of course. Even so, to be so completely ignored was, to say the least, dispiriting. Disconsolately, she returned to her cabin and stood, still wearing her coat, looking out from her portion of the stern-castle as the *Harbinger* made her way out into Lyme Bay and thence to the open waters of the Channel.

She hardly heard the door open, and when a familiar voice said, 'Mandala?' she turned in surprise.

Deveril stepped towards her. 'Haddenham owns this ship. You could not be here without his connivance,' he told her. 'Tell me the truth, Mandala. What part have you played in my freedom?'

'What did Nathaniel Haddenham tell you?'

'He didn't implicate you, if that's what you mean. I was not entirely convinced by what he said. Now I know why. You must have been involved.'

She nodded. 'Poor Nathaniel! He came to thank me for getting him released (something that would have happened anyway, as I subsequently learned) and found there was a price to pay. The scheme was mine, though, in fairness, most of the details were his. I rather fancy he quite enjoyed his temporary lapse from the straight and narrow path,' she added, as it suddenly occurred to her that Nathaniel, once his initial distaste had been overcome, had thrown himself into it unreservedly, revealing an unexpected aptitude for the task.

'So you came here while he and Mark took all the risks?'

'No, not quite.' Briefly and without dwelling on details, Mandala recounted her part in his rescue, and then, as she observed the deepening lines of disapproval on his face, wished she hadn't.

'You must have found it second nature to play that

part,' he said bitterly. 'Can you be sure your exalted lover will approve?'

'You misjudge me. I did not find it easy—quite the contrary, in fact. It just had to be done. The soldiers had to be distracted for as long as possible.' Mandala chose not to refer to his final question. The less said about Judge Jeffreys, the better.

'Why did you do it?' he asked. 'Haddenham was entirely innocent, but I wasn't—and you knew that. Why go to so much trouble on my behalf?'

She glanced up at him, an appeal in her eyes, and then looked away again at the infinity of waves that stretched behind the ship. 'Does it really matter?' she whispered.

He stood behind her, his hands on her arms. 'It matters to me,' he said softly.

She looked at him then, turning in his light clasp. 'I couldn't bear the thought of not seeing you again,' she said, lowering her head as if in shame. 'I knew you would not be able to stay in England, of course, but the Low Countries are not so very far. I thought . . . I hoped . . . I supposed it was the possibility that this way I might sometimes see you,' she finished dejectedly.

'Does that matter to you?' he asked gently.

'Oh, yes, it matters,' she said.

Gently he removed her coat, sliding it down her unresisting arms and then tossing it aside. He drew her to him, and his kiss was gentle and long so that her arms crept up and round his neck while his in their turn held her close. Such a kiss in the warm enclosure of his arms was something Mandala had dreamed of, and her mouth beneath his instinctively opened to seek a deeper satisfaction which his tongue did not hesitate to provide. His hands cupped her face in a tender gesture and then, so gently that she was scarcely aware of it, they loosened her shift and eased it from her shoulders so that it slid quietly to the floor and she stood before him, naked and vulnerable, her whole body welcoming the increased intimacy of his embrace.

Swiftly he lifted her in his arms and laid her on the bed, covering her lightly with the counterpane until he was ready to join her. Then he lifted the coverlet and gazed down at her and was surprised that innocence was a word that sprang to his mind. Since the first time he had seen Mandala, she had intrigued him, and he had recognised a voluptuous maturity which now was his for the taking, and his desire burnt with an increased passion. Something—some instinct, some consciousness of that inexplicable air of innocence—held him back from immediately gratifying his desire, and when he lay down beside her, the narrowness of a ship's bed making instant contact with the warmth of her body unavoidable, it was with the instinctive wish to bring her gradually to a physical fulfilment that would be with her for ever.

Her senses already heightened, the gentlest, whispering touch aroused the sensuality which Mandala had been hardly aware she possessed. Her whole body responded, seeking always to be closer to his. His lips and his hands together caressed the thrusting, pulsing ivory orbs of her breasts, and when his fingers strayed down across the inviting curve of her belly to her thighs, she sighed. Her legs parted at his fingers' invitation, and her body told him she must be approaching the apex of her need for him. She gasped in shock at his first entry and cried out with the brief pain before the thrusting mutual crescendo burst like gale-driven waves on a sea-shore, and then a lagoon of calm engulfed them both.

Accustomed to leaving a conquest as soon as it had been achieved, Deveril found he had no desire to do so this time and held her to him, his lips in her hair, until her uplifted face in mute appeal received the gentle, reassuring kisses it sought. The flood of desire abated, Mandala snuggled into his arms, his scorn and derision for her imagined past forgotten. They lay together thus for a long time. Words were superfluous. Their bodies had said all that needed to be said, and the calmness of the seas outside was echoed in the mood within the cabin.

Finally Mandala stirred in his arms. 'I did it because I love you,' she whispered.

Deveril smiled and kissed her eyelids. 'Did what, dear heart? Executed your ingenious plan or gave yourself to me?'

'Both. Do you mind?'

'Only a madman would mind.' He kissed her lips, and it was a long time before either felt any need to speak. 'What will you do when we land?' he asked suddenly.

Mandala hesitated. 'I don't know. I have nothing with me—no clothes, very little money, no maid. Martha can be sent for eventually, but I've given no thought to what I do in the meantime.'

'You could throw in your lot with me,' he suggested.

'Would you like that?' Mandala asked doubtfully.

Another kiss, long and lingering, was the answer, and Mandala found it not one to argue with. When at last Deveril slackened his hold slightly, she said tentatively, 'I will try not to bore you, you know.'

He chuckled. 'I fancy you'll never do that. You're no Isobel Courtenay. We'll find a clergyman as soon as we land. At least the Low Countries are Protestant, so there should be no difficulty.'

Mandala's heart leapt. Could he mean what he seemed to be saying? 'A clergyman?' she repeated. 'What for?'

'I may have taken you out of wedlock, my dear, but I'll not live with you in that state. I don't think I could survive Martha's disapproval.'

Mandala flushed. 'You're very kind, but—but you don't have to.'

'I'm well aware of that. Would you believe that I want to?' Hope flooded into Mandala's face, and Deveril thought it would be a brutal man indeed who could disappoint that hope.

'Are you sure?' she said doubtfully.

He kissed her. 'Believe me, my love, I have tried very hard not to love you, and when I realised how you had escaped the stake, I almost convinced myself. Until I found you were on board, I thought I had succeeded.'

'My escape was not achieved in quite the manner you believe,' Mandala began, but another kiss stopped her explanation.

'I don't want to hear about it,' Deveril said, his voice unexpectedly harsh. He knew she could give a satisfactory explanation only if she lied, and he had no wish to hear lies from the woman he loved.

Unaware of what was in his mind but grateful to be released from the necessity of revealing her secret, Mandala put her arms round him, drawing him to her once more, yearning for the exquisite delight of feeling him once more within her, and when he entered her again it was subtly, satisfyingly different this time, as if the knowledge of the years of nights that lay ahead removed the urgency of uncertainty.

He rested afterwards, his head in the valley between her breasts, his lips a small kiss away from the invitation of her nipple, and, as he rested, a small, persistent demon pricked and stabbed at his mind and at the love he knew he bore her. He fought to vanquish it, and failed. He thought he knew what the answer must be even though a part of his mind told him her body's response indicated something else. He knew that, if his fears were justified but Mandala lied for his sake, he would never know for sure whether she had lied or not. Only if she admitted to what he suspected, could he know she told the truth. Even so, he had to ask. The demon had done its work well.

He raised his head and kept his voice deliberately light, almost teasing, as if that might betray her into the truth. 'I trust you found me as satisfying as your former lover,' he said.

The question came as such a surprise that Mandala had, for a moment, no idea what he meant. 'My former lover? What lover?' she asked.

His face clouded. 'Don't take me for a fool, Mandala! I mean the Lord Chief Justice of England. Who else? Or is he so accomplished that any other man is cast into the shade?'

Mandala's puzzlement vanished and her face cleared. She chuckled, and felt him stiffen. 'Oh, him!' she said. 'As to that, I've no idea. You'd have to ask Maman, and I'm afraid she's dead.'

Deveril raised himself on one elbow, totally bemused by this entirely unexpected answer. 'What has your mother to do with it?' he asked.

Mandala reached out a hand and rested it upon his cheek. 'Lord Jeffreys is my father, not my lover. That's why I was able to exert some influence on him. Of course, he would infinitely prefer it not to get out and I have just broken my promise to him not to tell anyone, but I think a future husband is entitled to know, don't you?'

'Even Judge Jeffreys could hardly quarrel with that,' he assured her, and caught her to him with a ferocity bred of overwhelming relief.

No shadows remained to come between them that night, and Captain Scratby was far too discreet to comment upon an unused bed in the other passenger cabin.